SKIN IN THE GAME

A MACKENZIE AND COLE PARANORMAL MYSTERY

WILLIAM MILLER

LITERARY REBEL, LLC

A NOTE ON AUTISM

My wife has autism. Let's get that out of the way right up front, because there are people who will read this book and then go on to publicly claim that I've somehow misrepresented autism, or that I don't know anything about it.

This novel is, in no small part, a love letter to my autistic wife, without whom this story would not exist but don't let that fool you, it's not a romance. The autistic character in this book is, to a very large degree, a near exact copy of my wife. In fact, some of the conversations are taken verbatim from conversations I've had with Kimberly. Not very creative, I agree, but it puts to rest the argument that I've somehow misrepresented autistic people.

It's not my intention to represent *all* autistic people. My wife lectures medical professionals on autism and she'll be the first to tell you; if you've met one person with autism, you've met one person with autism. All autistic people are different, just like neurotypicals. The character of Jessica Mackenzie struggles with a fictionalized version of my wife's particular autism symptoms.

As to the inevitable claim that I don't know anything at all about autism, reread the first sentence.

1

My second case with Jessica Mackenzie came just two weeks after the first. It was mid-November and autumn had a chilly grip on Manhattan. I was standing on a sidewalk in the upper west side, staring at the body of a young gangbanger who had been stabbed through the chest with a screwdriver. A cold breeze off the Hudson whipped through my hair. I was bundled in a beige wool coat with the collar turned up and my chin tucked in the folds of a scarf, wishing Lincoln "Little Boy" Whatley had been stabbed someplace warm. There were spots of color in my cheeks and the breeze kept tugging my coattails, but all in all, I was doing a whole lot better than the stiff at my feet. I gathered the ends of my coat and hunkered down for a better look.

Little Boy—his banger name—had a flat-bladed screwdriver jammed in his chest, up high on the left side. The screwdriver had missed his heart by inches but nicked an artery. Whatley had run from his attacker and finally dropped dead on a sidewalk outside a brownstone not far from the iconic apartment where the Ghostbusters had done battle with Zuul in the famous movie. One of the residents found Whatley when he stepped outside for his morning jog. At first he'd thought Whatley was just another derelict sleeping it off, an easy mistake to make from the way the body was positioned, but upon closer inspection, the jogger had realized Little Boy was dead and he phoned the police.

I was back working homicides, thanks to luck or maybe the Man Upstairs, but still without a partner, which meant I was catching the bodies nobody else wanted. One look at Whatley, face to the wall with his hand loosely cradling the murder weapon still jammed in his chest, and it was easy to see this was a pop and drop. Or more correctly, a stab and drop. Pop and drops are notoriously difficult crimes to solve. One gangbanger stabs another while nobody is around to see. Even if there are witnesses, they usually aren't talking to the cops, which meant my only hope of solving this murder was pulling prints off the screwdriver, and if the banger who jousted with Little Boy Whatley was even halfway intelligent, he wore gloves.

I inspected the body for anything helpful. Little Boy was dressed in baggy blue jeans with hip-hop patches and a puffy red coat. His sneakers were scuffed and there was dried blood on the soles. Droplets trailed off down the sidewalk. There wasn't much, just small circular splats here and there. The screwdriver had acted as a plug, stopping the leak even as it killed him. If he had gotten to a hospital he might still be alive. I decided to follow the droplets. At least Id' know where the altercation took place. Maybe if there were street cams I'd actually have the murder on tape, but I wasn't hopeful. I stood back up, wondering how far Little Boy Whatley had run and told the waiting techs, "Okay, be sure to bag his hands and the handle of the screwdriver. If we're lucky, he's got his killer's DNA under his fingernails."

"And if we're not lucky?"

I shrugged. "Pray there was a camera wherever Whatley was stabbed, or a witness. If not, this will be just another unsolved gang murder."

Unsolved was probably not the right word for it. Whatley was a well-known Crypt. The killer was probably a Blood, or MS-13, or any of the other myriad gangs in NYC.

I stepped backward, careful not to walk on any of the droplets, and let the techs do their thing. I was wondering how long Whatley had been laying there. I was also thinking about breakfast. I'd gotten the call about the DB before I'd even had a chance to shave and because I wanted to impress Lieutenant DeSilva, I'd rushed out the door to make sure I got here before the crime scene people.

The photographer was hanging out near the ME's van, chatting up a pretty red-headed medical assistant. I waved him over. "Gonna follow these droplets and see if I can find the spot where Whatley was murdered. I'll need you along to take photographs."

He motioned for me to lead the way.

In a smaller town, police might have roped off the crime scene and put down evidence markers on each and every droplet, but in Manhattan hundreds, if not thousands of people had already walked through the crime scene. Finding the spot where Whatley had been stabbed would help my investigation, but any forensic evidence I pulled from the area would be tainted. At least that's what a good defense attorney would argue. It was slow work. I had to stop and wait for the photographer to document every single droplet from multiple angles.

We hadn't gone half the block when I spotted Jessica Mackenzie coming up the sidewalk, bundled in her familiar Navy peacoat with her chestnut hair pulled back in a pony-tail and her hands shoved deep in her pockets. She had worn two different color socks today. Her eyes were narrowed and her mouth was a curious little frown. She was following the same blood trail, only in the opposite direc-tion, and nearly walked right into me.

When she looked up and saw me, her hands came out of her pockets and danced on the air. There were small pink roses in her pale cheeks. She said, "Detective Cole. I'm glad I located you. I require your assistance on an investigation. Where's your car? I want to examine the crime scene before the forensic techs disturb anything."

2

"**G**ood to see you too, Special Agent Mackenzie," I said by way of greeting. The sarcasm was lost on the FBI's autistic investigator. I first met Mackenzie in late October when a group of friends made a pact with Satan and started dropping dead, their bodies burned from the inside. Mackenzie had been instrumental in solving the case. I had done my part, of course, but we'd still be chasing the Devil if not for Mackenzie.

She nodded and, without looking me in the eye, said, "We should hurry. The medical examiner will be there soon, if he's not there already, and the nature of the incident means the media will be interested. It's hard to work when reporters are asking questions."

I let out an exasperated sigh. "In case you hadn't noticed, I'm in the middle of a murder investigation here, Agent Mackenzie."

Her brow scrunched.

I waved an arm at the body still laying face to the wall. The coroner's people had yet to bag the corpse and a small crowd of rubberneckers were gathered on the opposite sidewalk.

"Are you sure it was a murder?" Mackenzie asked.

"Guy's got a screwdriver in his chest."

"That doesn't necessarily mean it's murder."

"What would you call it?" I asked. "When a guy gets stabbed in the chest with a screwdriver, it's murder."

She chewed her bottom lip and frowned. "I need your assistance in another matter. Isn't there someone else in your department who can handle this?"

The photographer had moved on, snapping photos of the droplets as he made his way up the sidewalk. I propped my hands on my hips. "No. It's a big city and we're a little short staffed. A gangbanger got himself stabbed and I'm working the case alone."

She craned her neck for a look over my shoulder at the body. "Shouldn't be too hard. Maybe you can work both cases at the same time."

"It's a pop and drop," I told her, a frosty edge to my voice. "These are some of the hardest crimes to solve. He's a gangbanger, so you can bet none of his gang buddies are going to talk to the fuzz, and likely nobody saw the attack. Hell, I don't even know *where* he was attacked. There's no telling how far he ran with that screwdriver in his chest."

"The blood trail stops one block up and one block over," Mackenzie said.

"That gets me one step closer," I said. "But I'm afraid I'm not going to be able to help you this time, Mackenzie. I've got a murder to solve and it's probably going to require all my attention."

It pained me to say it. Part of me was pleasantly

surprised to see her. We had paired up briefly to solve the case the media was calling, *the Devil's Daughters*. Rumor had it some big time Hollywood producer had plans to make a movie. Nobody had contacted me for an interview so I doubted I'd be getting any royalties. Too bad. Another part of me cringed at the thought of working with Mackenzie. As an autistic investigator, she was not easy to get along with. She could be emotionally distant and logical to a fault. Her inability to navigate social situations meant she tended to step on people's toes and it led to a lot of misunderstandings.

She peered at the body, a silent battle taking place on her face. Her fingers fluttered against the legs of her corduroy trousers and her mouth worked into funny shapes.

I left her and followed the photographer to the corner while Mackenzie went for a closer look at the body. The blood trail went down the block and around the corner, then just stopped right in the middle of the street. The photographer was standing there, camera in hand. He said, "Must have happened right here. I can't see any other droplets."

I nodded, propped my fists on my hips and cast around, hoping to find something, anything that might help me close this case. It didn't add up. I was standing on a residential street, apartments on both sides, and cars lined up along the sidewalk. It wasn't normally the kind of neighborhood where you expect to find gangbangers stabbing each other, but this is New York City. That kind of thing can happen just about anywhere.

"What do you think?" the photographer asked.

"I think it's going to be a miracle if I close this case." I motioned to the surrounding apartment buildings. "None of these buildings have cameras and I'm betting the working-class stiffs didn't see anything. Whatley probably got himself stabbed late last night after all these people went to bed, or early this morning."

I waved to the street in general. "Get plenty of wide shots of the neighborhood."

If this ever went to trial, the prosecutor would want to show the jury where it happened. Not that it would help much. The only evidence that a crime was committed were seven little red drops on the cracked asphalt, and they were so small they might have been left behind by a carpenter who accidentally smacked his thumb with a hammer.

Mackenzie returned, hands in her pockets and her shoulders pulled up around her ears. Her chestnut ponytail was dancing on the wind. She stopped at my side, scowled at the empty street and then brought her phone out of her pocket.

"What are you doing?"

"Helping you close this case," she said. "Then you can help with mine."

"It's that easy, is it?" I spread my hands. "You're just going to solve my pop and drop in the next sixty seconds so I can go off and help you? Well, thank God you're here. What would the NYPD do without brilliant minds like yours?"

Mackenzie wasn't paying attention. She had her phone out, tapping at the screen.

I felt my temperature start to rise. "You know, Mackenzie, random violence, especially gang-related violence, often goes unsolved. The nature of the crimes means no motive and seldom any witnesses. Which means this is probably going to end up a cold case. But I have to give it my due diligence all the same."

She was nodding as I spoke but never looked up from her phone.

The photographer said, "We done here?"

"Yeah, thanks Phil."

He waved. "I'll have the prints uploaded for you by the end of the day."

"Wait," Mackenzie said and pointed to an empty spot between a Cadillac SUV and a Toyota Camry. "Take a picture of this spot. This is where the crime happened."

"This is where Whatley was murdered?" I asked.

Mackenzie shook her head. "He wasn't murdered. He killed himself."

3

I had heard enough. Mackenzie was prone to the occasional wild theory, but this one beat all. I propped my fists on my hips and said, "You're telling me that my vic, Lincoln "Little Boy" Whatley—a rap sheet as long as my arm—got depressed with his gangbanger lifestyle, decided to commit suicide by stabbing himself in the chest with a screwdriver, then walked a block and a half before laying down to die?"

"I didn't say he committed suicide. I said he killed himself."

The crime scene photographer watched our interaction with interest.

"Okay," I said. "I'll play along. What bit of elusive evidence brought you to this miraculous solution?"

"At three-forty-seven A.M. a resident of this building"— she pointed to the brownstone—"called police to report the attempted theft of a silver Lincoln Navigator. The vehicle's alarm went off, waking the man from sleep, and he called 911 before going downstairs to check on the car. The thief

SKIN IN THE GAME

had broken into the vehicle but fled after the airbag deployed."

"How do you know that?"

She held up her phone. "Checked the crime blotter."

I turned my attention to the empty space, just big enough for a Lincoln Navigator. My mouth turned down in a frown. The blood trail Whatley had left stopped where the Lincoln would have been parked. I said, "What are you thinking, Mackenzie?"

She turned up an eyebrow. "What do you use to hotwire a car?"

"A screwdriver."

She nodded. "It's simple really. Whatley broke into the Lincoln and used the screwdriver to pry open the ignition. He was working on the wires when the airbag unexpectedly deployed."

"And he accidentally stabbed himself." I mimicked the action of holding a screwdriver and imagined a big oversized balloon suddenly exploding. It would have driven the blade right into Little Boy's chest, just above the heart. I shook my head. "So, Lincoln got himself killed trying to boost a Lincoln."

The crime scene photographer said, "Poetic."

"What's poetic?" Mackenzie asked.

He scowled at her.

I told him, "She's irony impaired."

He motioned to his camera. "You still need me?"

"No," I said. "I think we're done here."

He waved.

"Can we go now?" Mackenzie asked.

"Not yet."

WILLIAM MILLER

I still had to confirm her theory. It didn't take long. A quick check with the tenant gave us the name of the auto-body shop. I called and after a short wait, one of the mechanics found dark drops on the seat and doorframe that might be blood. "Want me to hold off the repairs?" he asked.

"Yeah," I told him. "I'm going to send a couple crime scene techs over for forensic evidence."

"How long's that gonna take, mac? I got a line o' cars waiting on repairs."

"Shouldn't set you back more than an hour."

He hung up with an indignant snort.

I pocketed my phone and turned back to Mackenzie. We were standing in the empty spot where Whatley had punched his own ticket trying to boost a set of wheels. She watched me expectantly, her eyelids blinking rapid fire and her hands dancing to a tune only she could hear.

She said, "We really should go now."

I held up a hand. "Now I have to clear it with my CO."

"I already talked to DeSilva," she said. "How do you think I knew where to find you?"

"You called DeSilva?"

She nodded.

"And he agreed?"

Another nod.

I fetched a heavy sigh.

"Loud auditory sigh," said Mackenzie and then, "That's a sign of exasperation. Right?"

"Right."

"Are you exasperated with me or DeSilva?"

"Both."

She considered that for a second before giving a little shake of her head. "We need to hurry."

I waved an arm in the direction of my beat-up Mercury Cougar. I had parked a block from the body. Just a few car lengths from the empty spot where Whatley had accidentally killed himself. It was blind luck that I hadn't taken the same spot. I said, "Your chariot awaits."

She frowned at the rusted-out Cougar. "You're still driving your personal vehicle?"

"The cruiser DeSilva issued me stalls out and smells like boiled potatoes."

"You should put it in for repairs."

"Oh I never thought of that." The humor went sailing right over Mackenzie's head. "I did put it in for repairs. They said it's going to be a week before they can even inspect it. How come you don't have a government-issue vehicle?"

She shook her head. "I don't drive."

"I know that," I said. "But I do. If you had an FBI car, I could drive it."

"It's against federal regulations for anyone but the designated officer to drive a government-issue sedan."

I rolled my eyes as I reached for the door. "What was I thinking?"

The driver's side opened with a loud shriek of age-worn hinges. The seat creaked and the springs groaned. I reached across and unlocked the passenger side so Mackenzie could climb in. She folded her lanky ballerina frame into the seat, knees hiked up to her chin and her arms wrapped around her legs. Her nose wrinkled. "It smells like old socks."

"Better than boiled potatoes."

The Mercury hitched and coughed and died when I turned the key. I tried again with the same results. Third time proved the charm. The engine came to life and I started to pull out of the space, only to have the Mercury stall out.

Mackenzie said, "Why aren't you driving your department-issue vehicle?"

"The difference," I told her, "is this one stalls and smells like *my* dirty socks. If I gotta ride around in a car that quits and stinks, at least it's my stink."

She cocked her head to the side. "I suppose that makes sense."

I got the Mercury started again and pulled out. The tailpipe gave a loud bang and Mackenzie flinched.

"On second thought," she said, "I'd prefer the patrol car."

"Yeah, yeah," I said. "The tailpipe is next on my list of repairs."

The car stalled out again, leaving us stranded in the middle of an intersection while yellow cabs blared their horns.

Mackenzie covered her ears. "Maybe you should fix the motor next?"

4

Thirty minutes later I angled the hiccupping Mercury into a spot in front of the Happy Time Dumpling shop in the heart of Chinatown. The engine died with a grateful cough and I seriously considered Mackenzie's suggestion that I tackle the engine next. The new transmission I had recently dropped in was supposed to solve most of my problems, but if anything, the old girl was worse. We had stalled out twice more on the drive over and by the time we reached Chinatown, Mackenzie was rocking in her seat humming *Jingle Bell Rock* under her breath.

"Maybe it's the fuel injection," I muttered as I cranked open my door. "Want to tell me what we're doing here?"

"Residents found a body and called police," Mackenzie said by way of explanation.

News crews were already on the scene and the neighborhood was in an uproar. Residents packed the sidewalk and heads poked from upstairs windows. A line of officers created a human barricade against a sizable crowd. Cameras flashed and reporters kept trying to get statements, but the uniforms probably knew as much as I did at this point. They ignored the reporters in favor of keeping the crowd in check. As is usual in Manhattan, curious youths kept trying to duck the crime scene tape and angry residents insisted they needed to get through to get home, but their complaints fell on deaf ears.

The smell of noodles and vinegar filled my nostrils as I climbed out of the Mercury. Just a little shy of two square kilometers, Chinatown is home to over forty-seven thousand official residents. Unofficially the number was probably twice that. Tourists are usually surprised at how small the neighborhood is, just a few city blocks, but it's so tightly packed that it would take the better part of a month to explore even half of what Chinatown has to offer. And it has some of the best eats in the city according to Detective Mike Cole's guide to Manhattan. My stomach was already rumbling at the tempting aromas.

Mackenzie sprang from the Mercury like a magician leaping from a deadly trap just before it slams shut. She took a moment to regather her chestnut ponytail and then followed the procession of crime scene techs and uniformed officers. We identified ourselves as law enforcement at the line of yellow tape and the media whores tried to mob us. One particularly obnoxious reporter stuffed a mic under Mackenzie's nose and started shouting questions. Mackenzie's arms snapped to her sides and her shoulders crept up. Her eyelids shuttered in time with the cameras. She was seizing up, standing stock still and didn't look like she could move under her own steam.

I had witnessed one of her meltdowns in a night club and didn't want the same thing to happen in front of reporters. That wouldn't be good for Mackenzie's already tenebrous reputation within the FBI. I pushed the microphone out of her face, put an arm around her shoulders and propelled her through the crowd.

A uniformed bull lead us around the corner of the dumpling shop, past a row of reeking dumpsters filled with decaying fish, and down a short flight of steps to an iron door set in a brick wall covered in decades of graffiti. We flashed our shields at a pair of officers guarding the door.

One of the uniforms said, "Your partner going to be alright?"

Mackenzie had her fingertips in her ears.

I said, "She hates the smell of dead fish."

The two officers traded a look.

One said, "I don't like it much myself."

The other said, "Why's she got her fingers in her ears?"

"It's a mind over matter thing," I told him and led Mackenzie through the iron portal into an underground tunnel of clammy stone.

A bare bulb dangling from a frayed electrical cord gave off a buzzing yellow light that turned our shadows into large black monsters on an uneven floor. Moths zipped and looped around the bulb. The temperature was ten degrees cooler down here. The smell was a mixture of wet earth and old stone. I turned to Mackenzie. "You alright now?"

"It's very loud," she said in a voice that echoed along the bare concrete corridor. Her mouth made a rictus grin, showing straight white teeth.

I made a calming gesture with both hands. "But it's not loud any more. It's quiet down here."

Mackenzie took a moment to master herself, nodded and with some effort, said, "I'm okay now. Thank you."

"No problem."

Mackenzie made like she was going to grab my arm but stopped herself at the last second. "I mean it. Thank you. Most people wouldn't have bothered to help."

"That's what partners do." I put a hand on her elbow. "They help each other."

She flinched from the touch and then relaxed. Sudden touch, especially light touch, alarmed her and I reminded myself not to make any fast movements.

We made our way along the dimly lit passage. The corridor twisted and turned. We passed several intersections, threaded our way through the basement of a Chinese dry cleaner, through the kitchen of a duck place that I'd never eat at again, and along a narrow underground footbridge made of cast-off two-by-fours spanning a slow-moving river. I could hear the rattle and hiss of a subway train. There were uniformed patrolmen every few hundred feet, giving directions. And still we got turned around twice and had to backtrack. We would have been quickly lost without them.

"I never knew these tunnels existed," Mackenzie remarked as we picked our way through a low-ceilinged room that looked like it had been used as community storage for all of Chinatown.

"These tunnels go all the way back to the prohibition days," I told her, happy to be the one supplying obscure knowledge for once. "They crisscross all of Chinatown. Rumor has it you can go from the East River to Broadway without ever seeing daylight. Triads use them pretty extensively for moving drugs and contraband. We busted an underground brothel down here a few years ago."

Mackenzie stopped and turned to me. We were in a section of tunnel so low we had to hunch over. She said, "If criminals use the tunnels, why doesn't the local precinct do something about it?"

I flashed a tight smile. "They try."

"I'll alert my Captain to the situation," Mackenzie said, as if the FBI might not be aware of the problem.

"I'm sure Fifth Precinct will be grateful for FBI help."

We moved on and after a few minutes Mackenzie asked, "Was that sarcasm?"

"Yep."

Five minutes later we finally reached the crime scene at a T intersection in a dark corner of the underground labyrinth. Two dozen techs were crawling over the area with flashlights, bluelights, and bottles of chemical spray. A pair of homicide detectives from the local precinct were there as well, along with their lieutenant, a career ball buster by the name of Upton. He was a fat, unhappy man with a walrus mustache, rotting teeth and bad breath.

Yellow plastic evidence tabs were scattered everywhere and a uniformed bull with a clipboard asked us to write down our names and badge numbers. I finished scrawling my signature and the patrolman said, "Hope you didn't eat breakfast."

I turned up an eyebrow, ducked the yellow bunting and got my first view of the body. Nothing could prepare me for what I saw.

5

The body lay in a large, wet slick of tacky blood. I couldn't tell if it was a man or a woman. It was just a skinless husk of glistening red muscle, lidless staring eyes and grinning teeth. I swallowed hard in an effort to keep bile from climbing my throat. I had never seen anything like it and I hope I never will again. Splashes of blood adorned the walls and there were bits of viscera everywhere. I had to be careful where I stepped. I instinctively gathered the ends of my long coat as I picked my way across the floor. A black storm cloud of flies buzzed around the corpse, making a lunatic symphony. Rats the size of house cats scurried along the walls, just beyond the electric hum of the portable lights, squeaking in indignation at this invasion of their subterranean kingdom. The crime scene techs had a full-time job just keeping the local wildlife at bay.

I pinched my nose shut and breathed through my mouth, but the smell got in anyway. It was a putrid odor that reminded me of maggots wriggling in spoiled food at the bottom of a dumpster on a hot day. A fly landed on my forehead and I waved him away.

Mackenzie pulled on a pair of nitrile gloves and squatted next to me, a look of intense concentration fixed on her pretty face. The first thing she did was drop down onto her belly, put her nose an inch from the tacky pool of dark red blood and sniff. If the smell bothered her, she didn't show it. One of the techs gave her a curious look before going back to his work.

I glanced around and spotted Tippy Lewis, all two-hundred and seventy pounds of him, conversing with one of the homicide detectives. Tippy had salt and pepper stubble on his double chins and the buttons of his coat strained against his belly. A peanut butter Twix bar was peeking from his coat pocket. He saw me and waddled over, breathing heavy. "Cole," he said by way of hello. His beady eyes flashed to Mackenzie and then back to me. "Still trailing after the feds?"

I shrugged. "Someone's got to be the go between."

He labored to kneel down next to me and I heard his joints pop. "I heard you were back on the murder boards."

"Yeah. First week back."

He waved his clipboard at the skinless corpse. "Hell of a way to start."

"You know me," I said. "Deep end. Feet first. What can you tell me about our victim?"

Tippy shook his head and breathed through his bulbous nose. It sounded like a winded buffalo struggling for breath. "Not much I'm afraid. Cause of death is unknown, but it looks like the skin was taken off in one clean motion. Like skinning a deer, it all came off in one piece."

I fought back a swell of bile in my throat. "Where is the skin?"

Tippy shook his head. "Gone."

"Your people took it away already?" I snapped. "You know that's not how it works. Did you at least photograph it first?"

"It's gone," Tippy said and then, "As in, we never found it."

"The killer took the skin?"

"You're the detective," Tippy said. "You tell me."

I gave a curious grunt and leaned forward, risked over-balancing and landing in the blood, so I could get a closer look at the corpse. "How did the killer manage that?"

"It wasn't easy," Tippy said. "Taking the skin off requires the right tools and knowledge of human anatomy."

"What about clothes?" I said. "You find any clothes?"

He shook his head.

Mackenzie had been crawling around the blood splashes on her hands and knees, using her phone as a flashlight, her face an inch from the dusty concrete floor. She said, "What are these three marks?"

Tippy levered himself up with a grunt, lumbered over and hunkered back down with another grunt. His brows bunched up and his mouth turned down. "What are you looking at?"

"See here?" Mackenzie pointed to a small divot in the stone.

Tippy shrugged and shook his head. "Just a pockmark in the floor. This passage is full of marks like that."

He was right. The age-worn concrete was cratered like

the surface of the moon, but Mackenzie shook her head and said, "This one is fresh."

"How can you tell?" I asked.

"Look closely at the inside of the mark. It's mostly clear of dust and other debris, meaning it was recently made or it would be full of grime. The rest of the floor is filthy. And that one"—she pointed to a small dry circle amid the pool of blood and viscera—"interrupts the blood pattern."

I did a funny crab walk over for a better look. She was right. There were three small divots and one of them was right at the edge of the blood, making a small cove, where blood had puddled around it.

"Something was here," I said.

"Three somethings," Mackenzie corrected.

"Get the photographer to take pictures," I instructed Tippy. "And make sure to put down evidence markers."

He nodded and signaled to one of the techs.

"Have we got an ID?"

"None," Tippy said. "Found him just like this."

"Are you sure it's a man?" I asked. The body was on its side, skinless face pressed to the ground and hips angled down at the floor.

"Pretty sure, but it's hard to tell with the way the corpse is laid out. I'll be able to say one way or the other once we move the body."

"Time of death?"

"That's going to be a lot harder," he said. "Normally I would take the temperature of the liver, but without skin the body will cool faster."

"Is there any way to know how long this body has been here?"

Tippy bobbed his head up and down, squishing his double chins like a pair of fleshy bellows. "I've got samples of the blood and intestine which I can use to measure bacterial growth and get an approximate time of death, but that requires me to get all this back to the lab."

"We'll need that information as soon as possible," Mackenzie told him.

"Anything for the FBI," Tippy said and made a mark on his clipboard. He gave me a look and I just grinned.

"The FBI hasn't got jurisdiction here."

I looked up.

The voice belonged to Upton and he was flanked by his detectives. I knew this would be a problem and was wondering when Upton would choose to make a scene. He stood with his fists propped on his hips and said, "This is an NYPD case and my precinct has jurisdiction. If we need any federal help, we'll be sure to let you know."

When your only knowledge of police procedure comes from television, you might think feds can take over a case whenever they want, but there are specific rules in place that dictate when the FBI can intervene in a case. More often than not, when the FBI gets involved it's because the police called them in. When that happens everything is copasetic. Unfortunately, when the FBI comes sniffing around a case where they aren't wanted, sparks fly.

Mackenzie was busy inspecting a grimy black smudge on the floor that might have been a boot print, or just dust and dirt collected over years. She said, "I'm not taking the case away from you, lieutenant. I am simply conducting a parallel investigation. I will of course share any evidence with your detectives."

"Parallel investigation my foot," Upton said.

Mackenzie frowned at the turn of phrase.

Upton said, "My guys are perfectly capable of closing this case."

"I'm sure they are," Mackenzie said. "Speaking of which, are all of your officers accounted for?"

"What the hell are you talking about?" Upton said.

Mackenzie turned her attention to the body. "I believe our victim is a law enforcement officer."

6

I t was like someone had dropped a bomb into the conversation. The mood in the tunnel instantly changed. The techs stopped their work. The pair of homicide detectives stared open mouthed and Upton scowled at Mackenzie like she had just suggested we all eat slug salad for lunch. There was a long moment of stunned silence, then Tippy Lewis said, "What makes you think that?"

Mackenzie pointed to the black smudge she had been studying. "This print matches the tread of boots issued to NYPD patrol officers. A man's size ten and a half, unless I'm mistaken. If you look closely you can see the distinct toe pattern."

I shifted my weight and put my nose less than an inch from the smudge. By the glow of Mackenzie's cellphone flashlight, I could just make out the pattern. She was right. It was the same boot I had been issued when I joined the department. Every NYPD officer gets two pairs. Some beat cops choose to buy different footwear, something better suited to their feet, but the boots issued by the

NYPD are pretty comfortable and last darn near forever. I still had mine. I said, "I'll be damned. Those *are* patrol boots."

Upton scrubbed his face with his hand. "Those prints could have been here for ages."

"Unlikely," Mackenzie said. "These tunnels flood when it rains. You can see the tide mark on the wall about two inches from the floor. And it rained just three nights ago. Whoever left this print was here in the last two days and there are small flecks of blood inside the print. This was made after the last rainfall and before the murder, meaning there is a very strong probability it belongs either to the killer or the victim."

Upton cursed under his breath, pulled out his radio and mashed the talk button. "Dispatch, this is command unit five-four, Lieutenant Upton. I need a situation on all our officers, pronto. And I mean everybody. Even our off-duty officers. If they're asleep, wake them up. I want to know where everybody is."

Fifteen minutes later we had the location of every cop in the department except two. Both were on vacation. One was on a commercial fishing trip in the Florida Keys soaking up beer and sunshine. The other was at a funeral in Nebraska.

I took Mackenzie aside and dropped my voice. "Looks like everybody is accounted for. You sure about this theory?"

Her eyelids fluttered up and down in quick time. "I'm certain those were left by NYPD issue footwear."

"A beat cop might have chased a suspect through here."

She nodded. "That's a possibility."

I sighed. "Well you just scared the hell out of everyone for no reason."

"Why would you be scared?"

"Because I thought a cop had been killed."

"And that scares you?"

I held my temper in check. "It doesn't so much scare me as upset me."

Her head cocked to one side. "Why?"

"Why? Because it's a terrible thing when a cop gets killed."

"Isn't it a terrible thing when anyone is killed?"

"Yes," I admitted. My anger was draining away as I remembered the autism and the analytical way Mackenzie viewed the situation. I said, "But cops take it personally when one of their own is killed."

"Why?"

I breathed through clenched teeth. "I can't explain why. Because we do. Okay?"

She thought about that for a moment and then said, "That doesn't make sense, but okay."

"Just do me a favor," I said. "Don't suggest any more cops are dead unless we know for sure."

"Okay," she said and returned her attention to the crime scene.

I waved Upton aside and spoke in a 'just between friends' tone. "Look, Lieutenant, we don't want to step on your toes here and I can promise you, Mackenzie isn't looking to take credit. She's just interested in the case, that's all. She'll share any evidence she finds."

"You're damn right she will," Upton told me. "I could make a stink, Cole."

By that Upton was telling me he could go up the chain of command and let the police commissioner know the FBI was snooping around his case without cause. It probably wouldn't be enough to get Mackenzie removed from the investigation—technically there was nothing stopping her from running a concurrent case—but it would certainly make my job harder.

"You won't have to," I promised. "I'll make sure Mackenzie plays nice."

"You'd better." Upton jabbed a finger in my chest. "I heard about you, Cole. You just got your gold shield back. I might not be able to do anything about your FBI buddy, but I can make sure you spend the rest of your career with the NYPD walking a beat."

I held up both hands in surrender. "We're just part of the team."

Upton gave me a hard look before turning and walking away. He summoned his two homicide detectives with a jerk of his head and spoke in whispers. I didn't have to hear what he was saying. His lead detectives would be keeping tabs on Mackenzie and me.

I caught Tippy Lewis's eye.

He waddled over, making scribbles on his clipboard and wheezing with every step. "What's up, Cole?"

"What can you tell me about Upton's homicide boys?"

He shook his head. "Don't involve me in inter-office politics, Mike."

"I'm not asking you to get involved," I said. "Just tell me what you know about them."

He frowned. "Names are Pottinger and Boone. They're capable detectives, but they aren't very creative. By the book kind of guys. In other words, the exact opposite of you."

I pointed to the candy bar in his top pocket. "I owe you a Twix."

"Make it a Baby Ruth."

"Deal," I said. "Who found the body?"

"Neighborhood girl," Tippy told me. "Works at one of the local eateries."

"Any good?" I asked.

Tippy Lewis had a reputation for knowing all the best restaurants in the city.

He shrugged. "Not bad. Try the dim sum."

I nodded. "Where?"

"At the dumpling shop," he said, as if that should be obvious.

"I meant where is the girl?"

"Oh." He waved his clipboard. "Sitting with one of the uniforms. Go down that way until you come to an intersection with a big low-hanging pipe. It's hot so don't touch it. Take a left-hand turn. There's a large room there."

I tipped him a two-finger salute and collected Mackenzie. She was on her hands and knees, crawling along the floor with her flashlight. I crouched down and whispered, "Let's interview the kid who found the body before Pottinger and Boone."

"Who are Pottinger and Boone?" she asked without looking up from her search. Her palms were dirty and the knees of her trousers were covered with a light coat of concrete dust.

"The homicide detectives."

She considered that a moment and then nodded. "Very well. I think I've seen all there is to see here."

"I've seen more than I ever wanted to see."

We made our way along the tunnel to the intersection with the big steam pipe. I could feel heat radiating from it as I ducked under. We found the local girl shooting dice with a uniformed officer. She pumped a fist in the air as we rounded the corner and said, "Pay up, sucka!"

7

The officer peeled a ten-dollar bill from a roll. The girl collected her winnings with a grin. She was fifteen or sixteen and looked younger. She wore a faded green military surplus jacket and ragged denims. Jet black hair poked out from under a Yankees ball cap. Without close inspection, she might pass for a boy. Probably intentional. Chinatown can be a rough neighborhood.

The uniform had his back to us and said, "Double or nothing?"

"You're on."

I cleared my throat. "Gambling on duty, officer?"

He straightened up and his eyes got wide.

I turned to Mackenzie. "I'm pretty sure that's against NYPD regulations. Isn't it?"

"Section seven-thirteen," she said. "NYPD officers are not permitted to engage in gambling, off-track betting, or other wage-based games while in uniform or in the commission of their daily duties."

"What's the penalty?"

Mackenzie said, "Depending on the severity of the offence, the imposed penalty can be thirty days suspension without pay and an official reprimand, to being relieved of duty, at the discretion of the commanding officer."

The color drained from the patrolman's face. He rubbed his hands together and said, "I was just... We were..."

"Community relations?" I supplied.

"Yeah," he said, latching onto my excuse. "That's right, sir. Just engaged in a little community relations."

"Your secret's safe with me," I told him. "Take a beat and get yourself a cup of coffee while we have a word with the girl."

"Yes, sir." He hurried off in search of a way out of the underground labyrinth. Good thing, too. It saved me having to show him my badge. He'd want to know why a cop from the nineteenth was poking around a body in Chinatown.

I waited until he was out of earshot before speaking to the girl. "Néih hóu. Sik jor fahn mei ah?"

The literal translation is; *Hello. Have you eaten lately?* In a country the size of China, where most people live on rice, asking if someone has eaten is a polite way of asking after their health and well-being. But there's a catch. If they say no, you might be expected to buy them a meal.

Her eyebrows went up. "Néih sīk-m̀h-sīk góng guǎng dōng huà?" *You speak Cantonese?*

I held up my thumb and forefinger an inch apart. "Wǒ shèng xì shi jiǎng shǎo shǎo guǎng dōng huà." *I only speak a little Cantonese.*

Mackenzie looked just as surprised as the girl. She blinked and cocked her head to the side. "You speak Chinese?"

"A little," I told her. "I was assigned to the Fifth right out of the academy and my training officer was Chinese. He taught me enough to get by."

"You're pretty good," the girl said. "For a white devil."

I laughed. "Mind if we switch to English?"

She stuffed the crumpled ten in her pocket, folded her arms across her chest and shrugged.

"I'm Detective Cole. This is Special Investigator Jessica Mackenzie. She's with the FBI. Can we ask you a few questions?"

"I already told the other police officers everything I know."

I bit back a curse. Pottinger and Boone had spoken with her already. So much for beating them to the punch. I said, "Yeah, well, we've got a few follow-up questions."

"What's the FBI's interest?"

I turned to Mackenzie. "Why is the FBI interested?"

"The Federal Bureau of Investigation routinely investigates murder."

"Yes," I said. "But why this murder?"

Mackenzie frowned. "I'm not sure how to process that question."

Come to think of it, I had never found out how Mackenzie became involved in the first case we worked. She had simply shown up at the crime scene asking for an NYPD liaison and, because the murder was so far from ordinary, we had been more than happy to accept federal help. I'd never met her ranking officer and, from what I had seen, her coworkers in the FBI mostly avoided her. I briefly wondered where Mackenzie was getting her marching orders.

"Not important." I waved a hand in the air and turned back to the girl. "What's your name?"

"Xu Yin."

She had to spell that for me. I wasn't even going to try the Chinese characters and used pinyin instead. I only know a few hundred words in Cantonese. The number of characters I can read and write is even less. I said, "So what were you doing down here, Xu Yin?"

"I use the tunnels all the time." She cocked the ball cap back on her head so she could look up at me. "I do deliveries for my family's restaurant. The tunnels are a great way to get around the city. You don't have to worry about traffic down here."

"Isn't it dangerous?" I said. "It's dark down here. Who knows what might happen? You could fall and break a leg or something."

She grinned. "You sound just like my grandfather."

"He sounds like a smart man."

She said, "I know these tunnels like the back of my hand."

Mackenzie's face scrunched. "What does the back of your hand have to do with it?"

"It's an expression," I said. "It means she knows these tunnels very well."

Xu Yin studied Mackenzie with a curious expression.

"She doesn't do idioms," I explained. "Approximately what time did you find the body?"

"Must have been a little after eight."

Mackenzie said, "What kind of food does your family's restaurant serve?"

I turned to Mackenzie. "Does it matter?"

Xu Yin apparently felt the same. She said, "Chinese food." As if that should be obvious.

Mackenzie said, "Does the restaurant serve breakfast?"

Xu Yin stuck her fists on her narrow hips. "You know anyone who eats Chinese food for breakfast?"

"I assume Chinese people eat Chinese food for breakfast."

Xu Yin turned to me for help.

I said, "What's your point, Mackenzie?"

"Most Chinese food delivery doesn't start until well after ten," Mackenzie said. "Closer to noon in fact."

"Yeah, that's right," Xu Yin said. "We start lunch deliveries at eleven thirty."

"You said you use the tunnels to deliver food," Mackenzie continued. "But you found the body, in your words, a little after eight. You weren't delivering food. What were you doing down here?"

Mackenzie had a point. I turned to Xu Yin and waited for an answer.

She crossed her arms over her chest. "Picking something up for my móuhchàn."

"Móuhchàn means mother," I told Mackenzie as an aside. But I knew Xu Yin was lying.

Mackenzie said, "What were you picking up?"

"None of your business," Xu Yin said. "It doesn't have anything to do with that body back there."

I gave her the hard stare all cops perfect the first year on the job. "Come on, Xu Yin. We're detectives. We'll find out sooner or later."

"I don't see why it's important," she said in a small

voice. She was inspecting the dirty floor and I could tell her secret was about to spill.

"Out with it, Xu Yin. What were you doing down here so early in the morning? And on a school day, no less?"

She fetched a heavy sigh. "I was taking money to somebody."

Mackenzie started to ask, but I held up a hand to stop her. "By somebody you mean the Triads?"

She nodded.

Mackenzie spoke like she was reciting from a textbook; "The Triads are an organized criminal organization responsible for illegal activities, predominantly active in Chinatown. Sometimes called the Black Hand."

"Yeah," Xu Yin said in the way all teenage girls do when they're copping attitude.

"The Triads are leaning on your family restaurant?" I asked.

"Of course."

"What does it mean to lean on?" Mackenzie asked.

"It means the Triads demand protection money from them."

"That's what they call an extortion racket," Mackenzie said. "Extortion is illegal. Have you notified the police?"

Xu Yin stared at her, like Mackenzie had suggested she use steelwool for toilet paper. "Like the police are going to do anything about it?"

Mackenzie nodded. "They are obligated to take action against any organization involved in extortion under New York City criminal code 252.1.7."

Xu Yin gave Mackenzie a blank expression.

I said, "Mackenzie's new in town."

She started to deny the accusation but I cut her off. "So the Triads are putting the squeeze on your móuhchàn and you were taking them a payment. Were you coming or going?"

"Going."

"And that's when you found the body?"

She nodded. "I came around the corner and found it there. I nearly puked."

"I can imagine," I said. "What did you do then?"

"I went back up to call the police," she said. "You can't get a cell signal down here."

"What about the money?"

"I delivered it while I was waiting for the police to show up," she said. "Then I led them down here. I been shooting dice with officer friendly for the last hour."

"How much did he lose?"

She stuffed her hands in her back pockets and scuffed the ground with a battle-worn sneaker. "A little over a hundred dollars."

I grinned. "How long you figure before he realizes you're using loaded dice?"

"You going to tell him?"

I shook my head.

Mackenzie said, "Did you see anyone else down here when you were going to deliver the money to the criminal organization?"

"No one," Xu Yin said. "Just me."

"What about sounds or smells?" Mackenzie asked. "Did you hear or smell anything unusual?"

"Smell?" Xu Yin's eyebrows walked halfway up her forehead. "I smelled rat poop."

"Seriously, kid," I said. "You might have been down here at the same time as the killer. Did you see or hear, or smell, anything out of the ordinary? Anything that might help us?"

"I saw a dead body and smelled blood," she told us. "But you won't find the killer. Even if you did, you can't catch him.

"Why not?" Mackenzie asked.

"How do you catch a ghost?"

8

I chuckled and shook my head. My training partner had been Chinese and believed in all manner of angry spirits. The Chinese seem to have a ghost for every day of the week. I said, "Are you telling us a ghost is the killer?"

"Not just any ghost," she said. "The ghost of Kwang Di."

"There's no such thing as ghosts."

Xu Yin crossed her arms. "Easy for you to say. You're not Chinese."

"Tell me about this ghost," Mackenzie said.

"Kwang Di was a magician in the first court of the Sun Emperor during the war of the three kingdoms. He could walk through walls and turn himself into mist."

"Like a vampire," I commented. "Our victim got skinned, not drained of blood."

"Kwang Di was no vampire," Xu Yin told us. "He was a sorcerer who could call down fire from the sky. He defeated the armies of the Shu empire by calling forth a flood from the mouth of a giant frog."

I laughed but Mackenzie was leaning forward, an eager expression on her face. She said, "What makes you think the ghost of Kwang Di is responsible for this murder?"

"Kwang Di was famous for skinning his enemies alive," Xu Yin said. "After a battle, the defeated army would be skinned by Kwang Di and his followers, one by one, and their skins turned into banners that Kwang Di's armies carried into battle."

I scratched an eyebrow. "Sounds like a swell bunch of guys."

Mackenzie was making furious notes on her phone and I said, "You're not taking this seriously, are you?"

She ignored me and asked, "How did Kwang Di die?"

"He was snaked by the emperor of the Yu kingdom and skinned alive, just like his victims. Before he died, Kwang Di promised to return from the grave and exact vengeance on the ancestors of those who had betrayed him in life."

I laughed. "So you think our victim is the ancestor of the Chinese emperor?"

"He must be."

"Now I've heard it all."

"Not by a long shot," Xu Yin said. "Kwang Di promised to exact his revenge until the streets ran red with blood. He claimed that when he returned, the blood of his victims would fill the vats of the nine hells."

"Then you think there will be more killings?"

Xu Yin looked confused. She said, "There already has been. Old Mei Tsu was killed two days ago by the ghost. And I know for a fact she was related to the emperor of Yu. She could trace her ancestry all the way back to the first empire."

"Skinned?" I asked.

Xu Yin's head bobbed up and down.

My eyebrows went up. I turned to Mackenzie for clarification. "You know about this?"

"Of course," she said, and to Xu Yin, "What else can you tell me about the Ghost of Kwang Di?"

"He's invisible and his eyes glow like green fire."

"If he's invisible," I asked, "how can you see his eyes?"

Xu Yin shrugged. "How should I know? He's a ghost. It doesn't have to make sense."

I cocked a thumb over my shoulder. "A ghost didn't skin that body back there. A person did. And we're going to find them. Isn't that right, Mackenzie?"

"I'll follow the evidence where it leads."

I threw my hands up.

Mackenzie said, "Why would the ghost of Kwang Di choose now to take his revenge?"

"Are you hearing yourself?" I said, but I was mostly excluded from the conversation at this point.

Xu Yin said, "This is the year of the Ox." As if that explained everything.

"I'm not sure I understand," Mackenzie said.

"I'm *sure* I don't understand," I added.

Xu Yin said, "Kwang Di was betrayed in 222 AD, during the year of the Ox."

"Oh, well, case closed," I muttered.

"That does seem compelling." Mackenzie tucked a loose strand of chestnut locks behind one ear. "Does anyone else in Chinatown share your convictions?"

"Everyone," Xu Yin told us.

I said, "I'll have the uniformed officers canvas the neighborhood for glowing green eyes."

"Do you have any familial connections to the emperor of the Yu kingdom?" Mackenzie asked.

"Not sure," Xu Yin admitted. "My family history is a little muddled. We lost most of our family records during the communist revolution when my grandfather fled to New York."

"Fascinating," Mackenzie said.

"Someone should write a book," I commented under my breath.

"I'd like to speak with your family if I may," Mackenzie said.

"You won't hassle móuhchàn about the payments to the Triads, will you?"

"Not if you don't want me to," Mackenzie said. "I'm only interested in the murder. Though I still think you should report these Triads to the local police."

I said, "Can you help us find our way out of here?"

"Of course," she said. "I know these tunnels like the back of my hand. I can get you anywhere in Chinatown. Follow me."

9

Ten minutes later we were back on the street. We emerged into the foul-smelling alley behind the Happy Time Dumpling. A phalanx of reporters had staked out the corner, thrusting their microphones at uniformed officers and crime scene techs as they came and went, demanding statements. We were far enough away that we went unnoticed.

It had taken decidedly longer to go down than it did to come up. When I asked Xu Yin about this, she told me again that she knew the tunnels like the back of her hand. She had tried to show the detectives from the Fifth a faster way, but the troop of crime scene techs kept getting lost and Xu Yin eventually had taken them by a longer, but less twisting, route to the body.

She led us through the back door of her family's restaurant into a kitchen thick with steam. Sweat instantly soaked through my shirt. It had to be ninety degrees in the narrow kitchen. Despite the uncomfortable heat, the unmistakable aroma of chicken fried rice coalesced around me and my stomach told me it was time for lunch.

Mackenzie had an altogether different reaction. Her arms clamped down against her sides and her nose wrinkled. Her brow twisted into a curious shape. I could tell she was fighting the urge to run. She looked like a cat in a room full of rocking chairs, searching for a way out.

I huddled close and dropped my voice. "You gonna be okay?"

She nodded, but it was a creaky, up and down motion that resembled a robot doing its best to copy human emotion.

An old Chinese woman in a sweat-stained silk shirt with little gold dragons embroidered on the sleeve was stirring a large wok and hollered. "*Ayeeyah!* Finally you're back. We've got orders." She spoke Cantonese. I only caught bits and pieces, but understood enough. Her sharp eyes flicked to me and Mackenzie. "Why did you bring the white devils here? They can't solve a murder from our dumpling shop! Tell them to go away."

"Careful mama," Xu Yin said. "The green-eyed devil speaks a little of our language."

I smiled at her, a big toothy American grin.

She flapped a dingy dish rag in my direction. "What you know, pale eyes? You speak Cantonese?"

"You've raised a respectable daughter," I said as proof.

"Ayeeyah!" the mother gasped and turned to the chef, Xu Yin's older brother. He was too busy chopping leeks to participate in the conversation. "Be careful around this one. He likes to pat the horse's rear end."

Xu Yin started to translate for me. "It means..."

"It means I'm only flattering her," I said.

Xu Yin gave me a sidelong glance and nodded. "You do speak a little of our language."

"Just enough to get myself in trouble," I told her.

Mackenzie forced us all back into English. "I'd like to ask you some questions about Kwang Di."

The mother's mouth dropped open. "What you know about Kwang Di?" She looked at her daughter. "What silly stories have you been telling?"

"I tell them the truth, mama. Everyone knows Kwang Di killed those people."

"*Pah!*" The mother flapped her dishrag and switched back to Cantonese. "They don't understand our culture. They'll never believe a ghost killed those people. They only believe what their pale eyes can see. *Ayeeyah!* It's bad enough you bring them here. Now you tell them about Kwang Di?" She clicked her tongue and shook her head. "Stupid, stupid child!"

I did my best to translate for Mackenzie but Xu Yin had to fill in some gaps for me.

The mother flapped her dishrag again and said, "No questions. No speakee English. Go away."

"Let the white woman ask her questions." An ancient Chinese man in a dirt-stained undershirt and black coolie slacks had hobbled into the kitchen, leaning heavily on a rattan cane. His head was perfectly bald. Light from the overhead fluorescents bounced off his scalp. His face was a topological map and his cataracts were so thick his eyes were nearly white. He waved the cane at Mackenzie. "This one sees with more than her eyes."

"*Ayeeyah*! Father, you know better than to talk to the police."

I turned to Xu Yin and asked, "Your grandfather?"

She nodded.

Grandfather waved his rattan cane at Mackenzie. "This one not police. She is true seeker."

Mackenzie was doing her best to tolerate the heavy, cloying steam and the constant *whack-whack-whack* of brother's butcher knife against the cutting board. Grandfather waved for her to follow. "Come with me, daughter. I have much that might interest you."

"Thank you," Mackenzie said and followed the old man out of the kitchen into the seating area where it was quieter.

Xu Yin's mother watched them go and shook her head. Then she grabbed a sack full of takeout from a counter and pushed it into Xu Yin's arms. "Don't just stand there! You want us to go broke? We have deliveries, stupid child! Hurry! Hurry!"

Xu Yin disappeared out the backdoor in a flash.

"You should go easy on her," I said. "She's a smart kid."

"Pah! She's lazy, like her brother. They try to drive me out of business."

Brother went on chopping onions without looking up.

"Triads are putting you out of business," I said. "Not your kids."

10

Momma Lo went perfectly still, like a poisonous snake had just slithered over her toes. Brother stopped chopping onions. A heavy silence settled over the small kitchen. In a quiet voice she said, "What you know about it, white devil?"

I shrugged out of my coat and palmed sweat from my forehead. "I know that until the people of this neighborhood band together and stand up to the Triads, they're going to bleed you dry."

Brother turned with the butcher knife clutched tight in one hand. His face was cut from stone. His eyes narrowed. For a moment, I thought he was going to come at me. My hand strayed toward my gun, but brother relaxed and I let my hand fall back to my side. His beef wasn't with me, and I knew that. It was with outsiders in general. The Chinese are a secretive people. They don't like outsiders interfering in Chinese affairs. Brother's reaction was an instinctive one. He exhaled, turned back to his onions, and brought the cleaver down with more force than necessary.

Thock!

I angled myself so I could watch his movements from the corner of my eye while talking to Momma Lo. "Look, I know the Triads are leaning on you for protection money. Maybe that body in the tunnels is another business owner, *heya*? Maybe someone decided they weren't going to pay and the Triads made an example of them?"

Brother muttered something under his breath in a regional dialect, a language all its own which I had no hope of understanding. Mandarin and Cantonese aren't the only languages spoken in China. The Chinese have hundreds of regional dialects which are all but impenetrable to outsiders.

Momma Lo said, "What do you care, *kwai lo*?"

"Believe it or not, I care," I told her, ignoring the insult. "This was my first beat. I know what the Triads are capable of. I know they soak up all your profits and leave you scraping to get by. Why not stand up to them?"

She wagged a finger under my nose like I was a naughty school boy. "You don't stand up to *Tai Pan*. You pay. Or you die."

"Then I'm right about the body," I said. "Is it someone who went against the Triads?"

She sniffed and shrugged. "Maybe."

"Any idea who?" I asked.

"None."

Even if she knew she wouldn't tell me and I'd find out sooner or later. No sense pushing her for an ID that I'd get in the next day or two from Tippy's autopsy. I said, "You mentioned a *Tai Pan*. Who is this *Tai Pan*? What's it mean?"

Brother said, "*Tai Pan* means supreme leader."

Momma Lo barked at him and he went back to work.

"Supreme leader?" I said. "Of the Triads?"

"You know too much already." She waved her dishrag. "You should go now, *kwai lo.*"

"Alright," I said. "I'll go, but take my card. If you think of anything, or you decide you want to make a stand against the Triads, give me a call."

I produced one of my department-issue cards and passed it over. She took it in both hands and gave a slight bow, a sign of respect. It would go in the garbage as soon as I was gone. I tipped my head and pushed through the beaded curtain into the seating area where Mackenzie was deep in conversation with grandpa Lo.

He was pointing to a painted mural on the wall, but his milky eyes were turned up to the ceiling. "That Shang Guo Chew, rightful emperor of the Qing empire who come to America in 1852 to avoid the Taiping rebellion. He die right here in Chinatown and was buried along with all his wealth. No one ever find his tomb, though many people try."

11

"A fascinating bit of history." I planted myself in front of the mural and pretended to study it for a second or two. The Chinse have long memories and they'll bore you to tears with tales of their ancestors. I knew from experience. When I had paused long enough to be polite, I shifted to Mackenzie and asked, "Learn anything?"

"Yes," she said, head bobbing up and down vigorously. "Shang Guo Chew is really quite interesting. He fled to America to avoid his enemies during the Taiping rebellion. It must have been a difficult adjustment for him, coming to America."

"Not that," I said. "Did you learn anything about our case?"

"Oh," she said. "Yes. Mr. Lo is intimately familiar with the history of the sorcerer Kwang Di as well. It seems most of the residents of Chinatown truly believe the ghost of the sorcerer is responsible for the killings. There have been a number of sightings as well."

I rubbed my eyes with thumb and forefinger. "Mackenzie, a two-thousand-year-old sorcerer did not come back from the grave to skin the local inhabitants of Chinatown."

She blinked. "How do you know?"

"Because I don't believe in ghosts," I said, and then to Mr. Lo. "No offense, Grandfather."

He hitched up one boney shoulder. "None taken."

"Why did you call him grandfather?" Mackenzie asked. "You're not related and he's not your grandfather."

"It's a term of respect in the Chinese community."

Mackenzie nodded and then said, "Just because you don't believe in ghosts, doesn't mean they aren't real. Mr. Lo certainly believes in spirits."

"And I appreciate and respect Mr. Lo's customs and culture," I said, walking the politically correct tightrope all cops are forced to balance if they want to retire with pay. "But I don't think we have any jurisdiction in the spirit world and I'm positive our superiors are going to want a more corporeal suspect. I can't go back to DeSilva and tell him we think a two-thousand-year-old ghost is skinning people in Chinatown."

"Why not?" both Mackenzie and Grandpa Lo said at the same time.

"Because I don't want to spend the next six months in a rubber room."

Mackenzie considered that a moment and then said, "The fact remains, there's more than enough evidence to support the idea of life after death and that the soul can continue on after the body has ceased functioning."

"Such as?"

"The first law of thermodynamics," Mackenzie said. "Energy cannot be created or destroyed, but merely changes forms. What happens to our body's energy when we die? It must go somewhere? What new form does it take?"

I scrubbed my face with both hands. "I'm here to solve a murder and ancient Chinese ghosts are way down on my suspect list. I think it's far more likely the local Triads are responsible."

Mr. Lo tensed and I felt the change. It was subtle, but evident. His lips narrowed and the wrinkled skin around his eyes pulled tight.

I dropped my voice and tried to sound sympathetic. "Want to tell me about the Triads, Mr. Lo?"

"What's to tell?" He shrugged. "The Triads take all of our profits and leave us fighting for scraps. Is always the same. My father start this restaurant because he want me to go to school, but no money for school with Triads. I work here instead and hope that my daughter can go to school. But no school for her either. I keep working and think maybe granddaughter Xu Yin go to school." He sighed and shook his head. "Triads take and they take. Now a big developer wants to buy the land and turn the neighborhood into high rise apartments. Soon, I have to sell shop and move out. Then what will become of Xu Yin? No college. No restaurant. I fear for her when I am gone."

"You said someone is trying to buy you out?" Mackenzie asked. "Who?"

"Big kwai lo McNab." He reached into his pocket, drawing out a folded brochure which he passed to me.

The advertisement was for a new development by McNab Properties. It showed a series of ultra-modern high rises. The crown jewel of the proposed development was a sleek shopping center which stood on the very same corner where the Happy Time Dumpling now stood.

I sucked my teeth and handed the brochure back. I had heard about Connor McNab's plans to revitalize Chinatown. Those plans mostly consisted of McNab holdings buying up the properties, razing the neighborhood and putting up expensive apartment buildings. It would drive most of the residents of Chinatown out and bring in a flood of hip young designers and artists who wanted to be able to tell their hip young friends that they lived in Chinatown. The villages was no longer the place to be. Chinatown was quickly becoming the hot spot for young up and comers.

"Conner McNab's trying to buy you out?" I said. "How much is he offering?"

"Not enough," Grandpa Lo told us. "But the other tenants say they will sell. What can I do? Between kwai lo McNab and the Triads, I must sell eventually."

Xu Yin's mother cleared her throat, loudly. I turned to find her standing in the doorway to the kitchen, a sour expression on her face. She was looking over my shoulder. I followed her gaze.

A trio of young Chinese men filed through the front door. The bell jingled. They stood watching us with stony expressions. One wore mirrored aviators. Another had fingerless gloves with shiny spikes on the knuckles. The third wore a sharkskin blazer over a punk rock shirt with Chinese characters that roughly translated; FEAR IS FOR THE WEAK. But I may have been reading it wrong. I read Chinese at a second grade level.

Grandpa Lo said, "I already tell you, kwai lo, we have nothing to say. Now to please leave."

"Yeah, alright," I said. "We'll go. Thanks for nothing."

"But..." Mackenzie started to say.

I caught hold of her elbow and steered her toward the door.

"I have more questions," she told me.

"You aren't going to get any answers," I said under my breath.

The hood with the studded gloves smacked a fist into his open palm as we passed. I gave him my best cop stare and we filed through the door onto the street. He didn't even blink, just watched us go with a dead pan look in his eyes.

12

After the stifling heat of the dumpling shop, the wet November air was a shock to my system. Cold wrapped me in an icy embrace, chilling the sweat into a sticky shell. I shrugged back into my overcoat and shoved my hands down into the pockets.

A mob of reporters were still camped on the corner. Crime scene techs were bringing up the body. Camera flashes shuttered, strobing the tableau in bright white bursts. The images would be all over the evening edition. Most of the stories would be focused on the rising tide of gang violence in Chinatown. Others would speculate on a serial killer. I was pretty certain none of the reports would run an op-ed on the ghost of Kwang Di.

Mackenzie had to adjust her ponytail. Her hair was a damp tangle from the steam. She shook out her chestnut locks, gathered them back up, and captured them with the simple black hair tie, then asked, "What happened?"

"You talking about the three hoods?"

"Hoods?"

"Bad guys," I clarified. "Gangbangers, skells."

She nodded. "Mr. Lo's energy changed as soon as they walked in."

"They're Triad enforcers," I told her. "They're making sure no one talks to the cops."

We were on the sidewalk in front of the restaurant. The Mercury was parked two spaces up and the reporters were screaming at Pottinger and Boone for a statement.

"Have there been other killings?" one reporter called out.

"Is it gang related?" another said.

"Do you have any suspects?"

Pottinger and Boone answered with terse 'no comments'.

I couldn't help but grin. Not being hounded by reporters was a nice change of pace. Let Pottinger and Boone handle the press. It would allow me and Mackenzie to focus on the case. And despite what I had told Upton, I had every intention of taking credit for solving the murder. This was exactly the type of case I needed to secure my seat at the homicide table.

Mackenzie was peering through the window of the Happy Time Dumpling. The trio of hoods were staring back at us. Mackenzie said, "If they're criminals, we should go back and make certain they are not hurting Mr. Lo or his family."

"They're gang members," I told her. "They'll be criminals as soon as I see them commit a crime, which they aren't likely to do with all these cops around."

Her brows furrowed. "I wish there was something we could do. Mr. Lo is a nice man."

"Maybe there is."

"What?" she asked.

"Got any cash on you?"

She reached into her front pocket and brought out a crumpled wad of bills. I wasn't surprised to learn she keeps her money in a confused jumble. She asked, "How much do you need?"

"Give me fifty bucks."

She sorted through the wad until she found two twenties and a ten.

I flagged down a pair of uniformed officers who had been blocking the reporters from entering the crime scene. Now that the body was gone and the crime scene techs were packing up, the press had lost interest. They'd be headed back to their respective papers to write up stories.

I showed the patrolmen my gold shield. "You fellas hungry?"

"Yes, sir." Both patrolmen nodded.

I handed over the cash. "Lunch is on me, but you have to eat at this dumpling shop."

One of the officer's made a face and looked up at the sign featuring a racially insensitive depiction of a smiling Chinese boy with a bowl of noodles. "Why here?"

"Ours is not to reason why," I told him.

"Free food is good food," the other said and tugged his partner's sleeve.

I watched them go, then turned to Mackenzie and grinned.

"It won't take them long to eat lunch," Mackenzie said.

"No," I agreed. "But it will give old man Lo some breathing room and frustrate the Triads."

Mackenzie nodded but glanced back over her shoulder at the shop. I could tell she wanted to do something. She was frustrated. It was a feeling all cops experience when we know someone is a criminal but can't do anything about it. Her mouth worked side to side and then she shook her head and said, "We should go see the original crime scene."

"Fine with me," I said, "But I already know who did the killing."

"Who?"

"The three Triads we just met in old man Lo's dumpling shop."

"How do you know they did it?"

"They did it," I told her. "Three marks at the murder scene. Three of them. Triad. I guarantee our investigation will prove it."

Mackenzie led the way to a nondescript door set in the wall around the corner from the dumpling shop and leaned on a buzzer. "You don't think there is even a possibility that a ghost is responsible?"

"You do?" I asked, mocking derision evident in my voice.

"I won't know until I gather more evidence."

"What is it with you?" I asked. "Why are you always so quick to believe in the supernatural?"

Before she could answer, the superintendent came over the intercom. We told him we were police and here to look at the apartment. He buzzed us in but didn't bother to meet us. We were left to find our own way up to the fourth floor.

Yellow crime scene tape was still strung over the door and there was a notice tacked to the frame inside a clear plastic baggy that said this was an active crime scene, anyone caught entering illegally would be subject to prosecution. I tried the knob. The door was unlocked. It swung in on old hinges that made a loud scree which echoed along the hall. I lifted the tape for Mackenzie. She ducked under and I followed her into the tiny apartment.

A short hall led us into a cramped living room with a rocking chair in one corner and a Chinese rug with a large bloodstain which seeped off the edge of the carpet and onto the scuffed hardwood. The sharp odor of copper hung heavy in the air and a fly buzzed against a grimy windowpane.

I waved a hand in front of my face and went to the mantlepiece for a look at a collection of old sepia-toned photographs. They all showed a good looking young Chinese girl in silk dresses at various parties, surrounded by young men in expensive suits.

Mackenzie crouched at the edge of the bloodstain. "Just as I suspected."

"What did you find?"

"Have a look."

13

I crouched next to Mackenzie, catching a whiff of vanilla shampoo. She was pointing to a pair of divots in the hardwood spaced about twenty inches apart. The sagging old floor was so scuffed and battered, covered in decades of scrapes and gouges, that I never would have seen them if Mackenzie hadn't pointed them out. The marks were small round indents, like someone had jammed an icepick into the blonde wood. It might have been something, it might have been nothing, and I told Mackenzie as much.

"Every mark tells a story." She stretched out on her belly for a closer examination.

"Oh really?" I pointed to a long curving scrape on the floor near a lacquered chest of drawers. "What's the story with that one?"

Without even looking she said, "The chest of drawers was pulled away from the wall when the picture frame on top slipped down between the wall and the chest."

I took a closer look at the scrape. It did coincide nicely with the leg of the heavy wood chest. "How do you know the picture frame fell? The owner might have moved it for some other reason."

"There is a slight dent in the lower left corner of the frame and a small crack in the glass where it hit the floor. The damage to the frame is consistent with the type of damage you see when a picture slides down between the wall and a piece of furniture."

"I think you're making this stuff up." I picked up the frame. Beneath the glass was a rather crude depiction of an ancient Chinese village. Coolies carried large rice sacks suspended on sticks and the women covered their faces with traditional fans. It was gaudy; the type of thing you find in any souvenir shop in Chinatown. The owner obviously hadn't cared much for it. The picture was upside down in the frame. And Mackenzie was right. The bottom edge of the frame was deformed where it had landed on its corner. There was a tiny crack in the glass, visible only when you tipped the frame at just the right angle.

I said, "You've been here before."

"No," Mackenzie said, still stretched out on the floor. "This is my first time at this crime scene."

"How did you spot the crack in the glass?"

"How did you not?" she asked.

I put the frame back and the cheap cardboard stand folded in, nearly sending the shoddy depiction down between the crevice, but I caught it in time and put it right.

Mackenzie popped up onto her feet, went to the edge of the rug and started rolling the carpet. "Help me, please."

I took the other side and together we rolled up the rug until we had uncovered a third divot in the hardwood.

Mackenzie nodded to herself. "Just like the other crime scene."

"This proves it," I said.

She frowned. "What does it prove?"

"Triads," I said and motioned to the marks in the floor. "Two victims, both skinned, and at both crime scenes we find three marks in the floor. The Triads are leaving their calling card. If you look, the indentations make a triangle."

"It's possible," Mackenzie said.

"Possible?" I said. "They practically signed their names."

"I can think of a number of other explanations for those marks."

"Like what?"

"It's a mistake to develop theories before you have all the facts."

"Granted, but I still think the Triads are responsible," I said. "Speaking of facts, have you got a name or any relevant info on this victim?"

She went on studying the marks for several seconds, like she hadn't heard me.

I cleared my throat. "Earth to Mackenzie."

She gave a little shake of her head and looked up. "What?"

"Relevant info on our first vic," I asked. "Have you got any?"

"Of course." She reached into her coat, brought out her phone and started scrolling. "Her name was Chin Mei Tsu. She was eighty-two years old."

"Why would the Triads want to kill an old woman?"

"*If* the Triads are responsible," said Mackenzie. "I'm not convinced."

"What else you got on Chin Mei Tsu?"

"She was born here in Chinatown. Lived here all her life. She was married twice. Outlived both husbands. She has no employment history, but she was arrested twice on solicitation charges. She never served any time."

"She was a prostitute," I said, turning back to the photos on the mantle. It was all coming together now. Mei Tsu was a good looking girl in her youth. She had made her living on her back. Her work as a pro would have put her in contact with Triads. The gangs get a cut of all illegal activity here in Chinatown. Mei Tsu must have learned something that got her killed. But what could it be? What secret would an eighty-two year old woman discover that was worth killing for?

I spelled out my suspicions for Mackenzie but she shook her head and said, "It's a mistake to..."

"Start forming theories before you have all the facts," I finished for her. "I've got enough facts to point me directly at the Triads and I say that's where we start. Mrs. Lo let slip that a new boss had recently taken over and all the shop owners are scared stiff. Called the new boss Tai-Pan, which loosely translates supreme leader. I think this Tai-Pan character is sending a message, letting the shop owners know he rules with an iron fist and anyone who goes against him will end up dead. Skinned."

Mackenzie was making notes in her phone. "How do you spell that?"

"T-A-I-P-A-N," I said.

"Your Chinese is very good."

I didn't bother to tell Mackenzie that Mrs. Lo had told me what it means.

We spent another hour going over Chin Mei Tsu's apartment from top to bottom. There wasn't much else to find. She had a collection of photographs from her glory days and a bunch of jade knickknacks cluttering the shelves. Her only real possession was a television and a rocking chair. It seems Chin Mei Tsu had led a pretty lonely existence at the end of her life.

When we ducked back under the crime scene tape, I spotted a face across the hall, watching us through the crack of an open door. I nudged Mackenzie and pointed just as the door snapped shut. "We might have found a witness."

14

I crossed the hall and rapped my knuckles against the flimsy wood. When no one answered I tried again. The walls in this building were so thin the neighbors probably knew each other's bathroom routine, not to mention their bedroom habits. Which meant whatever had happened to Chin Mei Tsu, someone had heard something. You don't skin a human being without making some noise. Unless of course it really was a ghost. Then all bets were off. But I kept reminding myself that I don't believe in spooks.

My fist made a loud hollow boom against the wood. "NYPD. Just want to ask you a few questions, sir."

The silence stretched and I was about to knock again when the knob rattled. The door peeled open an inch, just enough for a small, middle-aged man with thick coke-bottle glasses to peer out. He tried the 'sorry, no English' routine. It was the whole reason I had made the effort to learn Chinese in the first place. When you work Chinatown, and all of your suspects are Chinese, the only way to get information is Cantonese, Mandarin,

Shanghainese, or any number of regional dialects. Fifth precinct spends a small fortune every year on translators.

Without missing a beat I told him, "That's okay. I speak a little Cantonese. We'd like to ask you a few questions if you have the time."

His eyes got big behind the coke-bottle glasses and his shoulders crept up, reminding me of a turtle.

Mackenzie held up her FBI credentials. "It will only take a moment." Then to me she said, "Can you translate that?"

"No need," I told her. "He speaks perfect English. Don't you, Uncle?"

The turtle explored his teeth with his tongue for a moment before ducking his head and opening the door.

"Why did you call him uncle?" Mackenzie asked.

"It's like grandfather for an older man," I explained. "It's just a term of respect."

The turtle waved one small hand at a teapot on a low table in front of a sofa. "Cha?"

"Ching."

We gathered around the coffee table. Mackenzie perched herself on the very edge of the sofa, back ramrod straight, hands twitching like live wires and her mouth pressed tight. Any time she sat down she looked like a five-year-old in desperate need of a toilet. Only when she was moving did she seem able to relax.

The turtle poured three cups. I took mine, held it a moment and breathed in the scent before taking a sip, bobbing my head up and down, and replacing the cup on the tabletop. I pronounced it very good in Chinese.

He smiled and spoke English. "Your Chinese is very good for a kwai lo."

I waved a hand in the air and went through the routine of denying any real skill. It was a play that I had performed hundreds of times. A few minutes later we got down to business.

Mackenzie said, "Did you know Ms. Chin Mei Tsu?"

He ducked his head. "Very nice older woman. Never bothered anybody. Never made a fuss. Very nice neighbor."

"How long have you been living here?" Mackenzie asked.

"Twenty-two years."

"Has she been your neighbor the whole time?"

"No," he told us. "Before the Chins moved in, the Wongs lived in that apartment. Very loud. Always fighting. I was happy when they moved out. Ms. Chin was very nice. Her husband was a good man as well."

"You knew the husband?" I asked.

He ducked his head and sipped from his tea before answering. "Yes. Chin Fong was a good man. He took good care of Mei Tsu. He died about eleven years ago."

"Did Chin Mei Tsu have many visitors?" Mackenzie asked. "Anyone who came to see her regularly?"

His face fell. "No. She was all alone. Poor woman. I used to go over there and play mahjong with her. Sometimes I would pick up groceries for her or help out when her toilet was clogged, but she was mostly alone. She would talk my ear off any time I was there. She was starting to lose it." He tapped his temple. "Going senile, you know. She'd talk about anything and everything for hours on end. Sometimes it was hard to get away, but I made an effort to check in on her at least once a week."

"Good of you," I said.

He shrugged and waved away the compliment.

Mackenzie asked, "Were you home two nights ago?"

"I was the one who found the body and called the police."

"Can you tell us what happened?"

A change came over the turtle. He wanted to climb deep down inside his shell and hide. He stared into his tea and his eyebrows bunched.

I said, "We just want to find out who killed Chin Mei Tsu and why."

A sad smile worked one side of his mouth. "How do you catch a ghost?"

15

The turtle was staring hard into the depths of his tea, but his eyes were looking into the past. A nervous tick jerked at the corners of his mouth. The expression on his face said he desperately wished he could unsee whatever it was he saw.

Mackenzie said, "You believe a ghost killed Chin Mei Tsu?"

The turtle nodded.

"The ghost of Kwang Di?" Mackenzie said.

Another nod.

"What makes you say that?"

He looked up at her. "I saw him with my own eyes."

"No offense," I said, "but were your eyes under the influence of any drugs or alcohol at the time?"

"You think I'm a crazy man?"

"I don't believe in ghosts," I told him.

"Up until two nights ago, neither did I." He waved a hand in the air. "I'm not some old-world Chinese mystic who believes the ghosts of my ancestors bring me good fortune, detective. I graduated from Syracuse with a degree in finance. I don't believe in the spirit world, but what I saw two nights ago..." He shook his head. "I can't explain it. And I haven't slept since."

The temperature suddenly seemed stifling hot and I wanted to get out of my coat. In fact, I wanted out of the apartment. All this talk of ghosts made the hairs at the back of my neck stand on end.

Mackenzie asked, "What did you see?"

"I was just getting ready for bed. It had been a long day and I was watching something on Netflix, I can't remember what it was." He chuckled. "Isn't that strange? I remember enjoying it, but now it's gone."

"Memory loss is a common occurrence in the aftermath of high-stress situations." Mackenzie nodded. "Please, go on."

"I heard something across the hall. At first I thought it was nothing, just Mei Tsu moving around, but then I heard a crash. I looked at the clock and realized it was well past her bedtime. She usually goes to sleep around nine. So I decided I'd better check on her." He picked up his teacup. His hands were shaking so bad hot liquid jumped around inside the cup, making tiny waves against the rim that sloshed over and trailed down the porcelain.

"Then what happened?" Mackenzie asked. Her thumbs were poised over her phone, furiously typing every word.

"When I got to my door, I could tell it was more than just Mei Tsu moving around in there."

"How did you know that?" I asked.

He made a helpless little face and shrugged. "I can't say how I knew. I just did. I opened my door and froze, overcome with a terrible sense of dread. I couldn't even explain if I tried. I was standing there, scared stiff, and I heard a loud thump across the hall and then something was being dragged over the floor. I wanted to do something but it was like my feet were frozen in place."

A weak laugh piped up his throat. "You always hear that expression but you can't understand until it happens to you."

"Been there," I told him, trying to be reassuring.

"I was so scared," he was saying. "I wanted to move but my legs wouldn't budge. I can't even explain what had me so scared. I just... I felt an evil presence coming from across the hall and it was all I could do to stand there holding onto the door. Then I heard it."

"What did you hear?" Mackenzie asked.

"This terrible ripping, tearing noise, like wallpaper being peeled from old wood."

"How long did that last?" Mackenzie wanted to know.

He gave a little shake. "I'm not sure. It seemed to last a terribly long time, but it couldn't have been more than a few minutes."

"Please try to be exact," Mackenzie said.

His shoulders went up. "Maybe five minutes."

She nodded and her thumbs flashed over the phone screen. "Then what happened."

"Then I saw him."

"You saw him?" I said. "You saw the ghost?"

The turtle's head went up and down and his eyes got big behind the thick glasses.

"You were standing in your doorframe," Mackenzie said, "the door open, facing Chin Mei Tsu's apartment?"

"That's right."

"And?" Mackenzie prompted.

"And I saw it," he said. "Everything got real quiet and I was just working up the courage to step out into the hall. I had started to think I must be imaging the whole thing, when her door opened."

I was on the very edge of the sofa now, leaning forward, my fingers laced tight together and my jaw clenched. My heart was doing a gentle tap-tap-tap on the inside of my chest. It was obvious he believed his story and, hearing him tell it, I was starting to believe too.

He said, "At first there was nothing, just a dark opening. Then a shadow detached itself from the darkness and I saw a pair of glowing eyes."

"If you saw the killer's eyes, you must have seen his face," I said.

He shook his head. "There was no face. Only a dark shroud, kind of like a deep hood surrounded by shadow. And it was cold. So cold. And those eyes flashed like jade fire."

Mackenzie's eyebrows had slow walked halfway up her forehead. She said, "What did you do then?"

"I didn't do anything," he said. "I was too scared to move. I tried to scream but nothing came out. I thought I was going to have a heart attack and die right then and there. I just stood and watched it go."

"Where did it go?" I asked.

"It sort of floated along the hall and vanished down the stairs." He put his teacup back on the table with a rattle and fetched a deep breath. "That's when I finally worked up the courage to step across the hall. The door was open and I saw

Mei Tsu's body laying there, without any skin, in a pool of blood. I don't know how long I stood there. Maybe a minute or two, just staring. Then I ran back over here for my phone and dialed the police."

He glanced up at me with a sheepish grin. "They didn't believe my story either. Think I'm just some crazy Chinese who believes in ghosts. Well, I saw what I saw."

His story had chilled me right to my bones. Clearly he believed he was telling the truth, and that went a long way to making me believe as well. But I wasn't about to admit that, so I didn't say anything at all.

Mackenzie still had her phone out and a slight scowl on her face. She asked, "How tall was the ghost?"

"What?" I said at the same time as our witness.

"How tall?"

The turtle stared, as if that was the craziest question he'd ever heard. He screwed up his face as he tried to think. "Um..."

"Taller than Detective Cole?" Mackenzie offered.

I stood up so he could get a better idea of my height.

He stood up as well and rubbed his mouth while he pondered the question. "Maybe a little shorter."

"Thicker or thinner?" Mackenzie asked.

"A little wider maybe."

Mackenzie said, "Could you make out any details at all?"

He shook his head. "My heart was racing so hard and my vision was swimming, almost like I was underwater. I was so scared I could barely credit my own eyes. I thought for a second I had gone insane. But then I saw the body and knew I had to call the police."

He raised both hands in a manner that said, 'what can you do?'. "The police thought I was a drunk Chinaman."

"What about smell?" Mackenzie asked. "Did you smell anything as the ghost passed you?"

He thought about that for a moment and then nodded. "You know, I did get a whiff of something rotten, like an open grave."

Mackenzie nodded to herself. "I'm going to leave my card. If you think of anything else, no matter how minor, please don't hesitate to call."

16

The turtle took Mackenzie's business card in both hands and gave a slight bow. I thanked him for the tea, followed her into the hall and dropped my voice to a whisper. "His story is pretty convincing."

"I doubt he's lying," Mackenzie said. She stopped in front of Chin Mei Tsu's door to examine the scuffed wood around the door frame, taking pictures with her phone of various scratches and scuffs, then proceeded along the hall toward the stairs, going slow.

"How do you catch a ghost?" I wondered aloud.

Mackenzie straightened up and cocked her head to one side. "No way of which I know."

"That leaves us with a bit of a problem."

"What do you mean?"

"It's our job to solve murders," I said. "If a ghost really did kill Chin Mei Tsu and the poor bastard in the tunnels, then we're going to have a tough time apprehending the killer."

"Our job is to solve murders," she said, "but we can only

apprehend human suspects. If it turns out a ghost killed those people, we'll have to file our report and leave it at that."

I snorted. "Are you telling me you're ready to turn in a report that says two people were killed in Chinatown by the ghost of an ancient Chinese sorcerer?"

"Yes."

"And you think your CO will be okay with that?"

Mackenzie frowned in confusion. "I have to report the truth. Whether or not he is okay with it is really beside the point."

I rolled my eyes. Mackenzie never worried about losing her job. Having a rich daddy helps. Her father was Alexander Mackenzie, of Mackenzie Industries; a multimillionaire with fingers in many pies. Why she spent her time working for the FBI was anybody's guess. If my father was loaded, I wouldn't be investigating homicides for the state of New York at a lousy eighty grand a year. I'd be sitting on the French Riviera. Mackenzie claimed she never took money from her father, but she owned a building in Queens that was well above a federal agent's paygrade, especially someone so young.

"Some of us don't have rich parents," I said. "We have to turn in results that make our commanding officers happy, and that means a flesh and blood suspect."

"I don't see what my father has to do with it." Mackenzie brushed a rebellious strand of chestnut tangle behind one ear. "He doesn't have any influence in the FBI."

"Rich people have influence everywhere," I told her. "Just by being rich."

"I earned my position in the FBI," she said and I could hear the hurt in her voice.

I put my hands up. "Okay, okay. I didn't mean to imply anything. I'm just saying my lieutenant is going to want something more substantial than Chinese ghosts. I can't tell DeSilva an ancient sorcerer is skinning people in Manhattan."

Mackenzie said, "Don't tell him anything yet. We haven't got enough to go on."

"We've got three marks at each murder scene which clearly implicates the Triads. I say we have a sit down with this *Tai-Pan* character."

"I believe it would be more beneficial to consult a reputable Chinese spiritualist," Mackenzie said.

I held up a hand. "We are *not* contacting any spiritualists. If it gets out that I'm consulting psychics to help with a murder case, I can kiss my career as a homicide detective goodbye."

Mackenzie was bent double, taking a picture of a smudge on the hardwood floor. Without looking up she said, "To kiss goodbye means to lose something, right?"

"Right," I said. "In this case, my livelihood. And I don't have rich parents."

We reached the end of the hall, found the door to the stairwell propped open, and the three hoods from Old Man Lo's dumpling shop blocking our path. I drew up short and my hand strayed toward the pistol on my hip. The guy in the sharkskin jacket eyed me with open disdain. I returned the sentiment.

They had us boxed in. It was three against two and I

knew from experience that Mackenzie didn't carry a gun, which made it three against one.

"Why did you stop?" Mackenzie asked.

I said, "I don't think they're going to let us by."

"We are duly sworn officers of the law in commission of a murder investigation," Mackenzie said. "To impede our progress could be considered thwarting an investigation, punishable by up to seven years in federal prison and a two-hundred and fifty-thousand dollar fine."

"I get the feeling these guys don't care."

The hood with the spiked leather gloves smacked a fist into an open palm.

I turned my right shoulder away from them, shielding my hand as it gripped my pistol, and spoke with more confidence than I felt. "All right guys, first one to make a move spends twelve months in Sing Sing for assaulting an officer, and I'll make sure the charges stick. Now why don't you clear out and let us by."

Sharkskin Jacket sneered at me.

Sweat formed large wet beads on my forehead. Three guys can quickly overwhelm one, even a guy with a gun. If they managed to tackle me and take my weapon away, it would be happy trails to Detective Mike Cole. I worked the fear into anger and opened my mouth to order them out of the way when the lights went out with a loud pop, plunging us into darkness.

17

Blackness descended like a funeral shroud. There were no regulation emergency lights in the stairwell and no windows in the hall. The darkness was complete. My pulse was a jackhammer in my own ears. I had my department-issue Glock out of the holster but nothing to shoot. I couldn't pull the trigger even if I wanted to. I couldn't see my own hand in front of my face. Walls don't necessarily stop bullets. If I fired in the dark, my shot might kill a resident. I felt, more than heard, Mackenzie beside me. She gave a sudden sharp intake of breath that sounded like a loud hiss in the dark. There was movement on the stairs—I could hear the hoods—but I couldn't make anything out. I started to backpedal, trying to put some space between us, so they couldn't overwhelm me.

An unearthly wail split the silence. It sounded like all the hounds of hell braying at once and made the small hairs on the back of my neck stand straight up. My skin crawled and my testicles tried to scramble back up into my belly. The ear-piercing shriek was followed by a heavy thud, like the entire building had just been hit by a falling dump truck. I felt the floor tremble beneath my feet. Dogs barked. Neighbors started to open their doors. Several had flashlights. Others had candles or lighters. Shadows stretched and groaned, twisting into fantastic shapes on the walls. Everyone wanted to know what had happened but no one had answers.

A moment later the lights snapped back on. I blinked and looked around. The stairwell was empty. The Triads were gone. I edged onto the landing and peered down through the steps, but the hoods were nowhere to be seen.

My arms and legs were covered in gooseflesh. My heart was knocking hard on the wall of my chest. It took two tries to holster my weapon. I said, "I'm starting to believe in ghosts."

Mackenzie was beside me, her shoulders drawn up and her fingers flicking against her corduroy slacks. Her face had bunched into a confused tangle. Her mouth twisted to one side. She said, "They left in a hurry."

"Can't blame them," I said. "You think that was the ghost of Kwang Di screaming a minute ago?"

Mackenzie considered the question. Really considered it. A normal person would have scoffed and said there's no such thing as ghosts. Hell, a few hours ago, I'd have said the same, but Mackenzie pondered the question with an open mind. "It's a possibility."

"Is there another possibility?"

"Several."

"I'd love to hear a few," I said with sincerity.

She took a moment to examine a rusting old iron radiator against the wall next to the stairs, then gave the heater a kick with her scuffed Converse. The unit let out a ghostly moan.

"That accounts for the screaming," I said. "But what about the lights and the loud thud?"

"The lights could have been a simple power outage," Mackenzie said. "And one of the residents might have turned over a bookshelf."

We were on the stairs now, making our way down. "I thought you were the ghost whisperer?"

She blinked in confusion.

"I thought you believe in ghosts?" I clarified.

"I never said that." She shook her head. "I only said I was willing to entertain the possibility."

"If that wasn't a ghost coming out of Chin Mei Tsu's apartment, then what did our witness see?" I asked. "And what scared away those Triad goons?"

We reached the front door and emerged into late autumn sunshine. A cold November wind put spots of color in Mackenzie's pale cheeks and turned her ponytail into a chestnut banner. She pointed. "That answers one of your questions."

I turned.

A news van had backed up and hit an electric pole, which had fallen and impacted the side of the building. The pole was now laying on the sidewalk, twisted and broken. There was a large impact crater in the side of the building and one of the black metal fire escapes hung at a drunken angle.

Some of the fear, which had crystalized in my belly, started to melt. I rolled my shoulders and reminded myself that I don't believe in spooks. Funny how quickly the dark can squeeze out science and reason. I said, "That's going to cost him."

"Cost who, what?" Mackenzie asked.

"Whoever was driving that van," I told her. "Or more likely his station will have to foot the bill."

"What does that mean?" she asked. "Foot the bill?"

I reminded myself not to use idioms around her and explained. "Foot the bill means to pay the bill."

Her cellphone came out and she made a note of that, along with all the other idioms she encountered. The list was full of things like:

Take one for the team = to do something unpleasant for the good of others.

Don't look the gift horse in the mouth = don't question a favor or free gift.

The cat's meow = something good.

There were others for which she had no definition. Things like:

Straight from the horse's mouth = ???

A cold day in hell = ???

Spit in the ocean = ???

I pointed to 'A cold day in hell' and said, "That one means it's never going to happen."

"Really?" Her brow knotted and she looked disappointed as she filled in the translation.

"Someone tell you that recently?"

She nodded. "My boss."

I winced, but didn't bother to ask. We had reached my car and I opened the door for her before circling the front bumper. Traffic was already stacking up because of the wrecked news van. Getting clear of the jam would be a pain. It didn't help that other news crews were gleefully filming the aftermath of the wreck. The pictures would be all over the evening editions. I said, "Where to?"

"Either the New York field office, or your precinct," Mackenzie said. "I need to do some research."

"Precinct house," I said.

The FBI's New York field office was closer, but I wanted to keep Mackenzie on my home turf. It took me three tries to start the Mercury and ten minutes to get us out of the tangle of police and news vans. We were headed north along Broadway when a call came over the radio. "All units, all units. Robbery in progress. Suspects are in possession of an armored vehicle, westbound on 23rd Street."

18

There was a burst of static and then other units started coming on the net to say they were inbound. I grabbed for the mic but Mackenzie laid hold of my forearm with both hands, a look of panic in her eyes. Her bottom lip was caught between her teeth. She said, "Don't respond."

My foot was already on the accelerator. The Mercury let out a growl and, driving with one hand, I maneuvered around the back of a Tesla. I said, "Come on, Mackenzie. They called all units. You know how it works."

She was shaking her head, her ponytail whipping back and forth. "There are ample police officers in Manhattan."

A flower delivery van honked, tried to muscle into the lane and I had to jerk the wheel. I said, "What's the New York law enforcement code have to say?"

She let go of my arm. "All active-duty law enforcement units not currently engaged in the intervention of an ongoing crime in progress are required to respond to an all unit call."

I thumbed the talk button. "Mackenzie and Cole, north-bound on Bowery, in pursuit."

I racked the mic and reached for the gumball.

"No sirens," Mackenzie said.

"Fine," I said as I cranked down the window and reached out to slap the gumball on the roof. "No sirens."

One of the hallmarks of autism, I had discovered, is sensitivity to certain sensory input. In Mackenzie's case, loud noises cause her to shut down completely. I learned this the hard way at a busy nightclub. We'd gone there to question a suspect and I found Mackenzie catatonic, curled up in a ball on the floor of the bathroom. I practically had to carry her out.

I switched on the light without the siren and weaved through traffic, listening to the chatter coming over the radio. Mackenzie had her knees drawn up to her chest and her arms wrapped around her legs, rocking back and forth, humming softly under her breath. I followed 4th onto Park Avenue and reached 23rd in time to see a Knight's Armored Courier go slaloming through the intersection.

The bank truck had to be doing sixty. The front end clipped a Prius and sent it spinning. Glass flew in all directions. Horns blared and brakes shrieked. People on the sidewalks had their phones out, taking video.

I cut the wheel, sent the mercury into a controlled slide, and rounded the corner with my stomach clenched.

The armored vehicle roared west on 23rd Street at breakneck speeds and I hammered down the accelerator in an effort to keep up. We screamed past the Flatiron building. The Mercury's engine growled and the tailpipe let out an earsplitting fart. Three police cruisers trailed behind me, lights flashing and sirens wailing. Mackenzie clapped her hands over her ears, closed her eyes tight, and hummed *Jingle Bell Rock*.

The driver of the armored truck smashed a Lexus out of his way. The sedan crashed into a parked SUV with a bang and the musical jingle of shattering glass.

One of the black and whites came over the radio. "Where the hell does this clown think he's going? He's headed straight for the water."

I gripped the wheel tight with my left and reached for the mic. "Who cares? We gotta stop him before he kills somebody."

Dispatch told us to cut the chatter.

The back doors of the armored truck flew open and a man in a ski mask leveled a shotgun at my windshield. I gulped and jerked the wheel. There was a deafening boom and the side window of a Taurus blew out. People on the sidewalk screamed and ran for cover. My heart was racing along to the pace of the Mercury's engine. Most cops never find themselves in a shootout. I personally had only been forced to draw my gun a handful of times. I'd certainly never dodged shotgun blasts during a high-speed pursuit through the heart of Manhattan.

Mackenzie was curled in a tight ball, shouting the lyrics to *Jingle Bell Rock* at the top of her lungs. One of the pursuit cars radioed to say we were under fire and dispatch informed us a helicopter was enroute.

The bank robber racked the shotgun and aimed another blast at the hood of my car. I swerved and buckshot skipped off the blacktop.

Mackenzie's rendition of *Jingle Bell Rock* reached a

fevered pitch. Her face was tight and bright red, and her hands were tiny fists beating at her legs in time with her singing.

Another robber appeared at the back of the armored truck with a large blue canvas duffle in his arms. He hefted the bag overhead and launched it. The duffle sailed through the air. I shouted a curse. The bag came down on the hood of the Mercury with a heavy thump that sent me into a skid. The duffle burst open and crisp new hundred-dollar bills exploded into the air like confetti, along with a neon blue dye pack.

19

B right blue ink burst against the hood, spraying the windshield of my Mercury. I stamped the brakes. Rubber screamed and the back end humped up in the air. Police cruisers shot past as we slid to a howling stop in the middle of 23rd Street and 8th Avenue.

Seconds later, dispatch ordered us to break off the chase. Brass now considered the pursuit too dangerous. They didn't want an innocent civilian hit by shotgun spray. I hammered a fist against the steering wheel and bit back a string of curses.

Mackenzie had her hands over her ears and her teeth clenched. Her face relaxed slowly once we had stopped moving and her hands dropped. She blinked like a woman coming awake after a deep sleep, unsure of where she was.

I threw open my door, stepped out and saw that I had managed to stop inches from the back of a parked BMW. In the street behind me, people were grabbing hundred-dollar bills floating around on the breeze. Cars had stopped and their drivers leapt out to join in the treasure hunt. I closed my eyes a moment, imagining the avalanche of paperwork in my future, and then braced myself for a look at the hood of my prized Mercury.

Day-glow blue painted the front in wild Jackson Pollock stripes and splashes. I groaned. "Look what those jerks did to my car."

Mackenzie leaned over from the passenger seat and said, "I told you to let someone else handle it."

"The hell I will." I reached back into the car for the radio. "I'm gonna nail those guys."

"Why are you so intent on catching a trio of bank robbers?"

"Because they broke the law," I said and figured that should be enough.

"We have our own case to work," Mackenzie pointed out.

"We can work both," I told her and then radioed dispatch to apprise them of the damage to my vehicle. I was told to stay put and wait for an investigating officer. I knew it would be an hour, maybe longer, so I pulled into an open spot and killed the engine.

"We might as well get some food," I told Mackenzie. "I'm starving."

"Dispatch said to wait for an investigating officer."

"That's going to be a while."

She twisted around for a look out the back window. "What about that? Shouldn't we do something about that?"

I cranked around in my seat. People were scooping up as much cash as they could carry and traffic had come to a complete standstill. A pair of large women with cornrows started a fist fight over an unbroken bundle. I said, "Like what? You want to get out and tell those people they have to give that money back?"

"It's not theirs."

"Tell that to them."

Mackenzie opened her door and climbed out. I sighed and stepped out to watch. The FBI agent went to a heavyset man in a chambray shirt and scuffed work boots, and she told him that legally he was not allowed to keep the money, that it was evidence in a criminal investigation. He just laughed, shook his head and went on stuffing hundreds into his pockets. Mackenzie went to another person, this one an elderly pensioner hobbling around on a cane, snatching bills from the hoods of parked cars. She waved her cane under Mackenzie's nose in a threatening manner before going back to hunting paper. I chuckled, crossed my arms over my chest and leaned against the side of the Mercury while Mackenzie went from person to person, explaining that they were committing a crime.

Ten minutes later, much to my surprise, a skinny punk rocker with a bright red mohawk and a nose piercing handed over his bundle of cash with a mumbled apology. Mackenzie made an accurate accounting, handed him one of her cards, and thanked him for being a cooperative citizen. A minute later the burly construction worker in the chambray shirt and work boots handed over his loot as well. Two more people came forward to give Mackenzie money. By that time the crowd had grown into an unruly mob. Word had gone out that there was a street full of hundred-dollar bills and police cruisers were closing off the area.

Mackenzie salvaged an old Taco Bell sack from a garbage can to use as a temporary evidence bag and kept a running total with a black marker. She'd managed to recover nearly seventy-thousand dollars by the time the uniformed officers got things under control.

"Love what you've done with your car, Cole."

I turned.

Lieutenant DeSilva was standing at the hood of the Mercury. He had white-blonde hair swept straight back from a high forehead, deep pockmarks from adolescent acne, and eyes the color of faded denim. He would make a good extra in a Hollywood movie about vampires. "You do this yourself or have it custom?"

"Har har," I said. "A perp tossed a sack of money out of the back of a stolen armored truck."

"Yeah," he said, nodding. "I heard. You're supposed to be investigating the body in Chinatown with your FBI girlfriend."

"She's not my girlfriend," I said. "And we are investigating the body. We just finished up at the crime scene when the call went out for all units."

"So you decided to take a Special Investigator with the FBI on a high-speed chase through the streets of Manhattan?"

"It was an all-unit call." I shrugged. "What could I do?"

"You can let the black and whites handle it."

"That's what Mackenzie said."

"You should've listened. You wouldn't have paint all over your personal vehicle. And why are driving your personal vehicle instead of a department cruiser?"

I explained about the mistimed engine and the smell.

DeSilva clicked his tongue and shook his head. "Still no

excuse. I'm not sure the city of New York is going to be able to reimburse you for this damage, Mike."

"Aw come on, Lieutenant!"

DeSilva shrugged. "Maybe if we had the bad guys in custody we could make the case for reimbursement, but since you let them get away..." He scraped at the paint on my windshield with a thumbnail and pulled a face. "That's not coming off easy."

FROM THE JOURNAL OF JESSICA MACKENZIE

I once again find myself working with detective Michael Cole on a most curious case. Unlike my last two assignments which were both entirely pedestrian and easily solved, this proves to be rather extraordinary. Perhaps even the proof I've been seeking, but we mustn't get ahead of ourselves. Two individuals have been found dead in Chinatown, with their skin removed, and local residents are quite convinced that the ghost of an ancient Chinese sorcerer is responsible. Fascinating to be certain.

Detective Cole did not seem particularly happy to see me, but perhaps that is because he was preoccupied by another case at the time, an entirely trivial matter which was quickly handled, though I have the feeling he was not at all pleased with my help. Then again, it could be he was irritated by something altogether unrelated, or I might have been 'reading' the situation wrong. NT (neurotypical) behavior is often entirely perplexing, unlike murder. Murder is logical in its own way. The reasons people kill are limited and predictable. Love, revenge, money, or to conceal another crime. Which brings me to the current case: Is it murder? Or mystical? Only time and evidence will tell.

20

Mackenzie and I worked late into the evening. She spent most of the time researching Chinese ghosts, of which there were legion, while I pulled all the jackets on bank and armored car robberies over the last two years. I had a stack of reports three inches thick. The gonks who trashed my car were in there somewhere and I was determined to find them. We called it quits some time after nine and I dropped Mackenzie off at her brownstone.

The next morning, I took the Mercury through a body shop in the hopes of getting the dye removed. I found out the windshield would need to be replaced. Until then, I was driving around Manhattan with my head hanging out the driver's side window like a dog on a car ride. My cheeks were windburned and my hair blown straight back by the time I arrived at the morgue.

Mackenzie was already there, dressed in a seafoam green lab coat and scratched safety goggles. She was helping Tippy Lewis with the cut. The heavyset medical examiner did not look happy about the arrangement. He grunted and wheezed as he moved around the skinless corpse, making notes on his clipboard.

The smell of formaldehyde and disinfectant smacked me in the nose and my shoes made small squeaking noises on the polished tiles. I snagged a smock and the best pair of safety goggles I could rummage from the bin, then shouldered up next to Mackenzie. She smelled like warm spiced pumpkin pie this morning, but the scent was mostly hidden beneath the sour reek of decomposition.

Tippy acknowledged my presence with a chin jut.

Mackenzie went on examining the corpse in minute detail, her nose less than an inch from the skinless muscles of the victim's throat, like she were searching for a vampire's mark.

I cleared my throat. "Morning Mackenzie."

She went on staring at the body like she hadn't heard me and just when I was starting to think she was ignoring me, she gave a little shake, glanced up and said, "Good morning, Detective Cole," before turning back to the body.

"Find anything interesting?" I asked.

"Other than a skinless corpse?" Tippy asked.

I grinned at the gallows humor.

"Your victim died from fright."

My eyebrows went up. "How's that?"

Tippy said, "He was dead before he was skinned."

"Thank God for that," I said.

Mackenzie stopped her inspection and turned to me.

I motioned at the corpse. "I'm not happy the guy is dead. Just happy that he wasn't alive when he got skinned. That would be a terrible way to go. He is a man, right?"

Tippy nodded. "Male, age fifty-three. He had a bad

ticker, probably why he died of fright before the killer started cutting."

"How was the skin removed?" I asked. "Any idea?"

"Whoever took the skin did a clean job," said Tippy. "They knew what they were doing. One cut right down the middle, then they peeled the skin off like peeling a banana."

"That's possible?"

Tippy bobbed his head up and down. His fleshy chins squished. "If you know where to cut."

"Think our killer is a doctor?" I asked. "Maybe a mortician or something?"

"Could be," Tippy admitted. "Could also be a hunter."

"A hunter?"

He nodded. "Hunters know how to hang up a deer or boar and take the skin off with just a few quick cuts."

"That narrows our list of suspects," I said. "There's plenty of game in upstate New York, but I'll bet there aren't many serious hunters in Chinatown."

Mackenzie said, "This could also be the work of a butcher. There are plenty of those in Chinatown."

I immediately thought of Xu Yin's brother and his skillful use of a butcher knife. I asked Tippy, "Could a butcher do this kind of work?"

His lips pursed and he looked down at the body. "Possible. Especially one who works with swine. Taking the skin off a pig is a lot like taking the skin off a human. We did a lot of practice on pigs in medical school."

"Glad we're finally looking at human suspects."

"You forget that he was scared to death," Mackenzie said.

I said, "Just because he was scared to death doesn't mean he was killed by a ghost."

"What could a grown man see that would scare him so badly?" Mackenzie asked.

"It was dark down there," I said. "Maybe he saw someone coming at him and didn't know what he was seeing."

"Perhaps," Mackenzie admitted.

I stuck my fists on my hips. "I thought we agreed the most likely suspects are the Triads? You're back on ghosts?"

Tippy questioned me with a look.

I waved away his inquiry.

Mackenzie said, "I'm going to follow the evidence. And all we know right now is that he died of fright before being skinned."

"Well," I said, "if he was killed by a ghost, it was a ghost with a corporeal body because he obviously knows how to use a knife."

"Assuming a ghost would need a knife to skin a body," Mackenzie said. "The sorcerer Kwang Di was rumored to take the skin off his enemies with a spell."

Tippy's mouth was hanging open now. He cleared his throat. "Sorcerer?"

I nodded. "One of the prevailing theories is that an ancient Chinese sorcerer has come back from the grave."

"I don't know about sorcerers or ghosts," Tippy said, "but whatever this guy saw must have scared him pretty bad to stop his ticker."

"Don't add fuel to the fire," I said, with a glance at Mackenzie who was bent over the corpse again. "You got an ID on this guy?"

"Oh," Tippy said, "almost forgot. Your partner was right. He was a badge."

"What?" I asked, stunned. "We checked all the unis and detectives in Chinatown. They're all accounted for."

"I said he *was* a cop," Tippy corrected. "He retired ten years ago. Been working private security since then. Name is Johnathan Chen."

The name hit me like a sledge hammer to the gut and the bottom dropped out of my world.

21

Mackenzie didn't notice anything was wrong at first. She went right on examining the body. Tippy did and he asked, "Hey, you okay, Mike?"

I felt myself nod. My hands and feet were distant memories. My body felt like a puppet. Someone else was pulling the strings. The room, the odors, the buzzing fluorescents, all receded into the background until I was floating inside a void. I must have walked over to a chair and sat down, because that's where I found myself, sitting in a hard plastic chair by the door, staring at the skinless corpse.

"Mike?" Tippy Lewis came over, put a hand on my shoulder and gave a squeeze. "Mike? You alright?"

I nodded but my words weren't working.

By now Mackenzie had realized something was wrong and she straightened up from her inspection, a worried frown creasing her pretty face. "Are you ill? The smell bothers some people."

I shook my head. "It's not the smell."

All the same, Tippy went to a cabinet for a handful of

smelling salts. He popped one open, waved it under my nose and the odor pulled me back from the void. I had a queasy feeling in my gut and my throat choked closed.

"What's up, Mike?" Tippy asked. "You need a doctor?"

I motioned at the corpse. "I know him."

"You know the victim?" Mackenzie's eyebrows crept up her forehead and she blinked. "How?"

"He was my training officer," I told her, "first year on the job. John taught me almost everything I know about being a cop. Taught me Cantonese as well."

John Chen was like an older brother. My first few years on the force, we'd been inseparable. He had taught me a whole lot more than just how to bust bad guys and speak the local dialect; he taught me about life. After a shift, we'd knock back a beer and then head to his place where his wife always had dinner waiting. John was a beat cop, through and through. He loved patrolling the streets, keeping people safe. It was his mission in life, until a bad ticker had forced him to retire. He had been there for me when I went through my divorce, he had believed in me even when I was popping pills, and he helped me get straightened out.

I sat in the hard plastic chair thinking of all those nights sitting around his dinner table talking sports and office politics in a mish-mash of Cantonese and English. Then I thought of his wife, Carol, and it was like someone had rammed an iron barb through my heart.

"I'm very sorry for your loss," Mackenzie said.

"This is horrible," Tippy said. "I'm real sorry, Mike. Let's get you out of here. You don't want to look at that."

He tried to take me by the elbow, to steer me out of the

room, but I brushed off his hand. "I'm alright. Has anyone notified next of kin?"

"Er..." Tippy said. "Not that I know of, but I think you should leave that to someone else."

"I'll do it," I heard myself saying. "Carol deserves to hear it from me."

22

Carol Chen lived on the third floor of a six-story walkup in Chinatown, less than three blocks from where John's body had been found. We were standing in the hall outside and I was staring hard at the green door. The paint was flecked in places, showing an older, faded blue underneath. At my feet was a red mat with the Chinese character for luck. Red is a lucky color in Chinese folklore. On patrol, John always wore a jade pendant on a red string. He claimed it brought him luck.

I raised my hand to knock and remembered I was wearing a white button down. White is the color of death in Asian cultures. I cursed myself for the lapse, buttoned my coat all the way up to hide my shirt, then rapped my knuckles against the wood. The hollow boom sounded loud and ominous to my ears. I hated playing the grim reaper. Always had. It's emotional torture to deliver the bad news to families. This time it was even worse because I knew the victim. I took a deep breath and waited.

Mackenzie stood next to me, hands fluttering on an imaginary breeze and eyelids flickering. She kept going up on her tiptoes like she wanted to dance and was just waiting for the music to start.

I heard the chain and the deadbolt, then the door swung open. Carol Chen looked out at me and her face went through an awful twist. First there was surprise, followed by confusion, then pain. One hand covered her mouth and her eyes shut. She stood there a moment, tears building on her lashes, then held up a hand for us to wait while she retreated into the apartment. I heard a sob from the kitchen and muttered, "I hate this part."

Mackenzie had her head cocked to one side. "Why is she crying?"

I lowered my voice to a hiss. "Because her husband's dead."

"She can't possibly know that. You haven't told her yet."

My mouth opened and closed a few times while I tried to figure out how to respond. Her autism made it difficult for Mackenzie to understand how neurotypical (a word I had picked up while researching autism) people behave. I kept my voice a whisper. "She knows."

"How?"

"She just does, okay?"

"How do you know that?"

I took a deep breath and let it out. "Because I do."

"But how?"

"Mackenzie," I said, "you're going to have to trust me on this, okay? It's a neurotypical thing."

I could practically see her calculating that in the

computer she called a brain and then she nodded. "Very well. Should we go inside or wait?"

"We wait," I said.

We didn't have to wait long. Carol was back in five minutes, her eyes rimmed in red and her mouth turned down at the corners. She clutched a crumpled tissue in one hand. The pain in her face made my heart ache. She could barely get the words out. "I knew when he didn't come home last night."

I stepped inside and put my arms around her. Carol laid her head on my chest and let out a single, heart wrenching sob. "I called his company this morning," she said, wiping her nose with the tissue. "They didn't know where he was and then I called the precinct but..."

"It hadn't been forty-eight hours," I finished for her.

She nodded and I could feel tears soaking through my coat. I hugged her tighter and put a kiss on top of her head.

"When he went into private security I thought it would get easier, you know? I thought I wouldn't have to worry so much."

I nodded. I knew. Every cop wife spends the day wondering if she'll ever see her husband again. It was just one of the reasons so many cops end up divorced.

We stood that way for a long time, then Carol pulled herself together, sniffed and said, "How did it happen?"

"We're looking into it," I said. Carol was a cop's wife. I didn't need to say any more. She knew the score. We're looking into it meant that John's death was an ongoing investigation. Which meant we didn't have the killer in custody.

A fresh wave of pain broke over her face and she dabbed her eyes with the tissue.

I motioned to Mackenzie. "Carol, this is Special Agent Mackenzie. She's with the FBI."

Carol grasped hold of her hand. "They brought in the FBI? That means a lot to me. Thank you for coming. You'll find my John's killer. Won't you?"

"I'll do everything I can," Mackenzie said. "Statistically speaking there is a better than average chance of finding the killer. Sixty percent of all homicides in New York city are solved eventually."

Carol turned back to me. "What's she talking about, Mike?"

"Uh..." I scrambled to come up with something. "You know the FBI. They're always careful with their wording. It's all the legal tape they have to wade through. Make's them overly cautious. We'll find John's killer."

"You can't say that with any certainty," Mackenzie said.

I glared at her. One eyebrow went up and my mouth formed a strict line. I turned back to Carol. "We'll find John's killer. I promise. I won't sleep until the bastard is caught."

Carol nodded and planted a kiss on my cheek. "Thank you, Mike. You were one of his favorites. He always said you would have made a great cop if you hadn't become a homicide detective." She ended with a humorless little laugh that dissolved almost before it had begun.

John had never forgiven me for becoming a detective. He claimed beat cops were the ones doing the real work of keeping the peace. Detectives, he always said, just arrested the bad guys after the fact.

Carol stepped back and straightened her shoulders. Her taciturn Chinese nature reasserted itself and she said, "Where are my manners? *Cha?*"

"*Ching*," I said. "That would be nice. Thank you."

23

Carol disappeared into the kitchen and I waved Mackenzie inside before shutting the door. Nosy neighbors had probably gotten too much information already. I didn't want Carol's misery to be the talk of the building.

Mackenzie had a look around the apartment and then hovered near the sofa like she meant to sit down, but stayed standing and said, "*Cha* is tea?"

"That's right," I said. "You catch on quick."

"And *kwai lo* is foreigner?"

I nodded. "Foreigner, stranger, white devil, ghost. It can mean any and all of those things. Mostly it means, not Chinese."

Mackenzie made a note of that in her phone, then crossed to a mantle with a framed photograph of me and John Chen together in uniform. She used her phone to snap a pic before asking, "Is this you?"

"Have I changed that much?"

She studied the picture, then me. "Your eyes are older

now."

I laughed at the unintended insult.

Carol came back carrying a tray of tea and she motioned us to the sofa. "It's been a long time, Mike."

"Too long," I said. "I should have come by sooner."

She waved that away and poured. It was black tea. Carol and John both drank green tea, but she had always kept black on hand for my visits. I thanked her as I took the cup and said, "I'm so sorry for your loss. If there's anything I can do, just let me know."

Carol bobbed her head up and down, staring into the depths of her tea. Her eyes were hard and her mouth tight. She didn't drink, just gazed at the steaming liquid like it might contain the answers.

"Is it alright if we ask a few questions?" I said.

She laughed and fresh tears welled up. "I'm a cop's wife, remember? I know how it works."

Mackenzie came over and perched on the edge of the sofa, her back ramrod straight. "Did anyone have reason to hurt your husband? Had anyone threatened him recently?"

"John is... was a cop," she said by way of answer. "Every bad guy he ever busted had an axe to grind."

I jumped in with a translation before Mackenzie could ask. "All the criminals he arrested wanted to do him harm."

She nodded. "Anyone in particular? Anyone recent?"

Carol thought a moment and then shook her head. "He had a run in with some hoods a few nights ago. He had to chase them away from the construction site where he was working. But that's all I can think of."

"Triads?" I asked.

Carol frowned. "I'm not sure. John just called them hoods. But you know John."

"I don't know John," Mackenzie said. "Please explain."

I said, "John called near everybody who wasn't a cop, a hood."

Mackenzie scowled and asked Carol. "Did he call you a hood?"

"No," she said. "Never. Why would he?"

I reached over and took hold of Mackenzie's elbow. She flinched at the sudden touch. "Not everyone, just anyone he interacted with on the job. Shoplifters were hoods. Gang members were hoods. Jaywalkers were hoods. It was his general term for anyone the police had to interact with."

Carol was watching Mackenzie closely, coming to the slow realization that there was something different about her. From the outside, you would never know anything was off. There are no outward signs. Mackenzie looked like any normal girl, albeit a girl with a particularly unique fashion sense. But once she started asking questions, people realized pretty quick that she was operating on another level entirely, maybe playing in a whole different field. Carol questioned me with an arched brow.

I said, "Special Agent Mackenzie has... unique talents."

Carol sipped her tea and watched Mackenzie, like she might display some of those unique talents any second now.

I said, "Did John tell you anything else about those hoods?"

Carol shook her head and frowned an unspoken apology.

"Was he having any trouble with the Triads?"

"Not that I know of," she said. "You think Triads had something to do with this?"

I said yes at the same time Mackenzie said no. I turned to glare, but Mackenzie ignored me and asked, "Who was your husband working for?"

"A private security company called Global Access Elite," Carol told us. "They mostly employ retired cops and ex-military."

"Do you have any idea why your husband would be in the underground tunnels?"

"That's where he was working," Carol said. "Is that where he... where you found him?"

I nodded. "What was he doing down there, Carol?"

"Global Access had recently been contracted by a big developer to provide security. They want to revitalize the neighborhood."

"You're talking about Connor MacNab Development and Real Estate?"

She nodded. "MacNab is pouring big money into Chinatown and wanted to protect his future investment."

"He must be pretty sure he can close the deal if he's hiring security already," I wondered aloud.

"Don't ask me to speculate on how *kwai lo* think."

"You're more than a little *kwai lo* yourself," I said with a smile.

Carol grinned. Her father had been mud blood American with sandy hair and blue eyes. She said, "But all the important parts are Chinese."

Mackenzie cocked her head to the side. "Which parts are Chinese?"

"It's a joke," I told her.

"I don't get it," she said. "Why is it funny?"

I didn't have time, or ability, to explain all the intricacies surrounding Chinese/American relations and the social political circumstances that would make an offhand remark like Carol's funny, so I waved it away. "Rumor has it there's a new Triad boss in town," I said. "Someone called Tai Pan. You know anything about him?"

"Tai Pan means leader, or boss."

"I know." I nodded. "People say this new Tai Pan is dangerous. Not someone to cross."

"The Triads are not an organization to cross," Carol said. "You worked Chinatown. You know that."

I inclined my head. "Anybody threatened you, lately?"

She frowned. "No. No one. Do you think I'm in danger?"

I shook my head. "Just covering all the bases. You know how it goes."

Mackenzie dropped a bomb into the conversation. "Did you and your husband have any marital problems?"

Carol looked stricken at the suggestion.

I blurted, "Mackenzie!"

She turned to me with a look of blank confusion on her face. "We have to ask all the usual questions. Statistically speaking, wives and husbands are usually the murderer in a case where the victim is married. You know that."

I held up a hand. "I think, in this case, we can safely assume Carol had nothing to do with this."

"You don't know that."

"Yes," I said, my voice taking an edge, "I do."

"You said yourself that you haven't seen her in several

years," Mackenzie said. "You have no way of knowing what she could or would do."

Mackenzie turned back to Carol. "Can you account for your whereabouts from midnight on the 6th until early morning on the 7th?"

Carol put her cup down. She had cold fury in her eyes. "I think it's time for you to leave."

24

"You're angry," Mackenzie said. A strand of chestnut hair had broken loose from her ponytail. Her hands were stuffed inside the pockets of her Navy peacoat and a worried frown creased her face.

We were standing in the hall outside Carol Chen's apartment and one of the neighbors was peeking through a crack in his door. I had my fists on my hips and a deep scowl on my face. My lips were tight against my teeth. I wanted to yell, but kept my voice to a dangerous growl. "What clued you in?"

"It's mostly your energy," Mackenzie said, "but also that's the face you make when you're angry. Are you mad at me?"

"Yes, I'm mad at you," I hissed, taking a step closer and lowering my voice. "Carol is an old friend, and you just accused her of murder."

Mackenzie shook her head. "I didn't accuse her of murder. I simply asked her to confirm her whereabouts so that we could take her off our list of suspects. She's the spouse of a murder victim. It's only logical that we would investigate her first."

"Carol Chen did *not* murder her husband."

"You don't know that," Mackenzie said. "We can't know that until we determine her alibi during the time of John Chen's death."

I held up a hand. "Listen to me, Mackenzie. Carol Chen is not a suspect. Do you understand?"

"Why?"

"Because I know her," I said. "She's not capable of murder."

"How do you know that?"

"Because I do."

She blinked. "That's circular logic and wouldn't be enough to clear her in a criminal proceeding. I think you're letting personal emotions interfere with your thinking."

More doors were opening along the hall and curious faces peered out. I took Mackenzie by the elbow and steered her toward the stair. "It doesn't have to hold up in a criminal case," I muttered under my breath. "Carol is never going to be on trial for murder, because she didn't do it."

"You still haven't told me what makes you so certain."

"I just know." I had reached the end of my patience. I was about to pop off. I didn't want to do that so I reminded myself that Mackenzie is autistic and took a deep breath.

"But *how* do you know?"

We reached the stairs and started down. I stopped at the turn, out of earshot of nosy neighbors. "It's not anything I can put into words. Some things you just know. I don't know how to explain it."

"Please try."

I took in some air and let out a heavy sigh, marshalling my thoughts. "How do you know when you love somebody?"

She shook her head. "I don't know," she said in all honesty. It was a tragic statement made without any guile, just fact.

"Let me try again. Some people are just not capable of murder. Take your sister for instance. Do you think she could ever kill somebody?"

A change came over Mackenzie. Her mouth tightened around the corners and her hands stopped their incessant flicking. She said, "I'd rather not discuss that."

She hurried down the steps and I was forced to keep up. I didn't say a word until we reached the bottom and emerged from Carol's building onto the busy boulevard in Chinatown. A cold autumn sun was shining down on us and a strong wind carried the smell of fish and brine. I said, "Have you ever had a case where you just knew, deep down in your gut, that someone was guilty?"

She stopped on the sidewalk, hands in her pockets and the breeze playing through her hair. "No. What does that feel like?"

It dawned on me then just how differently autistic people think. Mackenzie didn't rely on instinct or gut feelings. She used facts and logic. I had to work at finding an answer. I felt like a man trying to explain human emotion to a space alien. I said, "It's a thousand little things that all add up to form a picture of a person and it lets you know what they are capable of."

"I find most people to be incredibly inconsistent,"

Mackenzie said. "I never know what they are capable of. People say one thing and do another."

"Granted," I nodded, "but there are some things you can rely on. When a homeless man walking down the street sees a dollar bill on the ground, what will he do?"

"He'll pick it up."

"Why?"

"Because he needs money," Makenzie said. "He hasn't got any."

"Right," I said. "Let me ask another question; why did you choose me to work this case with you?"

"Because you are the only partner who didn't request a transfer when you learned I was autistic."

"Sure," I said. "But we also worked well together. Doesn't that have something to do with it?"

She cocked an eyebrow. "I hadn't thought of it in those terms, but I suppose so."

"And when you needed someone to partner with you on this case, you knew I'd be a good fit."

"I guess that makes sense," she said.

"So you see? Sometimes you just know things," I said. "That's how I know Carol didn't kill her husband."

"That makes no sense," Mackenzie said. "To compare one to the other is illogical, but for the record, I feel it highly unlikely that Carol Chen killed her husband."

I threw my hands in the air. "If you agree with me, why did you press her for an alibi?"

"Because we have to use all the bases," Mackenzie said.

"You mean *cover* all our bases?"

"Right." She nodded. "It's a baseball metaphor."

I rubbed my forehead. "Look, we'll get Carol's alibi, and

I'm sure it will be rock solid, but we have to do it my way. We can't just ask her flat out. We have to be subtle about it."

"Finesse," Mackenzie said.

"Right," I said. "We have to finesse it out of her."

She frowned. "That's not one of my strengths."

"I noticed." There was a noodle shop across the street and I pointed. "Let me handle Carol Chen. That is, if she ever speaks to me again."

Mackenzie followed my finger and asked, "What do you want from there?"

"Lunch," I said. "I'm starving."

25

Thirty minutes later I was sitting on a park bench at a little square of green nestled in the heart of China-town, with a takeaway box of lo mein balanced on my knees and a pair of chopsticks in hand. I stuffed noodles into my face while an ancient Chinese man in khaki slacks and a parka practiced Tai Chi in the grass. The noodles had turned to icy strings, but the shop had been too noisy for Mackenzie, with shouting cooks, clashing cutlery, harried customers and the discordant strains of generic Chinese music coming from the speakers. She had turned into a block of wood so I opted to carry my lunch outside into the cold.

Mackenzie sat next to me on the bench watching every bite I took with intense interest. Her hands were knotted together in her lap and her head thrust forward.

I spoke around a mouthful of food. "Problem?"

"How do you do that?"

"Do what?"

"Open your mouth so wide?"

I swallowed. "What do you mean? I just open my mouth and put the food in."

"Yes," she said, "but you open your mouth so wide when you put the food in. I could never open my mouth that wide."

Then she tried, stretching her jaw as wide as she could. She tested the action several times and then said, "I've never understood how people eat things like hamburgers and hotdogs. I can't figure out how to get my mouth around it."

"Thought you didn't eat hotdogs."

"I don't. Even if I did, I couldn't bite into it," she said. "How do you do that?"

I laughed, stuffed more noodles in my mouth and said, "Magic."

I went on eating and Mackenzie went on watching. At last I said, "You going to watch me eat my lunch?"

"Does it bother you?"

"A little," I said. "Yeah."

"Sorry." She turned her eyes to the old man slowly going through the motions of his Tai Chi routine and said, "If John Chen was killed by a ghost, how would we prove it?"

"He wasn't killed by any ghost," I said. "He was killed by Triads. Probably the same three that cornered us in that apartment building."

"How do you know he wasn't killed by a ghost?"

"Because there's no such thing as ghosts."

"That's an opinion," Mackenzie said. "You refuse to examine evidence to the contrary. How do you explain the extra-phenomenal happenings in the Tower of London, the infamous Harwick Hotel in Innsmouth, or the ghostly apparitions frequently witnessed at the Lyceum Theater in New Orleans by staff and guests?"

"Crackpots," I said. "I don't have to explain any of it because all those people are crackpots. They see ghosts because they *want* to see ghosts."

"You don't think there is even a remote possibility?"

"No," I said. "I don't believe in ghosts because I'm a big boy and I'm not afraid of the dark. I do believe in gangs and organized crime however, and I'm telling you right now, the Triads killed John Chen."

"That is a possibility," Mackenzie admitted.

"It's more than possible," I said. "It's likely. How else do you explain the three marks at both crime scenes?"

"I'm still thinking about that."

"It's Triads marking their kill," I said. "I'm going to find the trigger man and put him behind bars for life. And I'm going to nail the shot caller as well."

"Trigger man?" Mackenzie questioned. "Shot caller?"

I put my frozen noodles aside and took out my phone.

"Who are you calling?"

"I have a friend in the gang squad who works Chinatown," I told her as I dialed. "He might be able to give us more information on this Tai Pan character."

While I phoned my contact, Mackenzie went over to the old man. I couldn't hear what they were saying over the gusting November winds, but five minutes later Mackenzie was happily following along to the old man's routine. He grinned and corrected her form, bobbing his head and smiling when she got it right.

When I finished, I hung up the phone and called out,

"When you're done pretending to be the Karate Kid, we've got a meeting down in the Battery."

Mackenzie thanked her new friend and he cupped a fist with one hand in the traditional Chinese greeting, bowing his head. She wandered back over and said, "He was nice."

The old man was watching her walk away with a smile on his face. I said, "I get the feeling he likes you too."

26

We stood at the railing, looking out over the water. A ferry was chugging toward Jersey, leaving a frothing trail of white foam in the green water. Pigeons wheeled overhead. A cold breeze put roses in Mackenzie's cheeks and played with her hair. I hunched my shoulders against the icy bite and watched a jogger go past. She had strawberry blonde hair up in a ponytail and tight yoga pants that hugged her curves.

"Do you think she's pretty?" Mackenzie asked.

Busted.

I felt the same way I did every time my ex-wife caught me looking at another woman. My stomach clenched and my mouth dried up. I had learned from painful experience that saying 'no' only proved I had been staring. Instead, I feigned ignorance. "Who?"

Mackenzie liberated a hand from her coat and pointed. "The jogger in the blue spandex. You were watching her. Do you think she's pretty?"

There was no accusation, only curiosity, and I reminded myself that I was divorced. I could look at any woman I wanted. I gazed at the jogger as she made her way along the esplanade and took a bold step for all mankind when I said, "Yeah. She's cute."

"Cute, not pretty?" Mackenzie asked.

"She's pretty."

"First you said cute."

"What's the difference?"

"That's what I want to know," Mackenzie said. "What makes one woman cute and another pretty? What about beautiful?"

"I don't know," I said, feeling like I was being interrogated by the female collective.

"What about me?" Mackenzie asked. "Am I pretty? Cute? Ugly?"

"You're not ugly," I said.

"Am I pretty?" she said. "You tried to kiss me last time we worked together. Do you think I'm pretty?"

"I uh... I'm not sure I wanna talk about this."

I didn't know where this was going and didn't want to get jammed up. Mackenzie was a federal agent; being involved with her could lead to a world of trouble. Besides, I had made my move and she had set me back on my heels. I turned toward the water and said, "Let's keep things professional, eh?"

Mackenzie gazed after the jogger, who was just a speck now. "I've always wondered what makes some women pretty, or beautiful, or gorgeous. Aren't all people beautiful in their own way? Everybody is unique, after all."

"I guess that's true," I said. "Beauty is in the eye of the beholder."

"I've never really understood that saying." She leaned her elbows on the railing and cranked her head over for a look at the water. The Hudson was choppy today. "People are people. They all look different and special in their own way."

"Haven't you ever had a crush?"

She questioned me with a furrowed brow.

"A boy you liked?" I explained. "Wasn't there ever someone you liked and wanted to go out with?"

Her pretty face pinched with a momentary pain. "Boys don't like girls like me. I'm different and strange. Boys like pretty girls, like that jogger. Normal girls."

"You're pretty," I said and added, "In a geeky chic sort of way."

"Geeky chic?" she said. "What's that?"

"It means you look like the type of girl who's smart and reads a lot of books."

"And guys like that?"

"Some guys."

She pondered that a moment and then shrugged. "It doesn't matter. I'm not really interested in a relationship. I have a hard enough time figuring out normal people while I'm working. I don't want to go through that at home as well."

"Relationships take work," I told her. "I speak from experience. I've destroyed more than one."

I spotted Benny Hoag making his way toward the sea wall and gave a slight nod. "That's our guy," I told Mackenzie.

Benny was a short bulldog with a thick neck and close-cropped hair. He was half black, half Chinese, and his eyes always seemed to be smiling. He had acne scars, a heavy gold chain, and a reputation as a bit of a playboy. He sidled up to the railing and said, "How's it hanging, Cole? Been a minute."

"Been more than a minute," I said. "I'm back working homicide out of the upper west. You still the man about town?"

"You know it. Who's your fine looking friend?"

"Special Agent Mackenzie." I made introductions. "This is Sergeant Hoag. He works Vice in Chinatown."

Mackenzie offered a hand. Benny took it in both of his own and placed a kiss on her knuckles. "A pleasure to meet you, Mackenzie. You can call me Benny. And you can call me anytime."

Mackenzie just blinked.

I suddenly felt like a dog protecting a bone. I said, "She plays for the other team."

"Is that right?" Benny said, still holding her hand. "What a shame. Well, if you ever change your mind, you know where to find me."

"Change my mind about what?" Mackenzie asked.

"She likes to keep things professional," I said before Benny could question her. "She's a real stickler for rules and such. You know the FBI."

Benny let go of her hand like it was electrified. "Hey, I get it, momma. It's cool. No offense, ya know?"

Mackenzie frowned. "Why would I be offended?"

I laughed, like Mackenzie had just told a joke. "She,

uh... It's... Let's talk about Triads. What can you tell me about Tai Pan?"

Benny's whole demeanor changed. All the humor ran away from his face and his eyes turned to chips of ice. He looked out over the water and said, "I know enough to scare me."

27

Benny glanced around before lowering his voice. "Why you asking about Tai Pan?"

"We're conducting a murder investigation," Mackenzie said.

"Got a dead cop," I told him. "Well, a retired cop."

He nodded. "Yeah, I heard. John Chen. He was a good man. I worked a few cases with him back in the day. You think the Triads are involved?"

"I'm positive," I said.

Mackenzie said, "It's a possibility."

Benny propped his forearms on the railing and stared out at the Hudson, motioning for us to close ranks. Mackenzie and I huddled close, one on either side. The wind nearly drowned out his words and I had to lean in. I got a whiff of his aftershave, a woody masculine scent, but he'd poured it on just a little too thick.

"Tai Pan took over the Black Dragon syndicate about six months ago," Benny explained in a whisper. "He made a name for himself by wiping out the Golden Sevens."

"When you say wiped them out?" I questioned.

"Killed their top leaders and put the foot soldiers to work for the Black Dragons."

"He took over an entire gang?"

Benny nodded. "That's the word on the street anyway."

I whistled low.

"Before six months ago no one had ever even heard of Tai Pan," Benny told us. "He took over when the old Hong running the Black Dragons kicked it, but if you believe the stories, it was Tai Pan who killed him. No one ever found the body. Word on the street is, Tai Pan garroted the old boss and dissolved him in acid, then killed all the top lieutenants to cement his leadership. And I know that part's true because we found the lieutenants. One of them was frozen in a block of ice, floating in the river. Another had been chopped into pieces. It was pretty gruesome stuff. All the murders are still open. We never found the perps. Probably never will."

Mackenzie said, "Why would he kill his lieutenants?"

"Not *his* lieutenants," Benny corrected. "The *old* lieutenants. He was trying to make a point. Out with the old, in with the new. Cross me and you'll pay. And he succeeded. The Black Dragons have all the local shop owners scared stiff and the other gangs running scared."

I said, "Tai Pan freezes one guy in a block of ice and dismembers another his first week on the job? Sounds like the type of psychopath who would skin people."

Benny winced. "John was skinned?"

I nodded. "Thankfully he was dead when it happened."

"Poor guy," Benny said. "What a way to go. How's his wife taking it?"

"About as well as you'd suspect."

"Do you know John Chen's wife?" Mackenzie asked.

"Sure," Benny said. "Met her a few times. Even had dinner with them once."

"Do you think she could have had anything to do with Officer Chen's death?"

"Carol?" Benny shook his head. "No way. No chance."

I leaned out so I could look past Benny to Mackenzie and said, "Told ya."

"How do you know?" Mackenzie asked.

Benny told her the same thing I had. "I just do."

His answer didn't seem to satisfy her and Mackenzie started making notes in her phone.

I said, "So this Tai Pan, you got a description?"

Benny's head went back and forth slowly. "Got nada. No one's ever even seen the cat. All we have is the moniker. Tai Pan. Means big boss or something like that in Chinese."

"Supreme leader," I corrected.

Mackenzie said, "If no one has ever seen him, how do you know he exists?"

"Got a string of bodies and word on the street," Benny said. "That's proof enough for me."

"How do we find him?" I asked.

"You don't," Benny said. "Tai Pan wants to talk, he'll find you. Take my advice and steer clear."

I shook my head. "You know we can't do that."

Mackenzie said, "He's a possible suspect in the murder of a law officer."

Benny only shrugged. "Your funeral."

"Come on, Benny," I said. "Give us something."

"I got nothing, man. If I had anything, Vice would make

a move. This guy is seriously bad news. Ever since Tai Pan came on the scene, we been chasing ghosts. Haven't got a whiff of the guy, other than rumors. You go after Tai Pan, take my advice, make sure your life insurance policy is up to date."

"Thanks for the vote of confidence," I said.

Benny spread his hands. "Gotta keep it real, brotha."

I turned around, put my back against the railing and crossed my arms over my chest, taking in the city. Somewhere in that concrete jungle was a Triad boss who liked to make an example of his victims. If he had killed John, I was going to find him and make him pay. He might get away with killing his own lieutenants, but I wasn't going to let him kill cops.

Mackenzie said, "Somebody must know how to find him. Have you asked any of the Black Dragon gang members?"

Benny laughed like she'd made a joke. "Sister, you've obviously never worked Vice. Those guys will do life in prison before snitching on the top dogs."

I said, "Well, thanks for the info."

"You know where to find me if you need me." Benny tipped a nod and sauntered off.

Mackenzie took his vacated space, closing the distance between us. "I'm still not convinced the Triads had anything to do with this murder, but I think we should at least have a talk with Tai Pan."

"Agreed."

"The only question is, how?"

"I might have an idea," I said. "You hungry?"

"You just ate."

I shrugged. "Yeah, well, now I'm in the mood for dumplings."

"Are you thinking of asking Mr. Lo at the Happy Time Dumpling?"

"Not the old man," I said. "I was thinking of someone a little younger."

28

I phoned the Happy Time Dumpling shop, placed an
order, and gave an address around the corner from
Carol Chen's apartment building. We sheltered from the
wind in a recessed door, watching a street vendor selling
knock-off Louis Vuitton handbags to gullible tourists while
we waited for Xu Yin. Mackenzie was bouncing from foot to
foot, like a grade school kid in bad need of a toilet. She said,
"You think a girl as young as Xu Yin knows about Tai Pan
and the Black Dragons?"

"Everybody in this neighborhood knows except the
cops," I assured her.

"I don't understand," she said. "Why don't they report
the criminals to the police."

"They would if they thought the police would do
anything." I rubbed my hands together and blew into them.
"Remember the Chinese, most of them immigrants, came
here from a communist country were everybody is corrupt.
To them, the cops are just as bad as the criminals. The
Chinese don't trust anybody except their own family and

sometimes not *even* their own family. John used to tell me; Chinese have three faces. One they show to the outside world. One they show to their family. One they show only to themselves. And one they hide from themselves."

"That's four," Mackenzie said.

"You noticed that, huh?" I tugged my coat a little tighter. "Point is, the Chinese are a complicated people with a complicated history. There's a lot going on under the surface. Nothing is secret in this neighborhood, except the thoughts you keep inside your own head. The only way the Chinese have survived all the wars and communism and invasions is to know everything about everybody. They just don't make a habit of telling outsiders."

"Don't they know we're here to help?" Mackenzie asked.

"No," I said. "They don't. And you can't tell them, you have to show them. And that takes time."

"How much time?"

"Several generations unless I miss my guess." I thrust my chin at the knockoff vendor. "See that guy?"

Mackenzie nodded.

"He made us," I told her.

"He what?"

"He knows we're cops," I explained. "In a few minutes he'll gather up his merchandise and clear out. A few minutes after that the entire neighborhood will know a couple of cops are hanging out on the corner."

"Will that put Xu Yin in danger?"

I hitched one shoulder. "Maybe."

The vendor eventually rolled up his blanket, along with all his handbags, and slunk off.

"What should we do?"

I glanced at my watch. "If she's not here in another minute or two, we'll take a powder."

I spent the next few minutes explaining to Mackenzie the meaning of 'take a powder' and by the time I'd finished, Xu Yin, in her oversized military surplus coat and baseball cap, rounded the corner with a sack of Chinese food in one hand. She was wearing earbuds, her head bopping to the music, and blowing a bubble with her chewing gum.

Soon as I saw her, I ran my hand down the line of buzzers next to the door. Someone inevitably buzzed us in without using the intercom. I pushed the door open as Xu Yin mounted the steps. A look of surprise spread across her face. She had one hand up for the buzzer and stopped. "You again."

I crooked a finger. "Right this way."

"I've got nothing to say to you," she said before following us into the small entryway. There was a row of mailboxes on one wall and a staircase on the other, and just enough room for the three of us to stand. Xu Yin passed the sack to me. "I already told you everything I know. I really shouldn't be talking to you."

"Because the Black Dragons warned you off?"

Xu Yin hitched up one shoulder and examined her scuffed sneakers.

"Look, kid, between the dragons and the real estate developer, someone is going to put your family out of business. Is that really what you want?"

She laughed. "You going to get the dragons off my grandfather's back?"

"There'll always be Triads in Chinatown," I said. "You know that."

"Then I don't see why I should help you."

"Because if you do, we might be able to put enough of them in jail to severely cripple their operation, and that will give your family some breathing room."

She shook her head. "You can put a hundred of them in jail and more will take their place. They're like a hydra."

Mackenzie said, "Did you know the FBI offers a substantial reward for information leading to an arrest and conviction in a federal murder case?"

"Reward?" Her interest was piqued. "How much?"

"Ten-thousand dollars," Mackenzie told her.

Xu Yin considered that and then her eyes narrowed. "What if you don't get a conviction?"

The kid was smart. Maybe too smart. I said, "You'll still be helping us take a few Black Dragons off the street and make your neighborhood a little safer. Isn't that worth it?"

She crossed her arms. "Not to me."

Mackenzie said, "What if I could promise certain tax-exempt statuses for your family's restaurant?"

Xu Yin turned to her. "No taxes?"

"No federal taxes. It wouldn't eliminate state or local taxes," Mackenzie said. "But it would remove a large part of your family's tax burden."

Her mouth went back and forth while she thought that over. "What do you want to know?"

"Tai Pan," I said. "Where do we find him?"

She laughed out loud like I had told a particularly funny joke.

"You don't," she said. "No one does. No one even knows anything about him."

"Somebody has to know something," I said. "How does the guy run his business?"

Xu Yin turned back to Mackenzie. "No federal taxes for life?"

"No federal taxes for ten years with an option to renew if your family continues to provide information to state and federal law enforcement."

"Deal." Xu Yin stuck out her hand.

Mackenzie shook it.

"Tai Pan runs a pachinko parlor off Elizabeth Street between Hester and Canal. If you want a face to face with Tai Pan, that's the place to go."

I said, "Thanks kid."

She pointed at the sack in my hands. "Someone has to pay for that."

I looked to Mackenzie.

She said, "I don't want it."

"The Federal Bureau of Investigation isn't good for an order of dim sum?"

"I'm not going to eat it," she protested. "Why should I pay for it?"

I dug money out of my wallet.

Xu Yin snagged the crumpled notes from my hand and backed toward the door. "I got your promise. A decade."

Mackenzie nodded. "I'll have it in writing first thing tomorrow."

Xu Yin pushed through the door and it slammed shut behind her.

I asked, "Can you really fix it so they don't pay federal taxes?"

"Of course," Mackenzie said. "You don't think I'd lie, do you?"

"That's a handy ace to have up your sleeve."

Mackenzie frowned and as we made our way back up the block to my Mercury I had to explain to her what it meant to have an ace up your sleeve. She walked beside me, making notes in her phone.

29

Stakeouts with Mackenzie proved to be an interesting experience. The FBI agent couldn't sit still more than five minutes. She was either pacing, rocking, flicking, or asking questions and it was starting to get on my nerves.

We were in the back of a dirt-streaked van with balding tires. Cosmato's and Sons Carpentry was stenciled on the side in flecked gold paint. None of that silly Flowers by Irene stuff you see on television. Mackenzie had requisitioned a surveillance vehicle from the New York field office, a process that required most of the afternoon and a small mountain of paperwork.

The sun was hovering above the horizon by the time we parked across the street from the pachinko parlor. The gambling den was wedged between a Chinese laundry and a gaudy gift shop. The opening was just a narrow door and a flight of steps leading underground. The shops on either side served as lookouts. The proprietors, a heavy-set woman in the gift shop and a spindly old man in the laundry, had closely eyed the van before making phone calls.

Inside the van was a small space crammed with electronics. It smelled like stale French fries and sweat. Most of the toys I had no idea how to operate; they were outside the NYPD budget. I was balanced on a rolling stool, a set of headphones clamped over my ears and one hand on the control panel. A series of monitors showed the entrance to the pachinko parlor, along with the gift shop and laundry. An ancient Chinese man in baggy black pants and a dingy grey t-shirt sat on a low stool playing dominoes with two younger men. A steady procession of people came and went. Some were well dressed high rollers; others were street toughs. All of them were known to the old man and his friends. No one got past without his nod of approval.

I said, "This is going to be a tough nut to crack."

Mackenzie was standing up, hunched over so she could pace the tiny space like a caged lion. She said, "I need to get out."

"You can't," I told her without taking my eyes off the monitor.

"Just for a few minutes."

"No way," I said. "They're watching the van. They'll see you."

She drummed her thighs with her fingers and her eyelids snapped like camera shutters. The stress of being cooped up in the van was showing on the lines of her face. "I just want to go for a walk around the block and then I'll come right back."

"It's not going to happen, Mackenzie. Take a load off and get comfortable. We're going to be here a while."

"We've been here for hours," she cried.

I glanced at my cheap Timex. "It's been thirty-seven minutes."

She moaned loudly and thumped her own head with a fist. "How can you stand just sitting around?"

"I'm practically a pro," I said.

"I have to get out of here," Mackenzie said. She offered up several gambits, including putting a bag over her head so that she could go for a walk without being seen. In the end, I was forced to put on a stern face and tell her, in no uncertain terms, that she wasn't leaving until we were done with our stakeout and that might take all night, so get comfortable.

After that she rocked and paced and sometimes hummed to herself, fingers flicking against her corduroy trousers and her mouth making funny shapes. She stopped and said, "What's that mean? Tough nut to crack?"

I had to think back to my earlier statement. "It means something that's difficult to do," I said, feeling like I should start carrying a Webster's dictionary of idioms around with me. I wondered if they made such a thing. If so, it might make a great Christmas gift. I said, "The Triads have got this operation locked up tight. No one goes in or out without being vetted by the old man, and the shops on either side serve as lookout. They're running a tight ship."

Before Mackenzie could ask, I said, "It means an organization that is well controlled."

"Unlicensed gambling organizations are illegal in the city of New York," Mackenzie said as she went back to her hunched pacing. "We have enough for a warrant. We should organize a raid and arrest the proprietors. We could offer them a reduced sentence in exchange for information on Tai Pan or any information leading to an arrest in connection with the murder of John Chen."

I snorted and shook my head. "You raid that place and Tai Pan will vanish in the wind before the SWAT team even reaches the front door. The employees aren't going to say a word. They'll be too afraid to talk."

"Then we need a plan," Mackenzie said.

"Sit here, waiting and watching, and hope we get lucky."

"We can't just watch them all night."

"Why not? We might get a look at Tai Pan."

"Doubtful."

"Why do you say that?"

"The Triads use the underground tunnels to move around the city. Tai Pan will use the tunnels to come and go."

She had a point. Especially since the gang knew cops were sitting right outside. I leaned back and stretched, nearly slipping off my stool. "Got a better idea?"

"We go inside and ask to speak to Tai Pan."

"Oh, why didn't I think of that? We'll just walk up and say, hello there boys. Mind if we have a word with Tai Pan?"

Mackenzie nodded.

"They'll give us the old 'no speakee engrish' bit," I told her. "And Tai Pan, if he's even in there, will vanish."

Mackenzie huffed, planted her small bottom on a stool and folded her knees up to her chest. "We have to do something."

Her impatience was going to drive me crazy. Stakeouts are hard work. Sitting and waiting is a skill, one that

Mackenzie obviously did not possess. I pulled the head-phones off. "Okay, there's nothing more to see. Let's get out of here."

I climbed into the cab and got the motor running.

"We need to get eyes inside," Mackenzie said. "Did I use that right?"

"You got it right," I said. "The only question is how?"

"We could go undercover," Mackenzie suggested. "Maybe we should dress up like plumbers."

"That only works in Scooby-Doo cartoons," I said. "But you might be onto something. We need eyes inside and I think I know just the guy."

30

We reached Times Square in the early evening. The sun had gone down, leaving the sky a velvet purple welt, and the bustling exchange of crossroads was crowded with sightseers, street musicians, and vendors—all lit by neon billboards. Not even the falling temperatures could keep the crowds indoors.

I had been forced to park two blocks away—I remember the days when you could drive through Times Square—and we navigated the hustle and bustle. Mackenzie had her shoulders pulled up around her ears and her hands tortured themselves into new and interesting shapes against her thighs.

I said, "You gonna be okay?"

She nodded but her face was a twist of pain.

I had my head on a swivel as we slipped through the crowds and asked, "Is it all noise? Or just certain noises?"

"Some noises are worse than others," she told me. The words jerked from her mouth, like each and every syllable took effort. "And it's worse when they're all jumbled together."

"Wish I knew what it felt like," I said absently. I hadn't meant it. It's just one of those things you say.

"Close your eyes."

I stopped and turned. Mackenzie's cheeks were mottled with pink and her thick dark brows pinched. Her eyes blinked non-stop. I said, "What? now?"

She nodded. It was a jerky movement. "Close your eyes."

I glanced around at the crowds and then sighed. "Alright, but if I get my pocket picked, it's on you."

I closed my eyes and Mackenzie said, "Now listen."

"I am listening."

"No," she said. "Really listen. Can you hear the wail of the siren?"

I nodded. "Of course I can. Everyone can..."

She pinched the inside of my elbow. Hard.

"That's what it feels like to me. It's a physical sensation and it hurts."

I winced and my eyelids fluttered open. "That must be awful."

"Keep your eyes closed," she ordered.

"People are watching us," I said.

"Keep them closed," she said. "And listen."

I shut my eyes again and let the cacophonous sounds of Times Square invade my ears.

"Hear the guitarist?" she asked.

I nodded. A homeless man was strumming a poor rendition of Tambourine Man on an ancient six string.

Mackenzie said, "His high E string is out of tune."

"How can you..."

She dug a finger into my side. I cringed at the sudden flash of pain.

"That's what it feels like," she said. "Do you hear the all the voices? All the conversations taking place at once? All the people laughing and raising their voices to be heard?"

There was a sharp flick against my ear and I flinched.

"Hear the jackhammer?" she asked.

I didn't want to know.

Mackenzie dug a knuckle into the soft flesh of my neck, just below my jawline. "That's what it feels like."

I opened my eyes again, but this time the sounds stayed. They didn't fade into the background the way sounds do when you're concentrating on something else. They stayed bright and painful and loud in my ears.

Mackenzie had tears standing in her eyes. "That's what it feels like," she said. "That's the way it feels, every day, all the time, and it never ends."

I reached out a hand to touch her and stopped myself. Adding any more sensory input would only make things worse. I said, "I'm sorry. I didn't know."

"Why are you sorry?" she asked. "It's not your fault that I'm autistic. I was born this way. It's just something I have to live with."

My respect for her went up a few notches. Given everything she had to deal with, it was a wonder she had ever graduated Quantico, or managed to hold down a job.

"Isn't there anything that makes it better?" I asked.

She shook her head. "Nothing that I've found."

"How do you do it?"

"Do what?"

"Cope with all the noise?"

"I run in the park or play my cello."

"Doesn't the sound of the cello bother you?"

"Not when it's in tune."

I turned for a look at the homeless man strumming his beat-up six string. He had finished butchering Tambourine Man and now he was mutilating All Along the Watchtower. He was doing such a poor job, I couldn't tell if it was the Bob Dylan version or Jimi Hendrix. I said, "Want me to break his guitar?"

"That would be mean."

I chuckled. "You're too nice. Come on. The faster we get this done the faster we can get you someplace quiet."

"What are we looking for?" she asked as we resumed our walk.

"Tell you when I find it."

We didn't have far to go. We were passing the Citizen store when I spotted Tight Fist Wu in a bright red puffer coat dealing three card monte atop an old milk crate for a small knot of tourists.

"Keep your eye on the lady," he said as he zipped the cards back and forth over the milkcrate. "Keep your eye on the lady. Where's she go? Where's she stop?"

He pointed to a heavyset man in a beige overcoat with a beanie pulled down over his balding head. "Take your pick my friend. Try your luck. Where is she?"

He pointed and Tight Fist flopped his card over, revealing a seven of hearts. "Oh! Too bad! You were so close. Tell you what; you look like a nice guy. I'll give you a chance to win back your money. Want to play again? Double or nothing? What do you say?"

I pushed through the knot of tourists and held up my shield. "This game is over and anyone caught gambling is going to spend the night in jail."

Wu's eyes opened wide at the sight of my gold shield. He made the money and the cards disappear like a magician's trick, and then he was running, pushing his way through the crowd, almost knocking over a young couple in his hurry to escape.

31

I kicked the makeshift card table out of my way. The empty wooden milk crate went tumbling across the sidewalk and the crowd of gamblers scattered. Someone gave a shout. One lady screamed. People turned to see what all the commotion was about and cellphones came out to capture it all on video.

Tight Fist Wu was tall and wiry with a track and field build. He dodged through the crowds at Times Square easily, quickly putting distance between us. I had to shuffle around a fat man and almost went down when I tangled with a group of Japanese tourists armed with state-of-the-art cameras. The fat man barked at me to watch where I was going and the Japanese bowed and apologized profusely, as if they were at fault. I hollered over my shoulder for Mackenzie but she was nowhere to be seen. Probably all the noise and commotion was too much for her.

Wu had pulled ahead and was rounding the corner on West 47th Street. My legs were already screaming with the effort of keeping up and my lungs were burning. Last time I had to chase a suspect on foot, I had promised to lay off the booze and get back to the gym. So far I hadn't made much progress on that goal and as I slid around the corner, spotting Tight Fist Wu already a block ahead, I reaffirmed my commitment to cardiovascular fitness.

Tight Fist was running like a gazelle, his long legs carrying him along the sidewalk with effortless grace, but I knew I'd catch him eventually and throttled down, slowing to a jog as I lumbered up the block.

A young hood in gang colors with a fade haircut tried to step into my path. He knew I was a cop and he was just helping out a fellow criminal. Who says there's no honor among thieves? I elbowed him out of my way like an NFL linebacker, sending him to the sidewalk, ignoring shouts of police brutality, and focused on my breathing. It felt like my heart was about to explode right out of my chest. My feet drummed the pavement. Sweat sprang out on my forehead and rolled down my face in fat wet drops.

Tight Fist turned down a narrow alley and I knew I had him. I just had to keep my aching thigh muscles moving and he'd be in my grasp.

I turned the corner moments later. Wu was nearly halfway down the long concrete corridor. He went skipping past a big green metal dumpster, past a row of dented plastic trashcans overflowing with refuse, and reached a small intersection. He slowed to look back over his shoulder, a smile on his face, and he was about take the turn into the smaller alley when Mackenzie stepped into his path.

She appeared like a phantom materializing out of the shadows and caught hold of Wu's wrist before he even knew she was there. His eyes opened wide. Next thing I knew, Mackenzie gave a loud, *"Hiya!"* and Tight Fist Wu went head over heels.

He came down flat on his back in the middle of the grubby little alleyway, landing in a puddle with a bone-jarring *whump*. All the air went out of his lungs in a loud exhale and then Tight Fist was rolling around, clutching his sides and coughing.

"Oh man, Cole, whatchu go letting her do that for man? Oh man, I think she broke something."

Wu had a high-pitched voice, made all the more effeminate by his pitiful moaning. He was clutching his sides and cooing like a dog with worms.

I looked at Mackenzie and spread my hands. "Why the hell did you do that?"

"He was resisting arrest and evading police," she said. "That's a class E misdemeanor punishable by up to six months in prison and a fifty-thousand dollar fine."

I cursed and stooped to help Wu up. He grabbed hold of me like a drowning man to a life preserver. I said, "You didn't have to throw him. Where did you learn to do that anyway?"

"I have a third degree black belt in judo."

"Good to know."

I helped Tight Fist into a sitting position. His face was scrunched in pain and he rubbed an elbow. "Whassa matter with you, Cole? Why you sick She Hulk on me man?"

"Sorry," I told him. "She didn't know."

"Know what?" Mackenzie asked.

"Wu is my CI," I told her. "Tight Fist Wu, meet Special Agent Mackenzie of the FBI."

"I wish I could say it was a pleasure," Wu grumbled.

"If he's your confidential informant," Mackenzie asked, "why did he run?"

I snorted. "You got a lot to learn about the street."

She peered down at the concrete beneath her feet as if I meant the literal ground on which she stood.

"Wu is a *confidential* informant," I said. "He doesn't want anyone to know he's passing information to the police."

"Bad for my street cred," Wu said, staring up at Mackenzie like she were some strange new breed of creature he'd never encountered before. He turned back to me. "She fresh out of the academy, or what? She don't know about informants?"

I said to Mackenzie, "Whenever I need information from Wu, he always runs, but he always lets me catch him after a few blocks."

"Once we're out of eyesight," Wu added. "I can't be seen talking to the cops."

"This was all a show?" Mackenzie asked.

"That's right," I told her. "We gotta make it look good."

"You made it look a little *too* good," Wu said. "My elbow is killing me. I should sue."

"She didn't know," I told him, and to Mackenzie I said, "Next time try not to injure my CIs."

"You didn't tell me he was a confidential informant," Mackenzie said. "For all I knew he was a criminal evading police."

"My mistake," I said. "Next time I'll let you in on the score ahead of time."

Wu said, "Try not to body slam me next time."

"I'm sorry," Mackenzie offered.

"If she's going to be your partner, Cole, I'm going to need health and dental."

"It's a temporary arrangement, if it makes you feel any better."

I helped him to his feet, peeling an old candy bar wrapper from his shoulder and tossing it. His bright red puffer coat was covered in muck. He arched his back and winced. "Small comfort."

"Come on," I said. "Let's get some ice for that elbow."

32

Tight Fist Wu was in the back seat of the Mercury with a bag of ice against his elbow and a burger in his lap, filling the car with the tempting aroma of grilled beef and melting cheese. He put the ice pack down long enough to chomp a bite and then replaced the cooling pack with a sigh of relief. He spoke around a mouthful of hamburger. "When did you start working with the feds, Mike?"

Mackenzie and I were in the front, turned around to face him. I said, "I'm not. Or... well... It's complicated."

"I'm sorry if I hurt you," Mackenzie said for the hundredth time.

He shrugged. He'd recovered from the shock of being body slammed by a hundred-and-ten-pound woman. The burger and fries helped. Since I had known him, Wu had always been a bottomless pit, able to eat anything and everything without putting on a pound. Nothing had changed. He'd devoured the fries and inhaled the cola before starting on the burger. He said, "I like a woman who plays rough."

The innuendo sailed right over Mackenzie's head and

Wu continued, "I haven't seen you in ages, Mike. How's the wife?"

"We're divorced," I told him.

"Sorry to hear that man." He took a bite out of the burger. "I always liked Michelle. What'd you do to screw it up? You get caught cheating?"

His eyes flashed to Mackenzie.

"It's none of your business," I said. My daughter had died of leukemia and I spiraled into a self-destructive tailspin fueled by painkillers and booze that only ended when I lost my gold shield and got busted down to patrol, but I wasn't about to tell all that to Tight Fist Wu. Smart cops keep a professional relationship with their informants. I liked Wu but he would sell his grandmother for the right price. I added, "And I didn't cheat."

"She cheated on you?" Wu guessed.

"No one cheated on anyone," I said and changed the subject. "We need a favor."

"Man, I haven't seen you in almost five years and now you show up asking for favors." Wu shook his head.

"We're investigating a murder," Mackenzie told him.

I looked at her and made a slashing motion across my throat. I didn't want Wu to know what we were investigating. It would be all over the street before the sun came up tomorrow.

"What murder? Who died?"

"The murder of Cole's former CI," I told him. "Never you mind what murder. We need someone who can get us inside the Black Dragon pachinko parlor."

His eyes got wide. "No way, man. No way. You know who owns that place?"

I nodded.

"Tai Pan," Mackenzie said.

"*Tai Pan,*" Wu parroted. "You know who Tai Pan is?"

"The suspected head of a Triad organization..." Mackenzie started to elaborate.

"He's the head of the Black Dragons," Wu said. "Not the pink dragons, or the fuchsia dragons. The *Black* Dragons. Those guys are bad news. And Tai Pan is worse. You know what Tai Pan does to anyone who crosses him?"

"We've heard tales," I said.

"He chops them up in pieces and burns them in acid!"

"Would you relax," I said. "All we need is someone to get us through the door."

"Oh, is that all you need?" He shook his head. "No way."

He reached for the door handle.

"Not so fast, Wu." I reached over the seat and caught his coat sleeve. "You're going to get us into that pachinko parlor or I'm going to run you in on all the charges I've let slide over the years."

His eyes filled with hurt. "You would do me like that, Mike?"

"A cop is dead."

He sat back in the seat, the leather creaking, and his expression changed. Even criminals and lowlifes know the score. When a cop gets killed the NYPD doesn't stop until the killer is brought to justice. Or on a slab in the morgue. He let out a long suffering sigh. "Okay, but I can't take you."

"Why not?" I asked.

"Because you look like a cop," he said and then turned to Mackenzie with a big smile plastered on his face.

33

"How do I look?" Mackenzie asked. She had shed the corduroys and oversized sweater for a slinky red dress that wrapped her slender frame like the label on an expensive champagne bottle. My eyebrows went up. I had been expecting something slightly off-kilter, maybe something a little old-fashioned, but Mackenzie had managed to change her appearance the way a sleight of hand artist swipes a wristwatch without the mark ever knowing, and she'd done it almost effortlessly.

We were in the back of the surveillance van again, parked a block over from the Black Dragon casino this time. Mackenzie had ordered us to turn our backs while she changed. It had taken ten minutes and I spent the time making sure Tight Fist Wu didn't peek.

I whistled and fumbled for my words. "You look... really... well... good."

Tight Fist Wu said, "You're a knockout."

Mackenzie didn't blush or thank us. She just blinked and asked, "Does it really look okay? I feel silly."

"Are you kidding?" I said. "You'll be the hottest girl in there."

"Is that flattery?" she asked. "Or do you really believe that?"

Wu gave me a nudge and a wink.

I said, "I really believe that. You look spectacular."

"I suppose I should say thank you," Mackenzie said. "It's the neurotypical thing to do, but I feel like a clown. I don't normally dress this way."

"I didn't think you owned any dresses like that," I admitted.

"I don't," Mackenzie told us. "This belongs to my sister. She left it along with some other clothes the last time she was in New York."

Tight Fist Wu said, "You'll have to introduce me to your sister."

"Okay," Mackenzie told him, completely unaware of the subtext behind his request.

Morgan Mackenzie was a high-profile socialite who spent as much time saving whales and rainforests as she did at cocaine-fueled Hollywood parties. She'd been in the press recently when she was photographed sunbathing nude on the French Riviera. The pictures had been on the front page of every tabloid and gossip mag. Morgan was the exact opposite of Jessica. You'd never catch her in anything but the latest styles, usually direct from Paris. She was a bottled blonde who never had a hair out of place and, I suspect, more than one operation.

I looked Mackenzie over and said, "I bet your sister never looked so good."

"I feel ridiculous."

"You look great." I picked up the small lavalier mic and said, "Time to wire you up."

She nodded, making her ponytail bounce. "How does it work?"

"You've never been mic'd before?"

Mackenzie shook her head.

"This part gets taped to your inner thigh," I said, indicating the small rectangular transponder unit. "And the mic gets tapped between your..."

"Breasts?" Mackenzie supplied.

"I'll do that part," Wu offered.

"You'll go sit up front and keep your eyes on the road," I told him.

He made a face like a scolded puppy and climbed into the front of the surveillance van.

I was suddenly alone with Mackenzie and the space felt cramped in all the right ways. I could feel my ears turning red. I held up the transponder. "Ready?"

She nodded and I thought I saw a small blush in her pale cheeks.

I pointed to the hem of her dress. "You're going to have to hike that up for me."

There wasn't much to work with. The hem of the red dress stopped just a few inches below her hips. I went down on one knee, like a man proposing, and fixed tape to the outside of the transponder. Mackenzie pulled her hem up and I got a glimpse of her panties. I grinned. She was wearing a five hundred dollar dress and blue cotton underwear with little white unicorns.

"Is something funny?" Mackenzie asked.

"No," I told her as I fixed the transponder to the inside

of her thigh, painfully aware of every contact between my fingers and her smooth white flesh.

"Why are you laughing?" she asked. "I look ridiculous, don't I?"

I shook my head. "I was thinking about a comic I read in the newspaper today."

"Which comic?"

"Dilbert."

"Why was it funny?"

"Dilbert is always funny," I told her. "Scott Adams is a national treasure."

When I finished making sure the transponder would stay put, I pulled her hem back down to cover the device and said, "If you sit down, be sure to cross your legs."

Then we worked together to feed the wire up through her dress. She slipped the shoulder straps down and my cheeks were on fire as I pressed the mic between the small globes of her breasts, just barely covered by the thin red material. When we finished, I was sweating and my heart was grinding.

"Are you alright?" Mackenzie asked. "You're breathing heavy."

I mopped sweat from my forehead. "Fine. Couldn't be better."

"Ready?" Tight Fist Wu asked from the front seat. He'd been watching the whole time.

"Almost." I reached behind Mackenzie to take her hair out of the ponytail. Brunette waves fell down around her bare shoulders. My stomach did a little somersault.

"I don't normally wear my hair down," Mackenzie said, running an exploratory hand through her locks.

"You should," I told her and reached for a necklace with a small video camera built into the pendant. The image quality was grainy under the best of circumstances but it was small enough to go unnoticed and it was better than anything the NYPD could afford. I said, "What's your emergency word?"

She blinked.

"Your emergency word," I said. "What are you going to say if things go south?"

"Why would I go south?"

"It means; if things go bad," I explained. "We need a code word for emergencies."

"Why not just say emergency?"

"Because that lets the bad guys know we're coming." I laughed. "How about steadfast? Can you remember that?"

She nodded and gave a thumbs up. "Steadfast. Got it."

"Hey," I said, taking her by the elbow. "If things get hairy—dangerous—say steadfast and I'll be through the door in less than a minute."

"Okay," was all she said.

Tight Fist Wu said, "Or you could just use your kung fu on them."

"Judo," Mackenzie corrected.

34

I parked myself on a rolling stool in the back of the surveillance van, my stomach in knots, watching the grainy video feed from Mackenzie's pendant and listening to audio shot through with static. Every time she moved, the dress swished against her breasts and it made a high rush of white noise that drowned out everything else. I did my best to fiddle with the dials, but I was only making things worse so I let the tapes record and hoped the important stuff would make it into evidence.

She and Tight Fist Wu were making their way along the sidewalk, arm in arm, and Tight Fist kept up a continuous stream of dialogue. I couldn't tell if he was talking for Mackenzie's sake, or because he was nervous, but it was starting to annoy me. If I had any way of communicating with them, I'd tell Wu to can it.

It was almost two in the morning and my eyelids felt like lead weights. I wanted to stretch out and sleep, but rubbed my face in an effort to clear away the cobwebs.

Mackenzie and Wu had reached the back door and

stopped in front of the old man with his mahjong game. Wu said something in a dialect I didn't understand. It wasn't Cantonese and I didn't think it was Mandarin either, but that was just an educated guess. It might have been Shanghainese or Haklo. I didn't like not being able to understand. Tight Fist Wu might be my informant, but he was still a criminal and there was no way to know if he was laying down the cover story we had agreed on, or selling Mackenzie out to the Triads.

And my camera angle wasn't giving me much. I could see the top of the old man's balding head and the iron gate, but not much else. There was some back and forth, and then Mackenzie was headed for the door.

The metal grate peeled open on well-worn hinges and clanged shut behind them, then they were headed down a dark stair into the basement of the building. The only light came from bare bulbs strung overhead. Wu leaned close to Mackenzie's mic and whispered, "We're in."

I winced and shook my head. Wu had seen too many movies. In real life undercover officers never make announcements into the microphone. It's a great way to blow your cover. And in the criminal world, it only takes a hint of suspicion to get an officer killed.

I took out my service weapon and pressed back on the slide to make certain there was a round in the chamber. If I had to go in, I wanted my gun close and ready for action. I prayed it wouldn't come to that.

I felt helpless as I watched them descend the stairs into the unknown. A moment later they emerged into a riot of sound and light that must have been hell for Mackenzie. There was the loud buzz and jangle of the machines and the raucous laughter of the players, along with the steady thrumming rhythm of hip hop music.

The camera image stopped. For a moment I thought the feed had frozen, then I realized it was Mackenzie who had frozen. She was standing there, her arms probably pinned to her side, like a statue. I remembered the way she'd jammed my neck in Times Square and knew she was fighting the pain from the avalanche of light and sound.

"Work through it," I whispered. "Come on Mackenzie. You can do it."

Wu was saying, "Hey, wassa matter? You okay?"

"Come on, Mackenzie," I said. "Don't crack up on me."

She managed to say, "I need the restroom."

"Right over there," Wu said and the camera swiveled. A moment later Mackenzie was hurrying through the casino, past rows of machines and tables, pushing through knots of people. She slammed through a door into the relative quiet of the ladies room.

I heard a toilet flush and glimpsed several ladies repairing their war paint in a long mirror. Mackenzie hurried past, found an empty stall and locked herself in. Then she was curled up on the toilet, sobbing, and my field of view was blacked out by her arms wrapped around her knees.

35

I dragged the headphones off my head and pushed up from the stool so fast it turned over, landing with a loud clang on the floor of the van. I was out the back door and hurrying along the sidewalk before I had anything resembling a plan. My mind was spinning and my legs felt like wet noodles. Mackenzie and I were undercover without official backup. If anything happened to an FBI agent, I'd be writing parking tickets until the day I retired. More than that, if anything really bad happened, I'd spend the rest of my life blaming myself. I knew she was autistic and I had let her walk into the lion's den.

I reached the old man and pointed at the iron gate. "You see a brunette in a red dress go through there?"

The old man and his friends stared at me with blank faces.

"She's my girlfriend," I said. "And she's with some other guy."

The old man shook his head and shrugged.

I spread my hands. "I know what goes on in there, okay.

I know there's gambling. Hell, I like to throw the dice myself. I don't care about that. She's my girlfriend and she's pregnant. And that guy she's with is a drug dealer. If I have to, I'll call the cops. I just want to get her and bring her out. Okay?"

The wizened old Chinese man watched me a moment and then nodded, almost imperceptibly.

I grasped the door and the hinges shrieked, then I was hurrying down the steps two at a time. I nearly fell flat on my face at the bottom. I pushed through another door into the raucous din made by the brightly colored machines all banging and whirring. It was almost too much for me. No wonder Mackenzie had gone catatonic. Who could blame her?

Looking around for the bathroom, I spotted Tight Fist Wu sitting at a table, watching the roulette wheel. His eyes locked with mine. I was here to save Mackenzie, but couldn't leave Wu in a pinch. If I barged in and carried Mackenzie out, Wu would have to answer some pretty tough questions. He might crack under pressure, or decide there was more money to be made selling out a pair of cops to the Black Dragons.

I put an ugly snarl on my face and said, "There you are you little weasel! Think you can just steal my girl?"

Wu was up off his seat, hands spread. "What are you tal..."

I plunged a fist into his breadbasket and he doubled up, then I grabbed him in a bear hug, like I was trying to put him in a headlock and said, "Get the hell out of here right now. Understand?"

He managed to nod. "Hey man, she called me," he said, playing his part. "Said she wanted to party in Chinatown."

"I ever catch you making time with my girl again and I'll kill ya! You hear?"

Wu shrugged me off and gave me a push that nearly sent me into the roulette table. "Whatever, *kwai lo*! Keep your hands off me!"

Then he was storming out.

A few people had turned to watch, but a surprising number went right on gambling. The dust-up wasn't their concern. I turned, searching for the ladies' room and spotted a door that resembled the one I had watched Mackenzie go through. There was no sign. Illegal gambling dens don't normally follow OSHA guidelines.

A pair of heavies had appeared out of nowhere. Both were bigger and taller than me, dressed in dark black suits with short buzz cuts. One of them had a nasty scar on his lip where someone had hit him with a bottle. He was not the type of fella I wanted to tangle with. If it came to a fight, I'd have to use my gun and things would go from bad to worse.

I pushed through the door into the ladies' and found the stall where Mackenzie was curled up, humming softly to herself. I rapped my knuckles against the flimsy plastic door. "Jessica? It's Cole. You okay?"

When I didn't get a response, I peeked over the top of the door. Mackenzie was curled up on top of the toilet, her knees pulled up to her chest and her cotton panties showing. Her face was buried against her knees. I said, "Hey, Mackenzie. We need to get out of here. Can you stand?"

She nodded but made no move to get up. When it was clear she wasn't moving under her own steam, I sighed, dropped onto my belly and wormed under the partition, getting decades of grime and filth all over my coat. I scrambled into the small space, managed to stand up, and unlocked the door before urging Mackenzie up.

"Come on," I said. "Stand up and walk with me. You're showing the world your underwear."

That got her moving. She stretched out her legs and pushed the hem of her dress down. Then we were out of the stall and headed for the door, but the pair of heavies in the dark suits blocked our path. One of them had a semi-automatic pistol in his giant paw. It wasn't aimed at us, it was hanging by his thigh, pointed at the floor, but the threat was very real. There was no way I could draw my weapon before he could lift his arm and shoot. I swallowed hard.

Mackenzie's eyes got wide. She said, "Oh."

"Come with us," the thug with the gun ordered.

"We were just leaving," I told them.

"Come with us," Scar said.

The first added, "We insist."

36

Mackenzie and I were seated in plush leather armchairs, in a spacious office with a deep piled rug underfoot. Several intricate Chinese tapestries hung on the wall. There was a whiff of incense in the air that reminded me of all those Sundays at Saint Marks. I could still hear the plink and ding of the pachinko machines, but it was muted and faraway.

The peace and relative quiet of the office helped calm Mackenzie. Instead of paralyzed by the overwhelming sensory input, she was paralyzed by two giant goons standing on either side of the door. The bigger of the two, Frick—I had come to think of them as Frick and Frack—still had a pistol in his massive paw. The other, Frack, stood with his muscular arms folded across his broad chest. He watched me with cold dead eyes.

I had my service weapon tucked in my holster at my hip. Frick and Frack hadn't bothered to search us, but I didn't dare go for it. I had a feeling Frick was waiting for me to try. It would simplify the situation for him and his partner.

I turned to Mackenzie and under my breath asked, "Thoughts?"

She was rocking back and forth in her chair, her fingers absently tapping out a tune on her bare white thigh. She said, "It's illegal to brandish a firearm in the county of New York and illegal to own one without a permit."

"Not sure he cares," I said.

"He should," Mackenzie said. "Possession of an illegal firearm is punishable by up to ten years in a federal penitentiary and a two-hundred and fifty-thousand dollar fine."

"Please don't tell him that," I said.

She did anyway.

Frick just stared at her like she were a mildly interesting piece of pottery.

We were in a jam. Fear was a tight fist squeezing my guts into new and interesting shapes.

The door opened and in walked a tall Chinese woman in a jade green dress with a slit up one thigh. Dark eyes took stock of us as she crossed the room. I watched her go past, watched her hips move, and the tantalizing glimpse of flesh through the slit in her cheongsam. There was a very good chance I'd die tonight, and still I was checking out a woman's legs. The male sex drive knows no limits.

The dragon lady crossed behind the desk and sat, took a moment to light a cigarette and breathed out a cloud of blue smoke before saying, "What have we here?"

I jumped in before Mackenzie could answer. I was afraid she'd tell the truth. She had a nasty habit of it. I said, "My girlfriend here got picked up by a low-life scumbag who brought her here and I came to get her. We don't want any trouble. Let us go and we'll be on our way."

Mackenzie turned to me with a confused frown on her face. "Girlfriend?"

"Yes, honey," I said, giving her a look that hopefully conveyed the dire warning I felt in my chest. "Let's not throw away everything we have over one little fight. I still love you."

"What fight?" Mackenzie asked. "Since when do you love me?"

The dragon lady watched me through a veil of smoke.

A nervous laugh rippled from my chest. "She's just upset," I said. "You know how women are?"

One finely manicured eyebrow arched. "Oh? Enlighten me."

"Well..." I shrugged. "That is to say... Not all women... of course... It's just..."

"Please," she said. "Spare me your lies. I know you are law enforcement."

She trained her eyes on me. "You are NYPD. That is a foregone conclusion."

My hand drifted to the gun hidden under my coat.

Her eyes swiveled to Mackenzie. "But I'm not sure what to make of you. You are not a cop. And I do not think you are a fed. Who are you and why are you here?"

"My name is Jessica Mackenzie," she said. "I'm a special investigator for the FBI. I want to speak to Tai Pan."

My heart sank, along with any chance I had of walking out of here. I shook my head and turned to Mackenzie with an exasperated sigh, but she was focused on our host.

The dragon lady sat back, took a drag, and shot smoke

up toward the ceiling. "The truth," she said. "How very bold of you. How do you know I won't have my men kill you both?"

Frick took a step forward.

"The murder of a federal officer is automatic life in prison," Mackenzie explained.

She laughed. It was a single short bark. "You must be incredibly brave. You came here, without any backup, and wish to speak to Tai Pan."

It was my turn to laugh. Only mine was forced and fake. I said, "What makes you think we haven't got backup?"

"Oh please." she waved away a cloud of smoke. "A SWAT team would already be breaking down my door. Let's dispense with the lies. Why are you here?"

"We're investigating a murder," Mackenzie said. "And we'd like to interview Tai Pan."

The dragon lady studied us from under heavy lidded eyes. "Very well. I'll give you five minutes."

37

Mackenzie blinked and cocked her head to the side. Her fingers temporarily stopped their drumming. "You're Tai Pan."

It was more a statement than a question.

My jaw was hanging open. Triads are not known for equal opportunity employment. In all my years working Chinatown, I'd never encountered a woman Triad. I'd certainly never heard of one taking the top spot. I heard myself say, "*You're* the head of the Black Dragons? How did that happen?"

She studied me with eyes rimmed in charcoal black liner. She had a shark's alien gaze. It was impossible to tell what was going on behind those eyes, but I had a feeling she was enjoying our surprise. She took a long drag from her cigarette and blew a cloud of smoke in my direction. I resisted the urge to cough and wave a hand in front of my face. She said, "Is that why you're here? To find out how a woman took the throne? Or are you here to ask about the death of John Chen?"

"How do *you* know we're looking into the murder of John Chen?" I asked. "If you know, then you must have something to do with it."

Tai Pan rolled her eyes. "Nothing happens in this town without my knowledge. And as to how I know you are investigating his death, that part is easy. A former police officer dies and now I have a pair of investigators in one of my clubs. It doesn't take a rocket scientist."

Mackenzie said, "How did you come to learn about Officer Chen's death?"

A small smile turned up one corner of her mouth. "I have my sources."

"What sources?"

"Reliable sources."

Mackenzie brought out her phone just like we were conducting an interview in an interrogation room. "Could you give me their names, please?"

Tai Pan laughed and turned to me, as if Mackenzie might be making a joke. But I wasn't smiling. She turned back to Mackenzie and said, "Surely, you aren't serious?"

"Of course." Mackenzie's thumbs hovered over the screen. "I'd like to interview them. One of them may be involved, or know more than they think. The information might lead us to the killer. Their names, please?"

"Everyone knows who killed John Chen," Tai Pan said.

"Is that so?" I asked.

Mackenzie said, "Who?"

"Kwang Di."

I clicked my tongue. "Not this again. You really expect us to believe an ancient Chinese sorcerer came back from the dead?"

"Think what you like," Tai Pan said. "It is the truth."

"Where have I heard that before?"

Mackenzie leaned forward. "You believe the ghost of Kwang Di killed John Chen?"

Tai Pan nodded. It was a subtle movement, barely more than a twitch.

"There's no such thing as ghosts," I said.

"Maybe not in your world," Tai Pan said.

"Not in any world," I said.

She leaned back in her leather office chair and studied me through slowly swirling eddies of cigarette smoke. "What makes you so sure?"

"Because I don't believe in ghosts," I said. "But I do believe in motive. John was a cop and a damn good one. You're a low life. You found out he was a cop and sent a couple of your bully boys to make an example of him. How's that sound to you? I'll bet a jury will buy it."

"What a jury thinks is quiet irrelevant," Tai Pan said. "I'm not on trial and I never will be. You, on the other hand, will be lucky to leave here alive."

Frick and Frack took a step closer, crowding my space.

Tai Pan said, "Make no mistake, officers. You are not in charge here. I am."

Mackenzie said, "You realize it's a crime to threaten a law officer?"

"How do you plan on pressing charges?" she asked. "If I decide to let you leave, which I'm honestly still debating, you'll never see me again."

I swallowed a knot in my throat.

Mackenzie said, "We're only interested in the death of

John Chen. You say you had nothing to do with it, but how can I believe you?"

She stubbed out her cigarette in a jade ashtray. "I had no reason to kill John. He was working for me."

"This is B.S." I growled.

"It's true," Tai Pan told us. "John had been hired by MacNab as part of a security team to protect his future investments. I'm a businesswoman and wanted to know how the deal with MacNab was proceeding. John was passing information to me."

I leaned forward, my hands curling into fists. My mouth turned down in a frown. "Are you telling me John was on the take?"

She smiled. "Are you surprised?"

"The John I know didn't take money from criminals."

"Perhaps you did not know him as well as you think," she said. "It's surprising what people will do to make ends meet in retirement. The NYPD doesn't pay that well, you know?"

I forced my hands to relax and asked myself the question; could John have been working for the Triads? I wanted to say it was impossible, but the rational side of me knew it was true. A little extra cash to keep the locale syndicate abreast of the *kwai lo* real estate developer's plans was an easy sell. After all, who did it hurt? Certainly not Connor MacNab. He was a billionaire. If this deal fell through, he'd be on to the next multibillion dollar deal.

Tai Pan watched my face as I came to the inevitable truth. She grinned. "As you can see, I had no reason to kill John."

Mackenzie said, "What can you tell us about Kwang Di?"

"Little more than the old man at the Happy Time Dumpling"

"I'd like to hear your own thoughts on the subject if you don't mind," Mackenzie said.

"I do mind," Tai Pan said. "This interview is over."

"I have more questions," Mackenzie said.

Tai Pan consulted a slim gold wristwatch. "I have important business elsewhere. You'll have to excuse me, and I apologize in advance for the rough treatment you'll receive on your way out."

38

I was shoved out the gate and went sprawling on the pavement, landing in a puddle of something wet and sticky that soaked through my shirt. Across the alley was a Chinese restaurant with a dumpster full of moldering refuse. The smell was a cross between rotting chicken guts and stale piss, and it made my eyes water.

Mackenzie was ejected as well, but with considerably less force. She staggered but was in no danger of face-planting. She said, "Are you alright?"

"Fine." I sat up and wiped sludge from my button down. The front of my shirt was covered in something dark green. "I don't think this is going to dry clean out."

Mackenzie helped me to my feet before turning for a look at the iron gate and the old man playing mahjong. He went on with his game as if we didn't exist. Mackenzie said, "Don't they know they can be charged with assaulting an officer?"

"They don't care," I told her.

"They should," she said and cited the penal code along with the potential penalties.

"That was a waste of time," I remarked.

"Not really. We now know the Black Dragons are not responsible for John Chen's death."

"Assuming Tai Pan is telling the truth," I said. "She might be lying. She's a criminal after all."

Mackenzie shook her head. "I don't think so."

"For the record, me neither. Which leads us right back to square one. A dead officer and no leads."

"I wouldn't say that."

"Please don't tell me you're back on the ghost of Kwang Di."

Mackenzie took a black hair tie from her small clutch and pulled her hair back into a ponytail. "Everyone we have interviewed from the owners of the Happy Time Dumpling to the head of the Black Dragons seem to think Kwang Di is responsible."

"There's no such thing as ghosts."

"You keep saying that, but you haven't provided any proof that they don't exist."

"I don't have to prove anything," I told her. "You're the one who thinks they exist. The onus is on you to prove they're real."

We were headed back toward the van. The night was turning cold and the sludge on my shirt smelled like rotting offal. I wanted to get home and take a shower but I knew we had to report this first, and that meant paperwork. Mackenzie said, "Dan Ackroyd believes ghosts are real."

"Dan Ackroyd?" I said. "The actor?"

She nodded.

"He lives in Hollywood," I said. "They're all nuts."

"Everyone in Hollywood is nuts?"

"Yes."

"I'm fairly certain that's not true," she said. "I think you're speaking hyperbolically."

"Trust me," I told her. "You tip America on edge and everything that's not screwed down right, rolls to California."

Mackenzie took a moment before she said, "That's a joke?"

"Yes," I said. "But also true."

"You can't tip America on edge."

"You're right," I said. "That would be impossible. The same way ghosts are impossible."

"Not impossible," Mackenzie said. We had reached the van and I opened the passenger side door. She climbed inside and her dress rode up, giving me a generous view of her legs. "They are very possible, but they've never been properly documented. Just because something hasn't been measured and classified, doesn't mean it's not real. At one time America was undiscovered."

"You're welcome to call up Dan Ackroyd and work on ghost documentation. I'm going to focus on the developer. Maybe someone at Connor MacNab found out John was passing information to the Triads and decided to shut him up."

"I can't call Dan Ackroyd," Mackenzie said. "I don't have his number and I doubt he would take my call. He's a big Hollywood star."

I settled behind the steering wheel and said, "It was a joke, Mac."

She blinked. "Mac?"

"Mac," I said. "Short for Mackenzie."

"I don't like that. Please don't do that."

"Fine." I held up both hands. "Mackenzie. Let's go file our report. I want to get home and take a shower."

Before we could put that plan into action my phone started buzzing. I pulled it out and saw Lieutenant DeSilva's name on the caller ID before putting the phone to my ear. "Evening Lieutenant. I was just about to call you. We've got a location on an illegal gambling den run by the Black Dragon crime syndicate. If we hurry, we can bust it up and put several of them behind bars."

"That'll have to wait," he told me. "There's another body."

FROM THE JOURNAL OF JESSICA MACKENZIE

My first ever undercover operation was a dismal failure. All I had to do was observe an illegal gambling operation and yet the lights and sounds were simply too much. It was like a drill bit in my frontal lobe, ripping at my sanity. I don't quite remember how I got there but I found myself curled up on a toilet. Or more correctly, Detective Cole found me on a toilet. In the moment, I was incapable of rational thought. All I knew was that I had to escape the noise.

At times like this I feel completely incapable of being an investigator. What kind of investigator turns catatonic because of loud music? I'm a dismal failure and if my department head ever hears of my incompetence, I'll be fired.

39

The corpse was in a shadowy space, too small to be called an alley, snaking between apartment buildings less than a block from the Happy Time Dumpling. A rusted iron fire escape crammed the space overhead, making me feel like a spelunker in an urban cave carved of concrete, brick, and steel. It was a little after four in the morning and the sun was still just a rumor on the horizon. The only light came from a naked bulb in a wire cage over a metal door. A cold wind ripped along the corridor, carrying with it the stench from overflowing trash bins and the decay that lurks just below the surface of any major metropolitan area; a smell of despair.

A glistening pink husk lay twisted on its side, face to the wall and arms stretched overhead. One hand still had the skin attached, along with most of the lower body. The scalp was intact as well. She had straight black hair, matted with dark blood.

Pottinger and Boone had arrived first. Both Chinatown

detectives stood over the body, hands tucked in their overcoats, brows furrowed. They were deep in conversation when Mackenzie and I ducked the crime scene tape.

"How'd you two get wind of it?" Boone wanted to know.

"Grapevine," I told him and left it at that.

The Chinatown detectives exchanged a glance. Boone said, "Heard you two been chasing Triads. How's that working out for ya?"

"We just came from a meeting with Tai Pan," Mackenzie told him, pulling on a pair of nitrile gloves.

Pottinger's brows went up and Boone said, "You actually met the Tai Pan?"

Mackenzie nodded.

"Dead end," I told them. "Tai Pan isn't our killer."

Mackenzie crouched down, peering at what remained of the victim. She was too busy examining the corpse to realize she was giving the detectives, along with the crime scene techs, a show. She was still wearing her slinky red dress and Pottinger studied her legs. His eyes trailed up Mackenzie's thighs, then shifted to me.

I levelled my best scowl at him.

He nodded at the stain on my shirt. "Date night?"

"Mud wrestling," I told him.

Tippy Lewis arrived ten minutes later, huffing and puffing. He went to work right away, bagging the hands and feet, and taking fiber samples. Pottinger and Boone had drawn away to confer in quiet while Makenzie and I stayed with the body. The number of techs swelled until the small space between buildings was a bustling hive. People had to shimmy past one another. I handed a uniformed officer a ten spot and asked him to fetch me a coffee. He looked green around the gills and was grateful to escape.

On the ground at my feet was a puddle of blood, drying into a tacky paste, just like the first victim, and Mackenzie discovered the same three marks. If I hadn't just come from a meeting with Tai Pan, I'd be absolutely certain it was a Triad calling card. But Tai Pan had impressed me with her frank honesty. If she was responsible for these murders, Mackenzie and I would be floating face down in the Hudson right now. The fact we were allowed to leave convinced me of her innocence.

By the time the uniform made it back with my coffee, news crews had started to converge. He passed me a styrofoam mug at arm's length, careful not to look at the body.

I thanked him and then thrust my chin at the gaggle of reporters clogging up the entrance to the narrow lane. "Get them back."

"Sure thing detective."

It gave him something to do and would keep him from upchucking all over the body.

"Got more to work with this time," Tippy told us. He directed his statement at all four detectives, careful not to take sides.

I sipped coffee. The caffeine helped drive out some of the cobwebs and I said, "A girl, right?"

He nodded. "Young by the looks. Mid to late teens."

I grimaced. It's always hard when someone so young dies. You can't help thinking about all the things they'll never get to do. She'd never go to prom, graduate high school, go off to college, never get married, or have children. What a shame. "How long has she been here?"

"Couple of hours at least." Tippy said. "Any trace of the missing skin?"

"None," I told him. "And we've searched this whole street. I've got uniforms doing a sweep of the neighborhood."

"Odd," Tippy said.

"What's odd?"

He motioned to the ground around the body. "There's no blood trail. The skin should be leaking blood all over the place after it's removed. I noticed the same thing at the other crime scene. It's like the killer removes the skin and somehow carries it away without leaving any blood trail. Like the skin just vanishes."

That thought sent a shiver up my spine. "What else can you tell me?"

Tippy shrugged. "Only that she's Asian."

"That doesn't give us much in this neighborhood."

"I'll have more once I get her back to the lab."

"Sure," I said and then looked in the direction of the reporters. The sun was coming up, casting the tops of the New York City sky scrapers in cold yellow fire, and the press was hollering for a statement. I said, "Make this your top priority, okay? We gotta close this case before the media starts a panic."

"You got it, Mike."

"I think I know the victim," Mackenzie said.

She was crouched near a line of dented trashcans covered in decades of gang tags and graffiti. The breath steamed out of her mouth in silver clouds, but she didn't seem to notice the cold. She held out a hand to Tippy. "May I borrow your pen?"

He passed it over and Mackenzie used it to lift the collar of a faded green Army surplus jacket from one of the metal trash bins.

40

It was almost noon. Mackenzie and I were in DeSilva's office and my brain was screaming for sleep. I had a cup of lukewarm coffee in one hand that tasted like sludge, but caffeine was no match for the fog creeping around my synapses. I couldn't remember the last time I had pulled an all-nighter. Cadets fresh out of the academy usually work the overnight, but those days were long past. And I'm creeping ever closer to middle age. My body just can't take the stress that comes with being up all night. It didn't seem to bother Mackenzie however. She was still in her dress, her hair up in a ponytail, looking like she could go another twenty-four hours.

De Silva's office was a small space decorated with a single accommodation. He sat back in his executive leather chair, his face long, one slim white hand resting on a folded newspaper. He had already raked us over the coals for the unwarranted operation into the Triad gambling den. Benny Hoag and his vice team had conducted a raid based on our info, but by the time they arrived the place was empty. A number of pachinko machines had been left behind, along with a handwritten note tacked to a wall advising the NYPD to '*suck it pigs*'. DeSilva read us the riot act, promising to bench us both if we pulled any more crazy stunts, before calming down.

"Any word on the girl?" he asked. His suit this morning was pinstriped and a baby blue pocket square matched his tie. "What did you say her name was? Sue?"

"Xu Yin," I supplied. "And none."

DeSilva frowned and shook his head. His eyes flashed to a framed picture of his wife and daughter propped on the corner of his desk. He muttered, "Shame."

I nodded.

Mackenzie and I had already been to the Happy Time Dumpling. Xu Yin had gone out last night, Momma Lo told us, and that's the last anyone had seen of her.

De Silva leaned back in his chair, causing the springs to creak. He said, "Tippy going over the body now?"

I nodded.

"He should have a preliminary in a few hours," Mackenzie said.

"Good," DeSilva said. "We need to find the killer and fast. Things are about to blow up in our faces."

"What makes you say that?" Mackenzie asked.

"You two obviously missed the morning edition." DeSilva unfolded the newspaper and passed it over. The headline read; FEAR GRIPS CHINATOWN. THREE DEAD. LOCALS BLAME GHOST.

Mackenzie and I put our heads together to read. One of the residents had told a reporter at the Times all about the dead sorcerer and his penchant for taking skins. I shrugged

SKIN IN THE GAME

and dropped the paper on DeSilva's desk. "No one reads print these days."

In answer, DeSilva brought out his cellphone and queued up a YouTube video of a shop owner telling anyone who would listen that the ghost of Kwang Di had returned from the grave to exact vengeance on the people of Chinatown. The video was trending with over two-hundred thousand views.

"Okay," I admitted. "That's bad."

"Why is that bad?" Mackenzie asked.

"It's going to cause a panic," I said.

"It already has," DeSilva told us. "I just got off the phone with Upton. He's not very happy with you two by the way. Says he should have been brought in on the illegal casino. You'll have to tread lightly around him."

Mackenzie started to ask what he meant by that but I warned her off and motioned for DeSilva to continue.

"Upton's had to call out the riot squads. All of Chinatown is in an uproar. The Triads have taken it upon themselves to act as community watch. They torched a white-owned business and beat up a few tourists. Things are getting out of hand."

"That's all we need," I muttered.

"Have you got any leads?" DeSilva asked. After a beat he added, "Any leads that don't involve ancient Chinese sorcerers from the afterlife?"

Mackenzie had her mouth open to speak but closed it.

"Yes, as a matter of fact." I told DeSilva about John Chen's work as a security guard for MacNab industries and his arrangement with the Triads.

"Sounds promising," DeSilva said.

My phone buzzed. I checked the caller ID and stood up. "Just got a text from Tippy. He's got something for us."

"Maybe you just caught a break," DeSilva said. "Keep me up to speed."

"Up to speed?" Mackenzie said as she rose and smoothed her dress. "What does that mean?"

DeSilva looked at her like she'd just sprouted a third eye.

I caught her elbow and steered her toward the door. "Come on. I'll explain on the way."

41

Tippy Lewis was shuffling around the skinned corpse in his white lab coat with a Mars Bar poking out of his top pocket. He had on plastic safety goggles and a scruffy five o'clock shadow covered his many chins. He glanced up as Mackenzie and I entered. "Good news and bad news."

"Start with the good news." I pulled on a sea foam green smock and sorted through the bin of goggles for a pair that wasn't so scratched it would be like looking at the world through an old dog's cataract. I was in desperate need of a shower and a shave. Whatever was on my shirt had turned a nasty puke shade of green and it smelled like someone mixed turpentine with horse manure before baking it in an oven at 400 degrees for days on end. The smell was so bad that I welcomed the formaldehyde and rot of the autopsy room.

Even Mackenzie was starting to show signs of fatigue. Her eyes were dull orbs and her mouth a tight line. Her constantly worrying fingers had frayed the hem of the red dress. I wondered about the price tag on a piece like that, and if her sister would even care. Probably not, I decided. The Mackenzies had more money than some small nations. For Morgan Mackenzie, a two-thousand dollar cocktail dress held no more importance than a dish rag to the rest of us. As for Jessica, well she probably had no idea how much the dress cost. From the look of her normal attire, Jessica shopped at thrift stores circa 1975.

"I've got enough here for dental records," Tippy told us. "I haven't gotten all the results back yet, but I can say with almost one-hundred percent certainty that this is *not* Lo Xu Yin."

My heart did a little leap. Xu Yin was a street tough smart-aleck, but I liked her. She was a good kid and I did not want to imagine her dead in a crummy alley in Chinatown with her skin ripped off. I said, "That's great news!"

"How can you be sure?" Mackenzie wanted to know. She was struggling with the ties on her smock and I helped.

"I was able to get Xu Yin's dental records from her dentist in Chinatown," Tippy said and I knew he had gone the extra mile to get the information so fast. No one likes to see a teen girl butchered, especially law enforcement. Tippy directed our attention to an x-ray clipped to the lightboard on the wall. A photonegative of human chompers glowed like a Halloween decoration through the black and white. "That's a copy of Xu Yin's most recent x-ray. It's a few years old, but still useful. See the left canine?"

"Pretend I'm not familiar with human dental vocabulary," I said.

Mackenzie circled a tooth in the x-ray with her pinkie

finger. "It's this one here." She was nodding. "It's decidedly crooked."

I had to squint and tip my head to the side. Reading X-rays had never been one of my talents. I thought I could see a snaggle tooth in the glowing black and white, but it was hard to be sure.

"That's right," Tippy said, clearly impressed with Mackenzie's ability to read and interpret data. He directed her attention to the corpse stretched out on the stainless steel slab. "Check out our victim's teeth."

Our shoes made peeling noises on the tile floor. Mackenzie bent over the corpse. Most of the skin had been taken off the face. The lips were missing, giving us a clear view of her dentals. Mackenzie said, "This person had braces. Recently."

"Right again," Tippy said.

"How do you know that?" I asked.

"There are certain tell-tale signs," Mackenzie informed me. "If you know what to look for. Could Xu Yin have had braces after that x-ray?"

Tippy shook his head. "Already checked with the family. The girl never had braces."

"Good work, Tippy." I crossed my arms over my chest and stared down at the skinless husk of slippery muscle and tendon, thankful I hadn't eaten any breakfast. I said, "But if this isn't Xu Yin, who is it?"

"I can't tell you that," Tippy said. "However, with these teeth, it's not going to be too hard to find out. I took an impression already and I'm checking with all the dentists in Chinatown. I should have a match for you in a day or two."

"That long?"

He shrugged. "We have to call each and every dentist and then wait for them to check their records. It takes time."

"How did she die?" Mackenzie asked.

"Glad you asked." Tippy took hold of the corpse's head and carefully, slowly, turned it to the right. "See this?"

He was pointing to a big ugly gash in the back of the skull. Looked like blunt force trauma. In layman's terms, someone had cracked the girl's noggin.

"She was struck?" Mackenzie asked.

He shook his head. "We found trace bits of skin, blood, and hair on the corner of a dumpster in the alley where we found the body. From the severity and direction of the blow, I think she either fell or was pushed."

"And smacked her head on the dumpster," I finished for him.

He nodded. "One last bit of trivia for you. This one was done in a hurry."

"What do you mean?" I asked.

Mackenzie answered for him. She was closely scrutinizing the body and said, "The skin was removed rapidly. The strokes are hurried and uneven."

"She's right," Tippy conceded, though he looked annoyed at having his thunder stolen. "With John the killer took their time, making sure the cuts were precise. With this one, the killer was in a hurry."

42

I was at my desk in the bullpen, my feet stacked on an open drawer and an old weathered football in my hands. I had found a change of clothes in my locker. The slacks were rumpled and the shirt had a slightly musty odor, but it was better than rotting garbage. I stared up at buzzing fluorescents and water-stained ceiling tiles, adjusting and readjusting my grip on the pigskin while I kicked over the facts.

While I called the Happy Time Dumpling to deliver the good news, Mackenzie had gone home for a change of clothes. She came back in her familiar corduroys and an oversized sweater with a cartoon bear on the front. The bear was wearing a bow tie and roller skates. Mackenzie seemed to think this was incredibly funny. Now she was pacing, her fingers dancing over an imaginary piano.

"The victims don't make any sense," I told her, staring at a water stain on the ceiling in the shape of the Madonna. "We've got an old woman, a security guard, and a teenage girl. How do they connect?"

"Why should they share a connection?" Mackenzie asked.

"Most murders aren't random," I said. "Killers usually have a purpose."

"But not a ghost," Mackenzie pointed out.

"Please don't start."

"If it really is a ghost," Mackenzie continued, "then the victims need not share any connection other than being Chinese and living in the area of the haunting."

"Keep your voice down, will ya?" I took my feet down, leaned forward, and spoke in hushed tones. "It's not a ghost. There's no such thing."

Mackenzie started to speak and I held up a finger. "Someone is killing and skinning people," I told her. "It's not a ghost. It's a person. And I'm starting to think we're dealing with some kind of serial killer."

Mackenzie frowned. "Serial killers normally have a type, a victim profile, and a reason for their behavior."

"Maybe we're overlooking the obvious," I said.

"Which is?"

"All the victims are Chinese."

"You think it might be racially motivated?"

"Possible."

The elevator dinged. Moore and Santiago stepped out. They had just closed a high profile case where a naked man in a ski mask had been robbing people at gunpoint. The papers were calling him the Streaking Bandit. Moore spotted me and said in a loud voice, "Well, if it isn't Peter Venkman. Catch any ghosts today?"

That line got a general chuckle from the bullpen. I gave

him the bird and said, "Heard you got your hands on the naked bandit. Bet you enjoyed that."

Moore's fists clenched and the muscles at the corner of his jaw bunched tight.

Santiago grabbed his shoulder and pulled him away. "Let it go."

"Why are they so mean to you?" Mackenzie asked.

"They're just jerks," I told her. "Some people are born mean."

"There has to be more to it than that."

I tossed the football into the open drawer and kicked it shut. "We've got history."

"What do you mean?"

"My first year as a detective, I uncovered evidence in one of their old cases that proved they had put an innocent man behind bars for murder," I said. "They've never forgiven me. And when I had my troubles, they pushed hard to get me fired."

Mackenzie blinked. "Why?"

"Pay me back for overturning their case."

"Why?" Mackenzie asked. "They made a mistake and you helped to find the right killer. Shouldn't they be happy?"

"Would you be?"

She nodded. "Yes."

"Of course you would." The way she said it left no room for doubt. She was here for justice. Whether she found the killer or someone else did, all she cared about was the truth, even if that truth made her look bad. Ego didn't factor into it. I shook my head and said, "Most people don't feel that way."

Mackenzie's head cocked to the side. "I don't understand that at all."

I returned my thoughts back to the problem at hand. "Three victims, no apparent link other than race, and now a missing girl."

"I've been thinking about that," Mackenzie said.

"And?"

"The jacket we found definitely belonged to Xu Yin."

"Agreed," I said. "So she was in the alley."

"Which means she's probably a witness."

"But where is she?" I said. "That's the question."

We had an APB out on the girl but Manhattan is a big place and she hadn't turned up yet. Momma Lo said it wasn't like Xu Yin to miss work. I leaned forward and laced my fingers together. "Maybe she's been kidnapped? Maybe the killer nabbed her?"

"Why?" Mackenzie asked. "Why not simply kill her?"

"I can't figure that part out."

"She was the one who found the body of John Chen," Mackenzie said. "And she was present at the next murder..."

"I see where you're going and I don't like it."

"Why not?"

"There's no way."

"What makes you say that?"

"You met her," I said. "Does that little tomboy strike you as a murderer?"

"You can't tell a murderer just by looking at a person."

"That's as may be, but I'm telling you right now that little girl isn't our killer."

"Then where is she?" Mackenzie asked.

"Either she was snatched by the killer," I said, "or she's running scared."

"If it really is the ghost of Kwang Di—"

"It's not," I interjected.

"—then it would explain why Xu Yin went into hiding."

A uniformed police officer stepped out of the elevator carrying a cardboard box full of plastic evidence bags. He made his way over to my desk and said, "You the ones working the Chinatown Ghost?"

"Yeah that's us," I groaned. The case had picked up a nickname. That's all we needed. A bunch of papers running the headline Chinatown Ghost.

He parked the box on my desk. "A canvas found this two blocks from your latest victim. We think it's the clothes."

After a cursory peek, Mackenzie and I carried the box down to forensics, logged the contents as evidence, and donned gloves before sorting the various bits of clothing onto a big table under the glow of fluorescent lights. Tippy joined us a few minutes later. We found a sweater with flecks of blood around the collar, a pair of denims with mud caked on the seat of the pants, and colorful tennis shoes with dry clay in the treads. Mackenzie asked Tippy to run soil samples.

"Along with DNA and fiber on everything," I added.

"What is this, my first day?" Tippy snorted at us.

From the bottom of the box, under a backpack stuffed with textbooks, gym clothes, and tampons, I pulled out a small periwinkle wallet with a gold zipper. Inside was a laminated ID card. "Our victim's name is Jennifer Kwan."

43

Two hours later, Mackenzie and I were standing on a street corner in Chinatown, huddling against a bitter November wind. The sun was throwing shafts of cold light between Manhattan high rises, but did little to take away the chill.

We had just delivered the bad news to Jennifer Kwan's parents. Mr. Kwan worked for a title company and Mrs. Kwan was a school teacher. Both parents were overcome with grief and it was a long time before we could get any information from them. In the end, neither had anything useful. Jennifer was a good daughter and a good student. She got into her fair share of trouble, what teenager didn't? But it was all minor stuff, cutting gym class to go clothes shopping with her girlfriends, throwing the occasional party while her parents were out of town. Nothing that would get a teenage girl killed.

It was all the things my own daughter would probably be doing if she were still alive, and it left a hard, cold knot deep in my chest. A pair of oxycodone and a Xanax would unravel the knot, but that was a temporary fix at best. I'd been down that road before and never wanted to go there again, so I took a few deep breaths and leaned my hips against the front of the Mercury. The only useful bit of intel we had gotten from the Kwans was that Jennifer and Xu Yin were classmates.

"I feel like every time we get a lead we end up right back at square one," I said.

There was a television crew two blocks away, parked in front of the small alley where we had found Jennifer Kwan's body. A reporter was doing a piece on the mysterious killings while locals milled about, gawking at the camera. The segment would be on the nightly news and would add fuel to the fire.

An undercurrent of fear and suspicion coursed through Chinatown. People passing by gave us curious sidelong stares and I noticed many of the shops closing early. I watched as the portly owner of a tea shop pulled down the metal gate and locked the front door before switching out the lights. It was barely dinner time and Chinatown was rolling up the sidewalks. No one wanted to be out after dark with a murderous ghost on the loose.

Triads had taken it upon themselves to police the neighborhood. Several knots of surly looking Chinese youths cruised the streets with short sticks, brass knuckles, and bits of chain. I could roust them for illegal weapons, but I'd spend the whole night rounding up Chinese gangsters and never get anywhere on the case. One group of toughs spotted Mackenzie and I on the corner and started across the street.

I swept my coat back to display my shield and gave

them my best cop stare, which sent them in the other direction.

There had already been several instances of gang and racial violence. Mostly it was Triads beating up *kwai lo*, and right now there was no shortage of *kwai lo*. More tourists than normal had flocked to Chinatown, drawn by reports of murder and ghosts. Everyone wants to say they were close to the chaos. The human penchant for the macabre is both fascinating and terrifying.

Mackenzie stood with her hands locked against her sides and her face going through a complicated series of expressions. It was her thinking face. I had come to recognize it and let her do her thinking in quiet. She finally pointed and I followed her finger. Halfway between us and the news crew was a three-story banner fixed to the side of a building that said: FUTURE SITE OF MacNAB DEVELOPMENT HIGH RISE LUXURY APARTMENTS.

I said, "Yeah, MacNab will buy up the property at a discount price now that the place is haunted."

Then it hit me.

I turned to Mackenzie. "You don't think?"

She nodded. Her words weren't working right now, but she managed to make her meaning clear by jabbing her finger at the banner. MacNab wanted to buy up the real estate and the stubborn locals, in many cases, refused to sell. What better way to force them out? I said, "I think we need to have a sit down with Connor MacNab."

We tried calling and got the cold shoulder from a receptionist who informed us Mr. MacNab was at his house in the Hamptons and that he *might* return our call when he had time.

I hung up the phone and said, "Want to go pay him a visit at home?"

Mackenzie nodded again and reached for the door handle.

"You going to be able to talk?" I asked.

She climbed inside. I circled the bumper and piled in beside her. It took her a minute to get her words working. She said, "I'll be okay. I'm just tired and I need a sensory break."

"A sensory what?"

"A sensory break," she told me. "A break from all the sensory input. Some place quiet."

I got the engine started and shifted into drive. "Want to stop by the Park?"

She nodded.

44

An hour in Central Park, strolling among the trees, set Mackenzie right and it was a good thing too, because she needed something to get her through the drive to Southampton. She spent the first half curled up in the passenger seat scrolling articles on her phone and making notes. She was researching ghosts and occasionally read interesting facts aloud.

"Did you know researchers at the University of Cambridge have been able to document changes in both temperature and electromagnetic field variations in buildings that were supposedly haunted?" I was noncommittal. I didn't want her going down that rabbit hole. I kept my responses to surly grunts and one-word answers.

"A team from Brown obtained audio graphs from an empty house in Savannah that clearly captures a child's voice followed by knocking sounds."

I gave a long *hmmm* that might be misconstrued as interest.

"Of course, all those things can be faked, but the question is why?"

"Why would someone want to fake paranormal evidence?" I said. "I can think of a bunch of reasons."

"Such as?"

"Money for starters," I told her.

"Why would anyone fake evidence of ghosts for money?"

"Researchers get paid big bucks from universities and the government," I told her. "If they admit their research is going nowhere, the funding dries up. I know this is going to be hard for you to believe, but a lot of people, most people, would rather fudge the results and keep the greenbacks rolling in than admit they have nothing."

"That doesn't make any sense."

"Maybe not to you," I said. "More importantly, most people have beliefs and they go looking for evidence to support those beliefs. When they can't find the evidence, people invent it. That's why America keeps electing career politicians."

"Like you," Mackenzie said.

"What are you talking about?"

"You don't want to believe a ghost killed those people so you're looking for evidence to the contrary."

"Because that's the truth."

"That's what you *want* the truth to be."

I rolled my eyes. "Think what you like. There's no such thing as ghosts. We're going to find John's killer and it's going to be a human."

"Maybe," Mackenzie said.

She spent the rest of the drive rocking back and forth and humming *Jingle Bell Rock* under her breath.

It was late by the time we pulled up to Connor MacNab's Southampton address. Stars were winking in a black velvet curtain and I could hear the crash of waves. MacNab's house was a sprawling, ultra-modern three-story mansion on the dunes surrounded by a high wall topped with security cameras.

We had come at the right time; there was a party and guests were just arriving. Cars were pulling up to the gates and we joined the queue. My beat-up Mercury Cougar with an explosion of neon paint baked on the hood looked out of place bumper to bumper with Teslas and BMWs.

"We may be in luck," I told Mackenzie.

"What do you mean?"

We had reached the front and a valet in a crimson waist coat hurried over.

I told Mackenzie, "We walk right in like we're invited."

"But we weren't invited."

"Nobody will know."

"We'll know."

"You want to talk to MacNab, right?"

Mackenzie nodded.

"Then follow my lead."

"But how do we..."

"Just act like you're supposed to be here."

She chewed her bottom lip a moment and then nodded and pushed her door open. I climbed out, passed the valet a crumpled dollar bill, and told him, "Make sure you scratch a more expensive car with her."

He grinned. "Yes sir."

45

My entire apartment would fit inside the entryway of Connor MacNab's Southampton house. In fact, there would be room to spare. It was a brightly lit cavern with pink marble floors and mirrored ceilings held aloft by roman pillars. The space was carefully designed to give testimony to the power and prestige of the man who owned it. Mission accomplished. I felt small and insignificant. Not to mention under dressed. I was struck by a momentary pang of jealousy and as we made our way into a vast hall lined with modern art, I decided Connor MacNab was probably guilty of something and that I should find a crime to hang on him just to spite. Don't get me wrong, I don't hate the rich or anything like that. I'm old enough and mature enough to realize it's the rich who start businesses and create jobs, but as I milled among the crowd, I decided Connor MacNab was the kind of rich bastard who liked to flaunt his success and needed to be taken down a peg.

A serving girl in a short black skirt with dark leggings wandered past carrying a tray of champagne. I caught one of the flutes and thanked her with a nod, which she ignored. The champagne was good, probably the best I've ever had, but I don't sip much champagne.

Mackenzie didn't seem impressed by our surroundings, but then she'd probably grown up in a house twice this size. We milled around, wandering from room to opulent room, until we laid eyes on the man himself; Zeus dwelling at the top of Mount Olympus. I had seen him before, in pictures and on the TV, but this was the first time I'd clapped eyes on him in person. He was the shortest guy in the room. Most of the women towered over him. No wonder he needed such lavish surroundings. The house and everything in it was trying to compensate for his diminutive stature. His suit was tailored, probably somewhere in London or the south of France, and his beard was well trimmed. He was shaking hands with a senator, flashing straight white teeth, and his eyes crinkled at the corners. "Good to see you again, Bill."

"Thanks for inviting me," the senator said. He was a representative from New Jersey. I'd seen him on the nightly news stumping for some political candidate or other. He'd represented Jersey for the last few years, and that's all I know about Jersey politics. I generally hold the opinion that you can tell a politician is lying when their lips are moving.

The fact that MacNab was on a first-name basis with politicians made me dislike him even more. I elbowed Mackenzie and we threaded our way through the crowd.

"Mr. MacNab." I stuck out a hand. "Good to meet you."

He looked at my hand and then at me. His mouth worked into a smile that forgot to notify the rest of his face.

His handshake was short and perfunctory. "Enjoy the party."

That was all he said before taking the senator from Jersey by the elbow and leading him away.

"Hello, sir," Mackenzie called after him. "I'd like to ask you a few questions."

But MacNab ignored.

I turned to Mackenzie. "What a swell guy."

"I think he was rather rude."

"I was being sarcastic."

"You know I have a hard time with sarcasm."

"Right," I said. "I forgot about our hand signal."

I put up the hang ten sign and said, "I really like him. He's great."

She smiled and returned the sign. "He's very polite and welcoming."

She said it in the same dry, matter-of-fact tone she used for everything else and if she wasn't using the hang ten sign, I never would have known she was trying to make a joke.

I laughed. "We have to work on your sarcasm voice."

"What's a sarcasm voice?"

"It's the tone you use when you want to be sarcastic," I told her and led her through the room toward a wet bar while I tried to explain the subtleties of tone.

A well-dressed young man was mixing drinks and cracking jokes with some of the other guests. I put my back against the mahogany countertop and scanned the room while I schemed up ways to trap MacNab into a private conversation. He had obviously taken my measure and instantly knew I didn't belong. Of course, that wasn't hard.

Mackenzie and I were the only people not dressed to the nines with diamonds dripping off our fingers.

"I really like Mr. MacNab," Mackenzie said, practicing her sarcasm. "He's swell."

"I see you've met my father."

I turned.

The young man at the bar was busy mixing a Manhattan and offered a sympathetic smile. I could see the resemblance right away. He had the same small build and light blonde hair, but he was nearly a foot taller. He probably got his height from his mother, no doubt a supermodel.

"Don't feel bad," he told me. "It took me nearly seventeen years to get my first audience with the king."

He passed me the drink and said, "The trick is you need to have something he wants, or he hasn't got time for you."

I accepted the Manhattan, setting aside the champagne flute, and sipped. My eyebrows went up. "This is really good."

He grinned and hefted both shoulders. "What can I say? I'm a bit of a chemist. I studied it at Harvard. I wanted to be a scientist. Ended up working for Dad in his chemicals division instead. I'm Bruce MacNab, by the way. Good to meet you."

We shook. It was a genuine pump accompanied by a smile. I said, "Mike Cole, and this is Jessica Mackenzie."

"Can I mix you up a drink?" he asked.

"No thank you," Mackenzie told him. "I don't drink."

Bruce narrowed his eyes. "We've met. You're Mr. Mackenzie's daughter."

She nodded once and her brow pinched. "I'm sorry, I don't remember you."

"It was at one of your father's annual Christmas parties," Bruce told her. "I was still in high school then and I was drunk at the time. I'm afraid I made a bit of a buffoon of myself. I was the guy dancing on a table wearing a lampshade for a hat."

"I remember that," Mackenzie said. "My father had you thrown out after you tried to dance with my sister Morgan. You didn't have any pants on at the time."

"Guilty as charged."

I said, "Remind me to get invited to one of your father's Christmas parties."

"They're very loud," Mackenzie told me. "And besides, I no longer attend."

Bruce MacNab said, "I heard you went to work for the police or something."

"The FBI," Mackenzie corrected.

"Then I take it this isn't a social call?"

Mackenzie said, "We'd like to have word with your father about one of his employees and some property that he is attempting to buy."

Bruce nodded. "Bet that went over well with his secretary."

"Like a lead balloon," I said.

"So you crashed his party."

"We didn't mean any harm," I said. I genuinely liked Bruce. He seemed like a good kid. He was obviously living in his father's shadow and trying to make up for it by being the life of the party. He probably spent freely and had few real friends. I could only imagine what it must be like to grow up the son of an aloof multimillionaire. I sipped my drink and said, "We were just hoping to have a conversation with him off the record, but we don't want to impose."

"Is he in some kind of trouble?" Bruce asked.

"Not that we know of," I said.

Bruce looked disappointed. "Too bad."

Mackenzie said, "One of his employees, a security guard, was murdered and we just wanted to ask him a few questions."

"This about those murders in Chinatown?"

I nodded.

"I heard about those," Bruce said. "And you say it was one of our people who was killed?"

"A former policeman turned security guard named John Chen," Mackenzie offered.

Bruce frowned. "That's a damn shame. Hate to think we put anybody in harm's way."

I sensed an opening. "Maybe you can find out why your father had security in the tunnels beneath Chinatown for us?"

He smiled and put his drink down. "I'll do one better, officer. Follow me."

46

Bruce MacNab led us through the house, shaking hands and greeting guests, until he found his father in a corner with a leggy supermodel wearing a black dress that left nothing to the imagination.

"There you are, father!" Bruce raised his voice to be heard. "I've been looking all over for you. Won't you introduce me to your new friend?"

Connor MacNab frowned and said, "Bruce, this is Claudia. She's with the New York ballet."

"Pleased to meet you, Claudia. You'll be happy to know my father, he's a great patron of the arts. Isn't that right, Dad?"

Connor MacNab flashed a tight smile.

"In fact," Bruce went on, "I'm sure he can get you into some very interesting positions, eh Dad?"

Claudia's face turned into a stony mask and Connor MacNab looked like he'd just swallowed a lemon. His nostrils flared.

The innuendo was completely lost on Mackenzie. She

watched the exchange with polite interest and was confused when the dancer excused herself with a frosty clip in her voice.

Connor MacNab fetched a heavy sigh. "What can I do for you, Bruce?"

"I have some people here who would like to speak with you, Father."

MacNab recognized us. "You two again. How did you even get in?"

Mackenzie opened her mouth and I knew she was about to tell the truth so I tapped my shield with a finger. "Keys to the kingdom, Connor."

"I wasn't aware we were on a first-name basis."

"Bad habit I picked up in public schools," I said.

"Well you might want to take your bad habits and vacate." Connor MacNab fixed a smile on his face for the other guests but his tone left no room for doubt. "This is a private event. If you aren't out of here in five minutes, I'm calling security."

"Don't be rude, Father," Bruce said in a voice just a little too loud. Heads swiveled in our direction. "These FBI agents have a few questions they'd like to ask. It's about the murders in Chinatown. Surely, we'll do everything in our power to back the boys in blue." As an afterthought he added, "And girls, of course."

Mackenzie thanked him with a nod.

The volume of chatter dropped several notches as guests stopped to watch.

Connor MacNab kept his smile in place. "Of course! Of course! Why don't you officers follow me right this way and I'll help in any way I can."

Bruce lifted his glass to us and muttered, "Good luck. Hope you find what you're looking for."

We trailed MacNab senior up a grand staircase to a private office on the second floor of the sprawling mansion. He opened a door and ushered us into an oak-paneled room with deep leather chairs and the rich smell of expensive pipe tobacco.

"Now what can I do for you officers?"

"Detectives," I corrected.

"We'd like to ask you a few questions," Mackenzie said.

"First let's start with who you are? Can I see some ID?"

"You already saw my badge," I said.

"But not hers." MacNab turned his attention on Mackenzie.

She produced her FBI credentials.

MacNab studied them and his eyebrows went up. It was the first genuine emotion I'd seen from him. He said, "You're Alexander Mackenzie's daughter."

"That's correct."

"I heard you joined the FBI," MacNab said. "Quite the career move. Your father must be very proud."

Again, the sarcasm was lost on Mackenzie.

I flashed the hang ten sign.

MacNab frowned in confusion.

Mackenzie said, "I'm not sure how he feels about my career in law enforcement, and I'm not sure I care. I'm here to ask you about a murder in Chinatown."

"So my son said." MacNab went to a wet bar against the wall and poured himself a drink. "Can I get you officers anything?"

"Detectives," I corrected. "And no."

"Then let's get right to it." MacNab took his drink, leaned his hips against his desk, and said, "You want to know if I have anything to do with the recent murders in Chinatown? It's a preposterous idea."

"Do you?" Mackenzie asked.

MacNab laughed and shook his head. "If I were innocent, I'd say no and if I were guilty, I'd still say no. What's the point of asking?"

"Gauge your reaction," I told him.

He sipped from his tumbler of scotch and put the drink down on the desktop. "And did you glean anything from my reaction?"

"Plenty," Mackenzie said, which was news to me. All I had learned was that Connor MacNab was a cool customer.

"You're unfazed by police questions," Mackenzie said. "Which means you are either certain of your innocence or certain that we have no evidence of criminal wrong doing. Given the nature of your business, it stands to reason that you're no stranger to law enforcement and you're used to answering difficult questions. You didn't immediately ask for a lawyer, and a man in your position certainly has lawyers on retainer, which means you feel free to speak to us without entrapping yourself. That goes a long way to proving innocence."

MacNab picked up his drink and tipped his head in Mackenzie's direction. "You're quick."

She blinked. "I'm not sure what my speed has to do with it."

"An employee of yours named John Chen was killed," I said. "Aren't you the least bit interested in who killed him or why?"

"I'm afraid I don't know who that is," MacNab said and I could tell it wasn't a lie. He'd never heard John Chen's name before in his life.

Mackenzie said, "He worked security for MacNab properties."

"We found his body in the tunnels under Chinatown," I said. "Someone had removed his skin."

"Nasty bit of business," MacNab said. "But like I said, I have no idea who John Chen is or why he was murdered. I don't hire employees personally and technically he didn't work for me, he worked for the security company which I contract through."

Mackenzie said, "And what security company is that?"

"Global Access Elite," MacNab told us. "You'll have to speak with them if you want more information on this James fellow."

"John," I corrected.

"Why did you have security in the tunnels?" Mackenzie asked.

"Protecting my investment." MacNab crossed around behind the desk and sat down. "I had plans to develop several blocks in Chinatown, bring in new business, new housing, revitalize the area."

"And to do that you needed to chase out the locals and their low rent business," I said.

"Manifest destiny," MacNab said.

"What does that mean?" Mackenzie asked.

I frowned and said, "That our friend here had plans to evict the local tenants and put the shops out of business so he could build his new development."

"Guilty as charged," MacNab said. "Is that a crime?"

"No," Mackenzie said. "You still haven't explained why you had security in the tunnels."

"The locals weren't happy with a white man taking over their neighborhood," MacNab said.

"What a surprise," I muttered.

"Let him finish," Mackenzie told me.

MacNab said, "Some of the business owners even went so far as to sabotage the plumbing and electricity in an effort to drive up the cost of development. We had security to make sure the locals weren't destroying *my* future property."

"Is it possible some of those locals were so opposed to the idea of a white man taking over that they killed John as a way of overturning the apple cart?" I asked.

"Maybe." MacNab leaned back and laced his fingers together behind his head. "If they did, there'll be hell to pay."

I arched a brow.

Mackenzie asked, "What makes you say that?"

"I was partnered with the local Triads," MacNab told us.

Mackenzie was leaning forward, practically on her tippy toes. She said, "Are you admitting to us that you were working with an illegal criminal organization?"

"I admit that I entered into a business deal with Tai Pan to make sure property was not destroyed or vandalized," MacNab said. "I never condoned any illegal activities and if Tai Pan is guilty of breaking the law..." He shrugged. "Well that's her problem and not mine."

"You've met Tai Pan," Mackenzie said.

"Of course," MacNab told us. "I never do business

without a face to face meeting. Why should Tai Pan be any different?"

"And she agreed to help you buy out the neighborhood?" I said. "I find that hard to believe. Why would she do a thing like that?"

MacNab smiled. "Tai Pan has ambitions beyond that of a petty crime boss."

"What exactly does that mean?" Mackenzie asked.

I said, "She wants to go legit."

MacNab nodded. "That's right."

"How do you know that?" Mackenzie asked.

"I know a lot of things," MacNab said. "In fact I know just about everything there is to know about the Tai Pan. Hell, she's not even Chinese. She's Filipino. Came over here a few years back and started taking over the Triad operations with the help of her top lieutenant; a former boxer with a cauliflower ear. Tai Pan is making a heroic effort to fuse the Triad income with more legitimate business practices."

"And you were going to help?" I asked.

He shrugged. "I promised Tai Pan if she helped me secure my foothold in Chinatown I would make her part owner in several of the storefront opportunities that would open up."

I said, "Giving the Triads a way to safely launder their dirty money."

Again MacNab shrugged. "I can't say, nor am I responsible for what they do with their business opportunities."

"So you were going to buy up real estate in Chinatown and then lease store fronts to Tai Pan in exchange for protection," Mackenzie said. "You own the high rises and Tai Pan owns the storefronts."

"That about covers it." MacNab spread his hands. "As you can see, I had no reason to want anyone dead and these murders have unfortunately put an indefinite hold on my plans for Chinatown."

I crossed my arms. "Meaning?"

"I'm pulling out of the deal," he told us. "The area is just too hot right now. I don't want any part of the negative publicity surrounding these murders and I certainly don't want high rise apartments rumored by the locals to be haunted. Can you imagine what that's going to do for rent prices? Just this afternoon I told my legal counsel that the Chinatown deal is off, for now. Maybe when things calm down a bit and everyone forgets about these murders we'll take another look, but for now I've refocused my energies on my new development in Boca Raton."

FROM THE JOURNAL OF JESSICA MACKENZIE

Curiouser and curiouser. We continue to interview suspects and the more people we talk to, the less we have to go on. Seems no one involved had reason to kill Officer Chen. Certainly no one seems to have a motive to kill an elderly pensioner. And yet I cannot help but feel that we are slowly, inexorably, drawing ever closer to the truth, despite Detective Cole's loud and frequent complaints that we have, in his words, "a whole lot of nothing".

I remind both him and myself that once the impossible is eliminated, what remains, no matter how improbable, must be the truth. And in this matter, we may be dealing with forces beyond nature. Detective Cole is adamant we interview the developer tomorrow first thing, but after that I have arranged for a meeting with someone who may be able to help peel back the proverbial curtain (an idiom which means to reveal missing information) on the supernatural elements of this case. I've not yet informed Cole of this meeting because I can fairly well predict his reaction.

47

The next morning we parked outside of Rothwell-Gornt. The contactor had a lot in the Bronx filled with heavy equipment surrounded by chain-link. A large weathered sign fixed to the rolling gate informed us that the lot was for authorized personnel only. NO UNAUTHORIZED ACCESS.

It was just after nine and the temperature had dipped overnight, promising an early winter. Frost rimmed window panes all over the city and steam billowed from every sewer grate. The Mercury clonked out before I could shift into park and the engine died with a series of soft ticking noises. I wrestled the gear shift into park anyway and turned the key

After Connor MacNab's party, Mackenzie and I had sat up late into the night discussing the case. We'd gone to Mackenzie's cramped Brooklyn apartment and laid out all the facts, but we were no closer to finding a killer than we had been when we'd started. We had three dead, all Chinese, one missing, and no apparent link other than ethnicity. Neither Connor MacNab, nor the Triads, had any reason to kill John Chen that we could find, nor any of the other victims. Our next, and only, move was to check MacNab's story so we decided to pay a visit to the contractor.

We climbed out of the Mercury and I spared a look at the hood of my car, still covered in a shock of neon paint. Wind was whipping down through the concrete corridors, carrying with it a smell of sewage, the all pervasive perfume of the Big Apple.

"Are you going to have that fixed?" Mackenzie asked. She had her hands buried in the pockets of her Navy coat and her hair pulled back in a ponytail this morning. She didn't look any worse for having stayed up half the night.

"Sure," I told her. "Just as soon as I can scrape together the money. Cheapest estimate was eight-hundred bucks."

"Is this car even worth eight-hundred dollars?"

"This is a classic," I said.

"But is it worth eight-hundred dollars?"

"It's worth a lot more to me," I told her with a hint of irritation.

We flashed our badges at a bleary-eyed security guard in a pillbox and he rolled open the gate for us. There was a trailer at the back of the lot with a set of steps and a sign tacked to the side that advertised the hours of operation along with a phone number. Satisfaction, according to the sign, was guaranteed. Decades of grime covered the mobile unit, along with colorful graffiti.

Mackenzie peeked in the bed of a mud-spattered pickup truck parked outside the trailer. The Rothwell-Gornt logo and website was stenciled on the side of the truck and the back was piled with hunting gear. I mounted the steps to the trailer, knocked briefly, and opened the door without waiting for an answer.

The inside was decorated in contractor vogue. The walls were plastered with posters of bikini models holding tools, a nudie calendar, and advertisements for construction equipment. A pair of desks were buried under mounds of paperwork and there was a pot of strong black coffee on top of a metal filing cabinet in one corner, giving off a rich aroma that helped mask the stink of sweat.

A fat man in a rumpled sport coat was parked behind one of the desks and his much younger secretary was parked in his lap. She leapt up as we entered.

"Can I help you?" the fat man growled. He had a bad combover and a jet-black pencil thin mustache.

I showed him my shield. "You Rothwell? Or Gornt?"

"If this is about the zoning permits in Battery Park you can talk to our attorney."

I shook my head. "We aren't here about any zoning permits, Mr...?"

The secretary smoothed down her leopard print skirt as she hurried back to her own desk and pretended to be busy.

"Cipriani," the fat man told me. "Nicky Cipriani."

"Sign says Rothwell-Gornt."

"Rothwell sold out his half to my father and Gornt died three years ago."

"How did he die?" Mackenzie asked.

"Face down in a plate of pasta primavera," Cipriani said. "What's this about? You looking into the death of Gornt? He was three-hundred pounds with a bad ticker."

I shook my head. "We're more interested in the death of the security guard," I said. "A man named John Chen."

"This again?" Cipriani shook his head. "I already told the other detectives everything I know."

Pottinger and Boone had already been here. I wondered if they were following the same track as us, or maybe it was the other way around. Maybe we were following them. I jerked my head at Mackenzie. "This is Special Agent Mackenzie with the FBI."

She held up her credentials.

The introduction of the FBI had the desired effect.

Cipriani held up both hands and said, "Whoa, whoa, whoa. What's the feds got anything to do with this?"

He pronounced it any*ting*.

Mackenzie said, "We're running a concurrent investigation into the recent string of murders in Chinatown."

"I don't know nothing about no murders."

"But John Chen was an employee?"

Ciprinai shook his head. "Technically he's an employee of Global Security Solutions, but he was working for us at the time. It's regrettable, but hey, what can I say? Bad things happen all the time. Especially in Chinatown. Those Chinamen are always bumping each other off."

"Hey!" My hands curled into fists and I felt my face turn red. I leaned across his desk and growled. "That *Chinaman* was a retired cop, and my friend. And he's got a name. You can refer to him as Officer Chen."

Cipriani held up both hands. "Alright, alright. But I can't tell you anything more than I told them other two cops. *Officer* Chen was working for us the night he died. He was guarding the tunnels where we planned to start the foundations for the new high rise. He didn't report in the next morning. That's all I know."

"We spoke with Connor MacNab last night," Mackenzie said. "He claims to have changed his mind about the deal, that he was no longer interested in purchasing the property in Chinatown. Do you know if that's true?"

"Yeah, that's right," Cipriani said. "Quite frankly, I'm relieved. The whole thing was too much drama for me."

"What drama?" Mackenzie asked.

"First the residents don't want to sell at a decent price, then you got the zoning commission." Cipriani ticked the problems off on his fingers. "The whole job was a nightmare from beginning to end. Between the Triads making a nuisance of themselves and Bruce MacNab constantly bickering with his father, the job was more hassle than it was worth. And that was only going to get worse after we broke ground. I'm glad MacNab backed out. I told him never to do business in Chinatown, but he wouldn't listen to me."

Mackenzie scrunched her brow and cocked her head to the side. "You said Bruce MacNab and his father were arguing?"

Cipriani turned to his secretary. "Stella, make yourself useful and fetch me some breakfast, will ya?"

Stella was busy filing her nails. She motioned to the mounds of paper on her desk. "I got all this paperwork to finish."

"It'll be waiting for you when you get back," he said. "Get me one of them sausage and egg burritos from the deli round the corner."

He looked at us. "Yous two want anything?"

Mackenzie shook her head. "No, but thank you for the offer."

A sausage and egg burrito sounded good but I said, "I'm fine thanks. You were saying, about MacNab and his son."

He waited for Stella to leave and then said, "Look, I don't want to talk out of school."

"What school?" Mackenzie asked.

I said, "It'll stay between us."

"Bruce was against the idea from the very start," Cipriani told us. "Kid went off to one of them big city colleges and got his head filled with all sorts of fancy notions. He said it was a shame to destroy the *culture and character* of such a historic neighborhood." Cipriani put the words in air quotes. "Bah, I was against it because I've worked Chinatown in the past and I know what a pain in the butt the locals can be. Anyway, Bruce and his dad had a real knockdown drag out over it, if ya know what I mean."

"I'm not sure I do," Mackenzie said. "What's a knock down drag out?"

"You ain't from around here," Cipriani said. "A knock down drag out is a fight."

"They were in a physical altercation?" Mackenzie asked.

"Verbal," I corrected.

Cipriani nodded. "Bruce tried several times to change Big Mac's thinking."

"Big Mac?" Mackenzie asked.

"Yeah," Cipriani said. "That's what we call 'em. Big Mac and Little Mac."

Mackenzie's face pinched. "I should think it would be

the other way around. Bruce MacNab is decidedly taller than his father."

I leaned in and lowered my voice. "Connor MacNab is the father and therefore older."

She thought it over and then shrugged. "Okay."

Cipriani studied her for a long moment and then spread his hands. "What else is there to say? Bruce was against the idea from the start, the locals were refusing to sell at any price, and the Triads were involved. The whole thing was a cluster from the word go and then you throw in a few murders. I'm glad it's over." As an afterthought he added, "Hey, I'm sorry about your guy."

I said, "Were the Triads helping pressure the locals into selling?"

Cipriani put up both hands. "Hey, I don't nothing about that."

"The deal fell through and we aren't investigating organized crime," I told him. "I'm just trying to solve a murder. Were the Triads working with MacNab to force out the residents?"

"I just do construction," Cipriani said, "but I get the feeling MacNab had an arrangement with the Triads."

"A feeling?" Mackenzie said.

He shrugged. "Let's just say a little birdy told me."

Mackenzie blinked.

"You didn't hear that from me," he said.

"Understood," I told him. "Thanks for your cooperation."

Mackenzie said, "This has been helpful."

We were almost to the door when Cipriani said, "Hey one more thing."

We stopped and turned.

Cipriani sucked his teeth a moment while he debated how much to say, and then shrugged. "Every time I was in them tunnels... It felt weird, ya know?"

Mackenzie shook her head. "Elaborate on that please."

One side of his face pinched in an embarrassed grin. "Look, it just felt spooky down there, like someone was always watching me. And none of the guys wanted to be down there alone. Maybe there's something to this ghost business after all. Like I said, I'm glad the deal is off."

48

Chinatown was in a state of chaos. News crews had camped out on every corner and reporters from all over the country were doing stories on the bizarre murders. Reports of the missing girl added fuel to the media firestorm. Posters of Xu Yin were plastered all over the neighborhood. Police were out in full force, directing traffic and trying to keep the peace. Half the residents had decided the ghost and the killings were the fault of the white man. An angry Chinese man banged on the hood of the Mercury as I stopped at a red light and shouted, "*Kwai lo* go home!"

He hurried off after I flashed my badge.

I pulled to a stop across from a nondescript building and leaned across the seats for a look at the address. It was a six-floor walkup in the heart of Chinatown with a tea shop on the ground floor and a decaying fire escape. The walls were blackened with age and the windows covered in grime. I said, "What is this place?"

"The home of Hap Sing," Mackenzie told me.

I pushed open my door on creaking springs. "Who's Hap Sing?"

"A Chinese spiritualist," Mackenzie told me.

"You're joking?"

She shook her head.

"You brought me all the way down here to talk with a medium?" I asked. "Are you hoping to summon up the ghost and arrest him?"

"Don't be silly," Mackenzie said. "I just want a better understanding of what we're dealing with."

"We're not dealing with a ghost," I said. "I can tell you that right now. And this guy, this Hap Sing, is a fraud."

"He's one of the most highly respected Taoist holy men in all of Manhattan."

"Manhattan is full of swindlers," I told her.

"Can we just see what he has to say?"

"Lead on."

We found our way inside and climbed sagging stairs to the third floor where we rapped on a flimsy wood door painted red and papered with numerous Chinese characters.

The chain rattled and a wizened old face peered out at us. Hap Sing was a diminutive man with a white fu man chu mustache and smiling eyes behind thick spectacles. He nodded his bald head and motioned us inside.

"Come in, come in, Ms. Mackenzie. Welcome to my home." He squinted at me. "And you must be Mr. Cole. Officer Michael Cole."

"Hang on just a darn minute," I said. "How do you know our names?"

He smiled, placed his palms together, and bowed. "Ancient Chinese secret, Mr. Cole."

My eyebrows went up.

He grinned. "Your partner called early this morning."

Mackenzie's face lit up at the joke.

I rubbed the back of my neck and felt my ears burning. "You got me."

"You do not believe in the supernatural," Hap Sing said.

I pointed at Mackenzie. "She's the spiritualist. I'm the realist."

"The spirit world and the real world are inseparable," Hap Sing said.

His apartment was an explosion of Chinese Taoist paraphernalia. There were red Chinese knots hanging on the walls, calligraphy scrolls, and several incense sticks burning. There was also a Weimaraner on a doggy bed in one corner. The pup lifted his graying muzzle and sniffed, then put his head back down and closed his eyes.

We gathered around a coffee table. Hap Sing lowered himself onto a cushion, poured tea and said, "Just because we cannot see the spirit world does not mean it does not exist. We cannot see oxygen either and yet we know it's there every time we take a breath. Without it, we would die. It is the same with the spiritual realm."

"If you say so." I sank into Hap Sing's molding sofa and reached for a cup of tea.

Mackenzie said, "We would like to know more about..."

Hap Sing stopped her with an upraised hand. "You are here about the ghost of Kwang Di."

Mackenzie nodded.

"Lucky guess," I said.

"I knew you would come." Hap Sing tapped his temple. "I saw you both in a dream. A pair of police officers, one a sceptic, the other a believer. You are destined to defeat the ghost and restore balance to the spiritual realm."

49

I rolled my eyes. The gesture was not lost on Hap Sing. He chuckled and shook his head. "You are not a believer," he said, "but you do not have to believe a thing for it to be true."

Mackenzie was perched on the edge of the sofa, her eyes locked on the old Chinese man in his slightly rumpled sport coat and mismatched necktie. "What does the ghost want?" she asked. "And why is he killing people? And how does he choose his targets?"

"All good questions," Hap Sing said. "First you need to understand Kwang Di."

"Are we really going to sit through a history lesson on a guy who's been dead for hundreds of years?" I muttered to Mackenzie.

She shushed me and motioned for Hap Sing to continue.

He got up, tottered over to a shelf crammed with dusty books, and selected an ancient leatherbound volume that looked like it had been printed around the same time

Kwang Di died. The old man handled it with care. Arthritic fingers traced Chinese characters as he read. "Kwang Di was a firm believer in ancestor worship. All Chinese believe the ghosts of our ancestors watch over us, imparting good fortune or bad. But Kwang Di paid special adherence to ancestor worship, and meted out strict punishment for any disciples who failed to pay proper respect to their ancestors."

"How does that help us?" I asked.

"There is a connection," Hap Sing said.

Mackenzie was nodding her head. "Modern Chinese people, especially those living in Manhattan, have largely abandoned the ancient rituals of ancestor worship, praying to the departed for luck or fortune."

Hap Sing ducked his head and smiled. "Quite right, Ms. Mackenzie."

I tossed my hands in the air. "Are you telling me this ancient sorcerer came back from the grave because he's mad Chinese people aren't burning incense in rice bowls?"

"The deaths will continue until my people learn to respect their ancestors once again."

"Oh, well case closed," I said. "We'll just go on the nightly news and tell all the people of Chinatown to pray to their dead grandfathers or Kwang Di will skin them."

"You joke," said Hap Sing, "but it is no laughing matter, Mr. Cole. The ghost of Kwang Di is angry and his anger will not stop until we return to the old ways."

"Look, Mister Sing, I respect you and your culture and your customs, even if I don't believe in it myself, but it's every Chinese person's right to be a shallow, self-absorbed, money grubbing, Twitter whore. We can't force Chinese people to return to ancestor worship."

"Then there will be more deaths," Hap Sing said.

Mackenzie asked, "How do we stop him? There must be a way?"

Hap Sing considered her words and then said, "There may be a way, but it will be dangerous."

"Are we really discussing this?" I asked.

Mackenzie frowned her annoyance and turned back to Hap Sing. "How?"

"First you must summon the ghost of Kwang Di," Hap Sing told her.

"How do we do that?"

"Ghostbusters?" I suggested.

Hap Sing said, "There is a summoning ritual which I can teach you, but it must be done in a place with special significance to the ghost, someplace it has been spotted before."

"The tunnels beneath Chinatown," Mackenzie said. "That's where we found the second body and the third victim was close to one of the underground entrances."

Hap Sing nodded. "If you can summon the spirit of Kwang Di, you may trap his essence in a rice bowl."

I closed my eyes and massaged my temples. "You want us to trap him in a rice bowl? You realize how crazy that sounds?"

"Not just any rice bowl." Hap Sing went to a cabinet, rummaged through a drawer and pulled out a chipped bowl of blue and white porcelain. "This has been blessed by a Taoist magician. It will contain the spirit of Kwang Di."

"Oh sure," I said. "I've got a few of those laying around my house. I should have thought to bring one."

Hap Sing ignored my quip and passed the bowl to Mackenzie. "Please, take it. It is my gift to you."

"But how do we summon the ghost of Kwang Di?" she asked.

"Ah," he held up a finger and smiled. "I have a summoning ritual that I will write down for you. It must be followed exactly, and you must use the proper ingredients. They can be a little pricey but I have most of what you will need right here."

"Let me guess," I said. "You'll sell them to us at a discount price."

Hap Sing gave a shrug. "Even Chinese spiritualists have to eat, Mr. Cole."

50

"I cannot believe I let you talk me into this." I was following Mackenzie along a darkened underground passage. We weren't far from where John Chen's skinless corpse had been discovered. The floor was cracked and uneven. A moldy odor, like loamy earth and wet paper, hung in the air. It reminded me of an attic in desperate need of sunshine and fresh air. Low-hanging pipes stretched overhead. The walls were clammy and sweating, and my shoes made soft scuffing noises in decades of grit. I said, "There's a murderer out there somewhere and you've got me crawling around a sewer trying to summon up the ghost of General Grant."

"It's not a sewer," Mackenzie said. "And we're trying to summon Kwang Di. Not General Grant."

"Sarcasm," I muttered.

"I'm not sure it's funny," she said.

"It's not," I told her. "But that's not the point."

"What is your point?"

"This is a huge waste of time."

Mackenzie held a bulky yellow plastic flashlight in one hand and a small spelunker's lamp was strapped to her forehead. Her brunette hair was pulled back in the usual ponytail. She ducked a fat, rust-covered pipe and said, "That's hot. Be careful."

I followed her under the pipe, my flashlight splashing across her bottom, and then over the sweating walls of the underground passage. There were ancient gang tags on the hewn rock, covered over by what passed as art in the graffiti world, and more gang tags on top of that. Some of it was Chinese or Korean. Most was English. One tag said; *bern the sistim.* If this were any indication of the general state of education in the United States, then it was easy to see why we were falling behind the rest of the world.

"We should be knocking on doors," I growled.

"You think the people of Chinatown are going to talk to us?"

It was a fair point. We'd tried to conduct interviews but all of Chinatown had suddenly caught a case of selective mutism. Even Xu Yin's family was done talking to us. I suspected the Triads had a lot to do with it. Word had gone out not to talk to the police. People feared the wrath of Tai Pan. Her illegal gambling operation may have vanished in the night, but that didn't mean the queen of crime in Chinatown was gone. She'd simply burrowed a new hole. Even with Tai Pan in hiding, her minions still patrolled the streets, and no one wanted to be seen talking to the fuzz. Despite that, I still thought tramping through these tunnels was a huge waste of time and I told Mackenzie as much.

"Have you got a better idea?" she asked.

I opened my mouth to bite off an angry reply and closed it again. We only had a handful of suspects and none of them had any solid motive to kill John or the girl, much less a kindly old pensioner in a rocking chair. In fact, as far as leads, we had a whole lot of nothing.

"If anyone in the department found out I was down here trying to summon up Zuul, I'd be committed to a rubber room. I just got back on the murder boards. If DeSilva finds out about this, I'll go back to walking a beat."

She stopped and shone her flashlight around an intersection with four halls branching off in different directions. There was a smell of rot, like something had died nearby, and a definite chill in the air. Mackenzie shook her head and said, "DeSilva can't put you back on patrol. He's not the one who had you promoted to homicide."

I turned my flashlight on her. "Wait a minute. Are you telling me, you're responsible for putting me back in homicide?"

She shielded her eyes with one hand and nodded.

"Why would you do that?"

"Because you're a talented investigator," Mackenzie said. "You're impatient, rude, often combative, and generally unwilling to believe anything you can't see with your own two eyes, but you're one of the better investigators I've ever worked with."

"I think that was almost a compliment," I said, and then, "I thought I earned my way back onto the murder boards."

"You did."

"DeSilva apparently didn't think so."

"He's bullish and overbearing," she said. "He's a good

commanding officer, but your talents were wasted in the bunko division."

"Is that why he's got such an attitude around you?"

Mackenzie shrugged. "I wouldn't know."

She was playing her light around the space and said, "This should do."

I looked around at the nondescript stretch of tunnel. "What's so special about this spot?"

Mackenzie pointed. "We found John Chen's body about two-hundred yards that way and, unless I'm very much mistaken, we found the body of the girl less than seventy-five yards in the other direction. It's a nice halfway point between the two murders. Hap Sing said to go where the ghost had been spotted before. This should work quite nicely."

I was still trying to work out how I felt about Mackenzie pulling strings. I was happy to be out of the bunko division —homicide was where I belonged—but at the same time I was painfully aware that Mackenzie had put me back on the boards for her own selfish reasons. She needed someone in NYPD and I was the only one who hadn't requested a transfer when I learned of her autism. I was both grateful and annoyed.

I shrugged the backpack off my shoulders. "Let's get this over with so we can go back to looking for real clues and solid evidence. I don't like it down here. These tunnels give me the willies."

Mackenzie placed her own pack on the ground, worked the zipper, and started laying out supplies. "If Hap Sing was right—"

"He's not."

"—this shouldn't take long."

"I'm telling you right now, we spent two-hundred bucks on nothing," I said. "Nothing is going to happen."

A cold gust of wind ripped through the tunnels with a mournful howl and my flashlight winked out.

51

My heart gave a little kick as the light blinked out of existence. Gooseflesh crawled across my belly. We hadn't been plunged into complete darkness, Mackenzie's flashlights were still working, but that didn't stop the small hairs on the back of my neck from standing up straight. I joggled my flashlight, gave it a thump, and the bulb came back to life. It was a solid body aluminum Maglite, the kind carried by law enforcement professionals the world over for their durability. And yet mine had chosen that very moment to go out.

I told myself it was coincidence. The flashlight had malfunctioned at the same time a strong wind, probably pushed by the Atlantic, had swept the tunnels. Nothing to worry about, and certainly nothing to do with ghosts. And yet my heartrate took a long time returning to normal.

Mackenzie was busy unrolling a large paper scroll with Chinese characters. She stopped, turned to me and arched a brow. "You were saying?"

"Okay," I said, "that was spooky, admittedly, but strong

winds and malfunctioning flashlights don't prove the existence of ghosts. Besides, it's been a year or more since I replaced the batteries in this thing. It's overdue."

"And the voice we heard?" She took out a small copper bowl and pestle, placing them down beside the scroll.

"I didn't hear any voice."

"Of course you did," Mackenzie said. "We both did. There were words in that gust of wind. You just don't want to admit it."

"There was wind in that gust of wind," I insisted. "Nothing sinister about a little wind."

"And where did the wind come from?" she asked. "We've never felt wind in these tunnels before."

"These tunnels open onto the Atlantic," I argued. "They used to be smuggling tunnels. Probably a wind off the ocean causes a breeze down here, or maybe there's an opening to a subway tunnel and that was a train going past. I can think of a hundred different explanations."

"And yet you refuse to believe the one most probable explanation despite all the evidence. Why is that?"

I crouched across from Mackenzie. She had laid out all of Hap Sing's ghost summoning kit, including a dried rat tail and a string of old copper coins, and now she sat cross legged in the dirt. I said, "Why are you so eager to prove the existence of ghosts and goblins?"

"I don't believe in goblins," she said. "I find the notion absurd."

I closed my eyes and let out a breath. "Why are you so eager to prove ghosts are real?"

"I'm not," she said, picking up the old coins and giving them a rattle. "I'm merely following the evidence."

"I've heard that before." I shined my flashlight behind me, making sure the passage was clear, before settling down on the cool stone floor. "But this is more than just following the evidence. You choose cases that have supernatural elements. Why?"

Mackenzie put ginseng into the copper bowl and crushed it with the pestle. "My birth mother disappeared when I was just five years old. Police never found a trace of her."

"I heard Mackenzie lost his first wife," I said. I had heard a lot more, but didn't bother to tell Jessica. The rumor mill claimed Alexander Mackenzie had done away with his first wife and police never found enough evidence to make an arrest. Mackenzie maintained his innocence and said he had no clue what had happened to his wife. He offered a two-million dollar reward to anyone with information, but no one ever came forward. Less than a year later the billionaire playboy mogul had remarried. There were people who still insisted he had gotten away with murder and others who claimed the first wife had run away with another man, along with a large chunk of her husband's money.

Mackenzie sprinkled the crushed powder of ginseng over the paper scroll and said, "So you know the rumors."

I nodded.

"What you didn't hear is that my mother was heavily into the occult," Mackenzie said. "Father kept all that out of the papers. Mother conducted research into the paranormal at the University of Stanford before she met my father. When I was little, her home office was filled with books on the occult and supernatural. She had been studying the idea of alternate planes of reality when she vanished."

"So all of this"—I waved my flashlight at the summoning scroll—"is about proving your mother right? You want to prove that the spiritual world is real, maybe even figure out what happened to her?"

Mackenzie cocked her head to one side; considering information she'd never encountered before. After a moment she said, "Perhaps. I'd never really thought of it in those terms. Investigating the supernatural is just my way of following in her footsteps, but maybe part of me wants to figure out what happened to her."

I reached across and gripped her wrist. "What if there is no explanation? What if you never find out what happened?"

She shrugged. "The work is reward enough."

I let go, not really believing her, but not ready to tell her any different. This might be one of those delusions people were better off believing. If researching the supernatural allowed her to believe she might uncover the mystery of her mother's disappearance, why not let her?

Mackenzie lit a candle, finishing the summoning ritual, and then we waited. Darkness seemed to press in around us and the silence was so complete that even the smallest movement sounded incredibly loud in the stillness of the underground passage. I could hear my watch slowly ticking. Seconds stretched into minutes. I was about to say something when another strong gust, accompanied by a tormented wail, swept through the passage, blowing out the candle along with all the flashlights, plunging us into total darkness.

52

There was a rustle of cloth and something rushed past me in the dark. I sensed more than felt it, like a whisper in the stillness. The skin on my arms turned to gooseflesh and my heart was going ninety miles an hour on an open freeway. I told myself over and over again that I don't believe in spooks while frantically shaking my flashlight. I tried the button several times. All I got was a muffled click.

"Mackenzie," I hissed, trying to keep the fear out of my voice. "Turn on a light, will ya?"

There was no answer and the dread creeping around the edges of my thoughts crowded a little closer, bringing me to the brink of panic. I gave the flashlight a violent shake, slapped it hard, and tried the button again. This time the bulb flared bright, casting a cone of light over the paper scroll and the empty spot where Mackenzie had been only seconds before. A streamer of black smoke curled up from the candle.

"Mackenzie?" I said and turned a circle, shining my light over the stone walls.

I was alone.

My heart was still thump-thumping inside my chest and my toes felt like little chips of ice. The temperature in the tunnels had plummeted ten degrees. Intellectually, I knew the cold in my fingers and toes was because my nervous system was rerouting blood from my extremities to my heart and lungs, but it was hard to convince my conscious brain, which was certain a ghost had just rushed past me in the dark, and taken Mackenzie with it.

Fear was an acid taste at the back of my throat. I forced myself to take a few deep breaths as I searched the ground for any sign of Mackenzie. There were a few scrapes and scuffs that might have been her shoes, or just random patterns in the dirt. I played the light down each tunnel, calling her name over and over, hoping for an answer. Next I tried my cellphone, but I didn't have any signal. I pocketed the phone wondering what to do.

Mackenzie was gone—*taken by the ghost*, my brain insisted—and I had to find her. But which way to go? I shined my flashlight on the tunnel at my back. Maybe that had been Mackenzie that went sprinting past me in the dark? It was the best, and only, thing I had to go on, so I started down the passage, calling her name. I told myself I'd search for ten minutes and if I didn't find her, I'd head topside for backup. I didn't like the idea of leaving Mackenzie down here alone. She was my partner and you don't leave your partner behind, but what else could I do? These tunnels were a labyrinth. I could spend a year crawling around down here without finding a single trace.

That thought sent a shiver up my spine. Mackenzie wasn't just my partner; she was a special investigator with the FBI. If anything happened to her, I was going to be in a jam. I had followed her into the underground without telling anybody where we were going or what we were up to. No one even knew we were down here.

"Stupid," I told myself in the dark. "Why'd you let her talk you into this?"

There was no answer from the darkness, which was just as well. I tried a few corners, but never strayed far from the intersection where the scroll and the candle were laid out. It was my only reference point and I was pretty sure I could still find my way out from there. I aimed my flashlight down the shadowy tunnels, yelled her name, and waited.

Minutes ticked past. I was just about to head back when I heard a soft scuff behind me. I wheeled around in time to see a shadowy figure flit past the intersection. It happened so fast I wasn't sure if I had actually seen something or if it was just my imagination. I hurried to the corner, thrust out my flashlight, and caught a glimpse of someone, or something, disappear into the darkness.

I gave a shout and took off at a sprint. A low pipe nearly sent me sprawling, but I managed to stay on my feet and pounded along the passage with my lungs burning and my thighs screaming.

"Stop!" I yelled. "Police!"

Like a ghost would care.

I rounded the corner and caught sight of the figure scrambling over a fat pipe. Ghosts don't have to climb over plumbing. I was chasing something with flesh and blood. My feet propelled me forward. I rolled over the pipe without slowing down, closed the distance on the fleeing suspect, and lunged. My fingers closed on the figure's waist-band as I fell. We both went down in a heap and the suspect's pants raked down around their ankles. I got a brief glimpse of blue cotton panties with little white cartoon bears.

53

I bit my tongue when I fell and the warm copper taste of pennies filled my mouth. I scrambled into a sitting position, one hand going automatically to my gun. My heart was scaling my esophagus.

"What are you, some kind of pervert?" Xu Yin barked as she hurried to pull her denims up over her narrow hips.

"What are you talking about?" I said. "I'm old enough to be your father."

"That makes it extra creepy," she said as she leapt to her feet.

"I thought you were..." I pushed up off the ground. I didn't want to say *a ghost*. Instead I said, "What are you doing down here? We been looking all over the city for you. Everyone thinks you're dead."

"I'm hiding," she said. "Isn't it obvious?"

"What are you hiding from?"

"The ghost. He's after me."

I trained my flashlight on her and she narrowed her

eyes. I said, "You were there when Jennifer Kwan was killed?"

"Why else would I spend all night hiding out in these tunnels?"

I said, "You saw the murder."

She nodded. Her eyes got big and tears gathered on her dark lashes. Some of the color drained from her face. "I saw everything."

I pulled her into a hug. She buried her face against my chest and the tears started to flow. I let her cry it out and then asked, "Why didn't you come forward? Why hide?"

"Because the ghost is after me."

"Are you telling me you actually saw a ghost?"

She disentangled herself from me and nodded. "He was... terrible. Just terrible. He's six foot tall with glowing green eyes. And he wants me next."

There was a cold hard knot in my chest. "How do you know that?"

"He was there for me," Xu Yin said. "Jen just got in his way. He bashed her head against the trashcan and I knew right away she was dead. The sound was awful. Then he was after me. He grabbed my coat but I slipped out of it and ran. I ducked into the underground and I've been down here ever since. Hey, you got any food? I'm starving."

"I left my salad in my other jacket. You're saying a ghost killed Jennifer Kwan?"

"Haven't you been listening?"

Another gust of wind went ripping through the tunnels, turning my hair into a cloud and tugging at the ends of my coat.

Xu Yin froze. Her eyes grew to the size of silver dollars

and the color drained from her face. Her hands hooked into claws. She pivoted on her heels, ready to run, but I reached out a hand and caught her.

"Where do you think you're going, kid? You're a missing person and witness to a murder."

"We have to go," she hissed. "We have to get out of here. He's coming. Don't you feel it? That's him! That's how you know he's coming."

I kept one hand on Xu Yin's collar, clamped the Maglite under my arm, and pulled my service pistol.

"A gun?" she whispered. "Really? I don't think that's going to stop him. He can walk through walls."

"There's no such thing as ghosts," I said, more to myself than Xu Yin.

"Believe what you like," she said. "I've seen him. I watched him kill Jenny. He's going to kill me next. I gotta get outta here!"

"Not so fast," I said. "My partner is down here somewhere and I'm not leaving without her. You know these tunnels better than anyone. Help me find her."

Xu Yin made a face. Her eyes were rolling in their sockets like a startled horse, trying to see everything at once. Her hands were fists. The breath exploded from her lungs in barely controlled bursts, but she nodded. "Okay, but if I see the ghost, I'm hauling butt."

"I'll be right behind you."

"Where did you last see Mackenzie?"

I cocked a thumb over my shoulder. "Back this way, I think. We were doing a summoning ritual, trying to scare up the ghost. Guess it worked."

She led the way and said, "Only a pair of *kwai lo* cops

would be dumb enough to try a summoning ritual. Where'd you even learn about the summoning?"

"Funny old guy named Hap Sing told us what to do and sold us the stuff we needed."

"That old goat?" She shook her head. "You know he's a fraud, right? Probably ripped you off."

"Tell that to my partner."

"If we ever find her," Xu Yin said. We reached an intersection and she looked around. "Maybe Kwang Di already got her."

"Don't say that."

She stopped and turned to me. "Is she your girlfriend?"

"No," I said. "But I don't want anything bad to happen to her."

"You sure she's not your girlfriend?"

"I'm sure."

She shrugged. "Too bad. You two would make a cute couple."

"What makes you say that?"

"You're both white," Xu Yin said and then broke into a cackle.

"Hilarious."

The laughter died and Xu Yin held up a hand for silence. I still had my gun out, my flashlight in my other hand. We had come to a fork. Xu Yin tapped an ear and I strained to listen. The only thing I heard was my own labored breathing. I shrugged. Xu Yin rolled her eyes and waved for me to follow. She took me along a narrow lane, around a junction littered with castoff furniture and an old engine block, and then through a low opening in a wall. I found myself in another passage, this one with a ceiling so low I had to duck, but there was definitely a light up ahead. Xu Yin and I crept forward, me in the lead, and together we peeked around a corner.

Mackenzie was stretched out on the dirt floor, her flashlight on the ground beside her. I gave a strangled cry and hurried forward. Dread filled my belly like battery acid, eating away at the lining of my stomach. I choked out, "Mackenzie? Are you alright?"

54

Mackenzie turned at the sound. She made a face partway between confusion and annoyance. "Why are you yelling?"

My feet slowed and my heart downshifted. I breathed out a jerking sigh of relief. "I thought you were dead. What happened? One minute you were there next to me, the next you were gone."

Mackenzie turned back around and put her nose an inch from the loamy soil. She was stretched out on her stomach, her sweater in the dirt and her fingers covered in muck. "I thought I saw a figure just before the lights went out. I heard footsteps, so I followed."

"And left me?" I stooped down next to her, my eyes roaming her arms and legs, searching for any sign of injury.

"I thought you were with me," Mackenzie said simply. "I yelled."

She pinched soil between her thumb and forefinger, rubbed it, sniffed, then dabbed a bit onto her tongue.

I sat down on the clammy concrete and ran a shaking hand over my face. "You really gave me a scare."

"Apologies," Mackenzie said. "I see you've located Xu Yin."

"She's been hiding down here ever since Jennifer Kwan was killed," I said. "She saw the attack."

Mackenzie rose up onto her knees, brushed off her hands, and said, "I'm relieved to know you are still among the living."

She said it the way other people speculate on rain. It was a flat voice that carried no emotional warmth, just a simple statement of fact. She sniffed the loamy handful of dirt one last time, then dusted her palms.

Xu Yin stuffed her hands in her pockets. "Good to see you too."

I said, "Xu Yin actually saw the ghost."

Mackenzie stood up and shook her head. "It's not a ghost."

"What do you mean?" I leapt to my feet. "Xu Yin saw it. She *saw* the ghost."

"The killer is a human," Mackenzie said. "And I can prove it."

"Is this a joke?" I spread my hands. "You're the one who's spent the last three days trying to convince me ghosts exist. Now you're saying they don't?"

"I never said that." Mackenzie shook her head and shone her flashlight around the tunnels, trying to get her bearings. "I only said that our killer is not a ghost."

"I saw him," Xu Yin said. "I watched him kill Jenny. I know what I saw."

"You know what you *think* you saw," Mackenzie said. "Which way to the nearest exit?"

Xu Yin pointed. "That way. What makes you so sure it wasn't a ghost?"

"All in good time," Mackenzie said. "Right now I need to re-examine the apartment of Chin Mei Tsu."

"Who?" Xu Yin asked.

"The first victim," I said.

"You mean Chin-Chin," Xu Yin said. "No one called her Chin Mei Tsu. If you want to get to her apartment, it's this way." She pointed back the way we had come.

"Lead on." Mackenzie passed her handheld flashlight to the girl and Xu Yin took us on a twisting tour of the tunnels, past what smelled like an underground laundry and a reservoir overflowing with brackish water.

"Why did you hide?" Mackenzie asked.

"Kwang Di is after me," Xu Yin said. "I figured I should hide."

"You didn't want to put your family in danger," Mackenzie said.

Xu Yin shrugged. "Yeah, I guess. Something like that."

"That was very brave," Mackenzie said. "Foolish, but brave."

"Thanks, I think."

I said, "A lot of her compliments sound like insults."

Five minutes later we emerged into a slightly musty-smelling basement with a series of storage lockers built against one wall. The space was lit by a bare bulb hanging from a chain. Moths swooped and circled. The wire cages were full of rusting old appliances, busted television sets, and broken toys. One of the doors had been wrenched off the hinges. Boxes and knickknacks were strewn across the floor.

"Where are we?" I asked.

"You wanted to see Chin-Chin's apartment," Xu Yin said.

"This is her building?" I asked.

She nodded.

My eyebrows went up. "How do you do that?"

"I told you," she said, "I know those tunnels better than anybody. I can get you anyplace in Chinatown."

"Know where Tai Pan set up her new shop?"

She shook her head. "No, and if I did, I wouldn't tell you."

Mackenzie stopped at the storage space with the busted door and inspected the ransacked belongings. "This is Chin Mei Tsu's storage locker."

I trained my flashlight on the wire cage but there were no apartment numbers on the spaces. "How do you know that?"

Mackenzie reached into the jumbled mess and pulled out a sepia photograph of a young Chinese girl in a cheongsam dress with a slit up one thigh. She showed the picture to Xu Yin, who nodded.

"Yeah," she said. "That's Chin-Chin. Wow, look how young she is there. She was really pretty back in the day."

I said, "The years go by fast, kid."

"You'd know."

"Hey, what's that supposed to mean?"

Xu Yin hitched up her shoulders and made an innocent face.

Mackenzie smiled and put the picture back. "Someone ransacked her storage space."

"But why?" I asked. "What were they looking for? And what's this got to do with our series of murders?"

"I think I know," Mackenzie said.

55

Chin Mei Tsu's apartment was exactly as we had left it, a puddle of dried blood on the floor and motes of dust dancing in the shaft of light through the window. Flies buzzed, landing in the pool of tacky red paste before taking off again, but the cold weather stopped them from breeding. If this were summer, the place would be full of them. The cold also helped with the smell. The building manager hadn't called in a crew to clean up the crime scene yet. Probably entertained notions of doing it himself. A lot of people thought they could clean the mess, until they started mopping up blood and offal. Then they gave in and called the professionals.

Xu Yin put a hand under her nose and made a face. "That's rotten."

"You should check out a murder scene in summer," I told her. "It's ten times worse."

"I'll take your word for it."

I said, "What are we looking for, Mackenzie?"

She crossed the living room, circling the dried blood,

and lifted the picture frame off the chest of drawers. "I'm so stupid," she said. "You had the answer to the mystery in your hands two days ago and I missed it."

"What are you talking about?"

"Look at the picture," Mackenzie said.

I looked and I shrugged. It was a large faded print of a traditional Chinese village with a bunch of dirt lanes twisting between the huts and temples. Tiny villagers with conical hats were frozen in time. It wasn't even a very good depiction. The roads seemed to be painted from a top-down view, while the thatched roof huts faced front. It reminded me of something tourists might pick up at a souvenir shop. And it was in the frame upside down. The old lady hadn't cared enough to make sure it was right-side up. "It's a crappy picture of a village. So what?"

Mackenzie shook her head. "It's not a village. It's a map. Look!"

I looked and saw a crude depiction of a Chinese fishing village. But Xu Yin's head started bobbing. She blurted an expletive, reached for the picture frame and said, "She's right." She turned it over so she was looking at it right side up and said, "This is a map of the tunnels."

"This is a bunch of lines on faded parchment," I said. "How can you be so sure?"

"Cause I know those tunnels better than anyone," Xu Yin said, examining the image. She pointed. "This stretch right here is where I found your cop friend, and over here is the passage to Lucky Wang's dry cleaner. This is the base-ment of the Chong Lu noodle shop. That goes to Wendy Song's tea shop and this bit over here..."

She trailed off but I wasn't really listening. I turned to Mackenzie. "How does this help us?"

"Don't you see?" Her face was lit up with excitement. "This is what the killer was after."

"How do you know that?"

"The scrape in the floor." She motioned to the very same curving arc in the hardwood I had pointed out the first time we were here. "Chin Mei Tsu didn't pull the chest of drawers out from the wall. Look at the size of it. She was in her eighties. She wouldn't have the strength to move a piece of furniture that size. It's solid wood, and lacquered. It must weigh eighty or ninety pounds."

I tested an edge. She was right. The big old chest of drawers was solidly built. There was no way a little old lady could move it. "I'll give you that," I said, "But it doesn't prove anything. The picture could have fallen ages ago and she had a nephew or someone move the chest."

"The neighbor told us Chin Mei Tsu was going senile," Mackenzie said. "She would talk and talk so that it was difficult for him to leave."

"You think she said something to someone that got her killed?"

Mackenzie nodded, a smile on her face.

"Something's not right," Xu Yin said. She pointed to a T intersection on the map. "There is a passage here that I've never seen before."

"You've never seen any of this before," I said. "It's all in your head. That's not a map. You're seeing what you want to see."

She narrowed her eyes. "I know my way around the tunnels. And this passage doesn't exist."

"May I?" Mackenzie asked, holding out a hand.

Xu Yin passed it back.

Mackenzie turned it over, worked the small catches on the frame and removed the faded paper. The back was covered in Chinese characters. Mackenzie said, "That's why it was upside down. The killer took it out of the frame for a look at the writing and then put it back improperly in his haste. Can you translate?"

She passed the parchment to Xu Yin.

"It's says Made in China."

"You're kidding?" I motioned to the paper. "All that says Made in China?"

She grinned. "It's a tale about an exiled Qing Dynasty emperor who supposedly came to the Golden Mountain."

"What's the Golden Mountain?" Mackenzie asked.

"It's what the Chinese call America," I explained, and then said to Xu Yin, "Are you sure?"

She made a face at me with all the attitude a teenage girl can muster. "Of course I'm sure. Think I don't know my own culture?"

I ignored her. I was frowning at the old parchment. It was a lot of speculation and little actual evidence. I said, "So Chin Mei Tsu told someone about an old map, but she didn't tell them where it was. First they searched her storage space in the basement and when they didn't find it there..."

Xu Yin said, "They came back and tortured her."

"Which means it's something worth killing for."

Mackenzie was studying the map. She tapped the spot Xu Yin had pointed out and said, "Can you take us here?"

"Sure." Xu Yin shrugged. "But I'm telling you that passage doesn't exist."

"All the same," said Mackenzie, "I'd like to see it."

"Hold up," I said. "She's still technically a missing girl."

"Not anymore," Mackenzie said. "We found her."

"Yeah, but her parents don't know that," I said. "First thing we're going to do is let her mother and grandfather know she's alive and unharmed."

A worried frown creased her face. "The ghost is after me. I don't want him to hurt my family."

"There's no ghost," Mackenzie said.

"I saw him," Xu Yin insisted.

"Ghost or no ghost," I said, "we have to let your family know. We're cops. We'll get fired if we don't."

Xu Yin twisted her hands together and chewed her bottom lip but finally nodded. "Okay, but promise me we'll dip at the first sign of the ghost."

Mackenzie said, "I have a feeling this particular ghost won't appear in public places."

56

The sun was bleeding into the horizon by the time we left Chin Mei Tsu's apartment. A cold gust ripped up the boulevard and dead leaves skittered along the pavement like dry bones, rattling over the cracked concrete. A group of Triad thugs passed us going the other direction but all they could do was stare because a patrol car was crawling along the street, spotlight swinging one way and then the other. Just as well because I was in no mood to tangle. I was tired and my stomach was growling. I was looking forward to some fried pork dumplings, but the Happy Time Dumpling was closed and we had to enter the back door through the kitchens.

The stoves were all cold and the cook pots were empty. Xu Yin's eyebrows went up in surprise. We pushed past the beaded curtain into the dining area where Xu Yin's mother and grandfather were sitting down with Bruce MacNab and a lawyer in a neatly pressed black suit.

"What's this?" Xu Yin asked.

Momma Lo leapt up from the table, tears beading in her

small eyes, and ran to her daughter. Instead of a hug, she gave Xu Yin a good drubbing, slapping her on the back of the head and pinching her ears. Brother chewed her out in rapid fire Cantonese, wagging a finger under her nose and shouting. It wasn't the homecoming you'd expect for a girl who had gone missing. Momma Lo wailed and shook her fist and slapped the girl some more. Grandfather was the one exception. He took the girl into his arms and gave her a hug, a rare occurrence for Chinese of his generation.

After they had recovered from the shock and the tears finally dried up, Mackenzie and I explained that Xu Yin had been hiding in the tunnels after being attacked and that she was now a material witness to the murder of Jennifer Kwan.

It was a half hour before the attention returned to Bruce MacNab and his lawyer, waiting patiently at the table. Xu Yin thrust her chin. "Who's this?"

Grandfather said, "Honorable MacNab has offered to buy our establishment."

Mackenzie's eyebrows danced. "I thought the deal was off?"

"It was," Bruce MacNab told us. He was slightly rumpled with sweat on his brow and dark bags under his eyes. "I was never on board with my father's vision of Chinatown. He wanted to tear down the buildings and modernize. I want to breathe new life into the neighborhood by protecting the history and culture, and I'm going to start right here."

He pushed up from the table and stuck his hand out. "Detective Cole? Am I right?"

I nodded.

"And agent Mackenzie."

"Hello again," she said.

"You'll have to excuse my appearance. I really tied one on last night."

Xu Yin grasped her grandfather's arm. "You're selling the business."

"Honorable MacNab wants to turn this block into a cultural center dedicated to the history of Chinatown."

"That's right." Bruce smiled his frat boy smile. "I want the history and culture to be front and center. People from all over America, hell, all over the world, will come here to learn about Chinatown and then spend their hard-earned money in the shops and restaurants. It's a win win. And I don't have to evict a whole neighborhood."

"Just me and my family," Xu Yin said.

Her mother put a hand on Xu Yin's shoulder. "MacNab has made us a very generous offer."

Xu Yin crossed her arms over her chest and pouted. "Generous for who?"

I peeked at the numbers on the contract and my eyes nearly popped right out of my skull. If anyone offered me that kind of dough, I'd take the money and run.

Mackenzie said, "You should retain a lawyer to go over the paperwork."

"Very wise." Momma Lo nodded and turned to MacNab. "You will not object?"

"Of course not," Bruce agreed. "With everything that's happened, I'd expect nothing less. I understand this is a very emotional time. There's no rush. Contact an attorney. In fact, if you don't have someone you trust, I have several law firms I could suggest. I'll even help offset the cost. Attorneys can be prohibitively expensive." He spared a glance at the suit sitting next to him.

The lawyer didn't rise to the bait.

Bruce continued, saying, "We'll leave these papers here with you. If you have any questions, don't hesitate to reach out."

With that, Bruce and his lawyer left, and I had the unenviable task of asking Momma Lo if the girl could accompany us back into the tunnels.

The idea went over like a lead balloon. Momma Lo had just gotten her baby back and didn't want to let Xu Yin out of her sight, but grandfather came to our rescue. Sitting on a stool, hands on his knees, in his filth-stained white t-shirt, he spoke a regional dialect that I couldn't understand and, after a lengthy back and forth, the mother turned to us and said, "If she get killed it's on you, *heya?*"

57

We stood before a narrow stair in the alley behind the Happy Time Dumpling. The rusty metal storm door was open and the slightly musty odor of dank earth wafted up from the yawning cavity. The sun had gone down, leaving the sky an inky black stain, but that wouldn't matter in the tunnels. A nasty, biting wind whipped between the buildings, forcing me deeper into my overcoat. I said, "Once more in to the breach, eh?"

"What's that from?" Xu Yin asked.

"I dunno." I shrugged. "An old movie, I think."

"Henry the Fifth," Mackenzie said. "Act three, scene one."

Xu Yin and I turned to her.

Mackenzie quoted: "Once more unto the breach, dear friends, once more; Or close the wall up with our English dead!"

I said, "Let's hope it doesn't come to that."

"Yeah," Xu Yin said. "If I get killed my mom will be pissed."

Mackenzie motioned to the stairs. "Lead on."

Xu Yin went first, with the map and a flashlight. Mackenzie was right behind her. I brought up the rear, one hand on my pistol. Mackenzie might not believe a ghost was responsible for the murders, but Xu Yin's testimony was pretty convincing. She had seen the ghost with her own eyes and even described it in gruesome details that included a shadowy form with glowing green eyes. I didn't know if bullets worked on ghosts, but it was the only tool in my arsenal, so I was going to keep it handy.

We trekked into the tunnels, taking a twisting path, hopping over a shallow waterway of open sewage, clambering over a warm pipe, and then down a flight of stone steps carved in the earth.

"We're a level below the tunnels now," Xu Yin told us. "I don't normally come down here unless I need to use the subway and my oyster card is empty."

"You can get past the turnstiles?" I asked.

She nodded and pointed to a buckled metal door with iron rivets. "That leads to the Broadway Line. You can hop right onto the platform. Just be careful you don't step out in front of a train."

Driving her point home, we heard a subway train go hurtling past, shaking the ground beneath our feet and raining dust from the low ceiling. It was like standing in the tunnel with the train thundering past an inch from your face. The sound was deafening. I could feel it shaking my teeth inside my skull. Mackenzie clapped both hands over her ears and screwed her eyes closed. I put a hand on her shoulder and squeezed hard. After a moment the click and clack of the underground train faded and silence returned.

The only noise was the air rasping out of my lungs and the steady drip-drip-drip of water.

Xu Yin had to rely on the map now, shining her flashlight on the ancient parchment and then peering around at the passages.

"Are we lost?" I asked.

"We're not lost," she said. "I know exactly where we are."

"I think she got us lost," I said to Mackenzie.

"Give her time to concentrate," Mackenzie said.

Xu Yin took us around a series of turns and down another stair. The temperature dropped ten degrees. We were below the level of the subway now, deep in the bowels of Manhattan. Xu Yin ducked a leaky pipe and said, "This is it."

I followed her under the pipe and said, "And we aren't the only ones."

Mackenzie nodded. "Someone else has been here."

58

Dust swirled and danced in the spill of our flashlights and a musty odor hung in the air, like freshly turned earth. A collection of tools were spread on a dirty tarp covering the stone floor, along with a battery-operated work lamp. A crude opening had been cut in the rock wall and old 2x4s had been used to shore up the entrance.

Mackenzie laid the back of her hand against the work lamp and said, "It's still warm. Someone was here quite recently."

My hand tightened on my pistol.

Xu Yin said, "Should we go?"

I shook my head.

"What if he's still here?" she asked.

"We're cops," I told her. "Bad guys generally split when we show up."

"He's right," Mackenzie said. "Whoever was down here probably heard us coming and made a hasty retreat. Is there any other way out?"

"Only about fifty," Xu Yin said.

"No sense trying to give chase," said Mackenzie. "Let's see what our suspect discovered behind this wall that's worth killing for."

She motioned at the opening.

Xu Yin's eyebrows went up and she shook her head. "I'm not going first."

I pulled my weapon from the holster and held it down by my leg. "I'll go. Xu Yin, you stay behind me. Mackenzie, bring up the rear. Have you got your service weapon?"

"You know I don't carry it," she said.

"She doesn't carry a gun?" Xu Yin asked.

"No. It's a sore spot between us," I said. "Next time we go wading through sewers in search of a killer, I want you to bring your gun."

"We're not in a sewer," Mackenzie pointed out.

It was no use trying to explain the semantically pointless difference and now wasn't the time. I ducked through the rough-hewn door with my gun in hand.

A short flight of steps led down to a chamber chiseled from solid rock with a high ceiling and walls covered in Chinese symbols. At the far end of the chamber was another door; this one had been covered by a large stone slab which now lay broken on the floor. The air was stale and old. The rock beneath our feet was covered in a thick carpet of dust.

Mackenzie stooped and shined her flashlight on a set of tracks. "Ghosts don't leave footprints."

"How do you know?" Xu Yin asked.

I looked to Mackenzie expectantly.

"A ghost is a non-corporeal entity," Mackenzie said. "It

stands to reason that without a body, they cannot leave footprints."

"Who made you an expert on ghosts?" I asked.

"I've studied most of the relevant literature on the subject by the top researchers in the field of paranormal studies," Mackenzie said. "Along with more esoteric volumes such as Tobin's Spirit Guide and Alhazred's works on the disembodied and fantastic, though admittedly the last two are more fanciful than scientific. Still, all the serious researchers seem to agree that spirits are disembodied beings who interact with the physical world through manifestations of ectoplasmic energies."

"The thing I saw seemed to float," Xu Yin said.

"What you *think* you saw," Mackenzie said.

She narrowed her eyes. "I know what I saw."

To avoid an argument, I pointed to the walls. "What do these inscriptions say?"

Xu Yin studied the characters cut in the rock face and frowned. "These are very old. They use an outdated method of calligraphy."

"Maybe your mother could interpret them," I suggested.

"I said they were old." She traced a hand over the inscriptions. "I didn't say I couldn't read them."

"So what's it all about?"

"It seems to be a history of Shang Guo Chew."

Mackenzie said, "The Chinese emperor who fled the Taiping rebellion?"

Xu Yin nodded without taking her eyes off the text. "That's right."

"How do you know that?" I asked.

"Xu Yin's grandfather told us all about Shang Guo

Chew," Mackenzie said. "Don't you remember? There is a mural dedicated to him on the wall of the Happy Time Dumpling."

"I remember the old man blathering on about some dead guy," I said. "I wasn't really paying attention. I was too busy trying to solve a murder."

"You really should pay better attention," Mackenzie admonished. "Mysteries often turn on the smallest detail."

"Somehow I don't think ancient Chinese history is going to crack this case."

"You never know," Mackenzie said. "Let's see what's in the next room."

At the end of the passage, I stepped into another, smaller chamber. This one had a low ceiling and alcoves cut in the walls, housing hundreds of jade figurines and enameled pottery. Four stone warriors stood sentry, stern expressions on their carven faces, with real polearms in their lifeless hands. One of the weapons had decayed and the steel blade lay on the floor. In the middle of the room was a low stone table, roughly six feet long and three feet wide. A pillar stood at one end, inscribed with fading red characters. There was a bowl filled with sand on one end of the low tablet. Two sticks stood at attention in the sand. On closer inspection, the contents of the bowl might have been rice slowly decaying into dust. I trained my flashlight on the pillar and said, "Is that...?"

Xu Yin nodded. "A headstone."

Mackenzie stooped at the side of the stone sarcophagus, her fingers lightly tracing cold rock. There were pink roses in her cheeks and a light danced in her eyes. "This must be the grave of Shang Guo Chew."

Xu Yin was reading the stone pillar and she ducked her head. "This is Shang Guo Chew's grave, alright. Holy cow! Just think. All these years, people have been searching for his resting place, and he's been buried under a dumpling shop."

"Someone found it," Mackenzie said. She pointed to a few empty alcoves with clean patches in the dust where a vase or other figurine had been removed. "And they've taken some of the artifacts."

Xu Yin said, "Maybe that's why the ghost is killing people? Someone disturbed the tomb and he wants the artifacts back."

"That doesn't make any sense," Mackenzie said.

"Makes perfect sense to me," I said. "Someone broke in and robbed his tomb. Now this dead guy wants his ancient Tupperware back."

Mackenzie shook her head. "This is Shang Guo Chew's tomb. Kwang Di died in China, long before Shang Guo Chew was even born. Why would an ancient sorcerer care about the tomb of an emperor in America?"

"Maybe they were related?" Xu Yin offered.

Mackenzie picked up one of the jade figurines, turned it over in her hands and said, "A possibility, however unlikely."

"I don't think you should touch that," I said. "You might make the ghost angry."

"There is no ghost," Mackenzie said.

A ghastly wail echoed through the stone passages, followed by a gust of foul-smelling wind. What happened next, I'm not sure. Fear gripped me hard. All the hairs on the back of my next stood on end and my heart squeezed inside my chest. The world turned kaleidoscopic. I felt the walls receding, getting further and further away, while the ceiling pressed down. There were tremors in the earth and terrible groanings that came from somewhere deep, somewhere dark. Shadows pressed in and the beam of my flashlight dimmed, threatening to extinguish. I locked a scream in my throat and before I knew what was happening, I was running headlong through the tunnels. My flashlight beam bounced and scrambled over walls and pipes. My world titled and my feet kept slip-sliding over uneven surfaces. The breath was coming up out of my lungs in ragged gasps. Then I felt something smack the back of my skull and darkness overtook me.

59

I swam up from the bottom of a cold dark lake, breaking the surface of consciousness, and found myself hanging upside down with a raging headache. It was a moment before I could make sense of my surroundings. I was still in the tunnels, but I had no idea where. The tomb, along with the Chinese artifacts, was gone. I was in a long room with a low ceiling and dirty plastic sheets hanging over makeshift openings. Graffiti covered every wall and shallow puddles of rancid water dotted the floor. A single bulb in a cage cast an anemic glow.

I let out a low moan. It sounded like a dog with worms. My head felt hot and heavy, and slightly too big, and I knew it was all the blood going to my brain. My feet were bound. I was dangling from the center hook in a metal tripod. Numb fingertips trailed the dirty concrete floor. I tried to speak but the words came out a drunken slur. *"Whasgoinon? Whereumi?"*

"You're in the deepest depths of the nine Chinese hells,

kwai lo!" The voice was an icy knife's edge that chilled me to my spine. "And now you're going to die."

I let out a strangled cry. Terror swirled and pressed down on me until I was sure my heart would explode inside my chest. I was twisting around on the tripod, trying to get a look at the speaker, but I was terrified to see the face that belonged to that ghastly voice. I bent double in a vain effort to free myself from the tripod, but I couldn't reach the hook and my fingers were too numb to do anything but flap around like wet noodles. I let out another senseless scream. This one echoed around the room; a shrill hollow cry for help.

Footsteps crunched in the grit behind me and I heard the sharp scrape of a blade drawing over a whetstone. The sound turned my guts to ice and my bladder threatened to let go.

"This can't be happening," I heard myself say. "Ghosts don't exist."

"Oh but they do exist," Kwang Di told me.

Then I saw him for the first time; a towering ghostly specter in whisps of dirty gray cloth that seemed to float on a phantom breeze. His eyes were glowing green orbs and his mouth was an open grave. My mind rebelled at the sight. I shut my eyes tight. Another scream, this one shot through with panic, ripped from my chest. My brain kept insisting this couldn't be real, that this could not be happening, but when I opened my eyes the ghost was still there, staring down at me with those hate-filled eyes. Phantom hands clutched a wickedly curved knife.

"Help!" I shouted so loud it felt like my lungs would burst. "Somebody help me!"

"No one is coming to save you," Kwang Di rasped in that sepulcher voice. The spirit drew the knife across a whetstone with a savage hiss and light winked on the blade. I knew I was a dead man. I bucked and squirmed but it was no use. I could only watch as the apparition came closer and closer. It all seemed to happen in slow motion. The ghost reached out a hand, racked my shirt up and poised the tip of the knife over my belly, ready to split me like a hog. I instinctively sucked in my gut, like that would do any good, and let out one last desperate scream.

I thought my time had come. My life went flashing before my eyes, clichéd as that may sound. I was a dead man. My brain clawed through all my memories, good and bad, drinking in the sweet and coming to terms with all the bad that had happened. My arms waved in the air, in a pointless attempt to ward off the knife, but I knew this was the end.

Mackenzie burst through one of the dirty plastic sheets and yelled, "Stop in the name of the law!"

60

She actually yelled that. She yelled 'stop in the name of the law' like she was a 20's era prohibition officer in pursuit of a bootlegger. And the ghost stopped. The knife paused and the phantom wheeled about. There was a ragged hiss from the disembodied mouth and then the ghost was running.

I reached out with numb fingers in the hopes of latching onto the non-corporeal form, like I might actually prevent him from escaping. Whisps of ragged cloth slipped through my fingers and the ghost vanished down one of the tunnels with a ghastly wail. My mind was still reeling, like I'd had too much to drink. Another paroxysm of fear gripped me and for no reason at all I was screaming bloody murder, twisting on the tripod in a futile effort to escape.

Mackenzie and Xu Yin tried to calm me down. Mackenzie was waving a hand in front of my face, forcing fresh oxygen into my lungs and Xu Yin was working to release me from the hook. I realized what she was doing and said, "Hey, wait! Don't..."

But I was too late.

Xu Yin found the release and I crashed to the ground with a bone-jarring thud. Lights danced in my vision. Mackenzie's face blurred and darkness swarmed. The next thing I knew I was waking up in the hospital. Harsh lights assaulted my vision and the sharp smell of disinfectant wrinkled my nose. My tongue felt too big for my head and someone had scrubbed my throat with steel wool. There was a steady *beep beep beep* in my ear.

"Owlong I beenout?" I slurred.

"Less than an hour," Mackenzie said with a look at her watch. She was perched on the edge of a plastic chair next to the bed, hands twisting together into interesting knots.

Xu Yin was there as well, along with a portly doctor who cranked my bed into a sitting position before shining a pen light in my eyes.

"No permanent damage," he said. "The effects of the gas should be wearing off soon."

"Gas?" I ran a hand over my face. My fingers felt foreign to me, like they belonged to someone else, and my face was numb.

Mackenzie nodded. "The killer uses, what I can only assume, is an hallucinogenic aerosol to induce panic in his victims. The FBI lab here in New York is running a tox screen on your blood samples to isolate the chemical compound. We should know the exact make up the hallucinogen in a few days."

"You mean I was drugged?"

"In effect," Mackenzie said.

"Drink this." The doctor thrust a cup of orange juice into my hand.

"Got any vodka to go with it?"

He didn't even crack a smile. "I'm afraid not."

I sipped, scowled, and downed the rest in one long gulp. I could feel the sugar going to work on my system, helping to wake me up. I put the cup aside and said, "So it wasn't a ghost?"

"Just a man in a costume meant to inflict fear in his victims. I've been doing some research and believe the outfit is called a ghillie suit. It's favored by military snipers and hunters for blending into a woodland environment."

She held up her phone and showed me a picture of a camouflaged suit covered in green and brown strips of burlap. In the dark, with a mind-altering drug coursing through my veins, it could very easily pass for a disembodied spirit. I probed a growing lump on the back of my skull and said, "What about the eyes? His eyes were glowing green."

"Yeah," Xu Yin said. "What about those eyes? You can't fake that."

Mackenzie produced another picture on her phone. This one was a bulky set of night vision goggles. She said, "The lenses in these early model night vision goggles sometimes produce a pale green glow which can only be seen from very close distance. That's how the killer moves around in the dark without a flashlight."

"And the tripod?" I asked.

"Hunters use them for skinning animals."

I worked myself into a sitting position, waved away a warning by the doctor to take it easy, and said, "You mean to tell me there's some guy out there pulling a Scooby-Doo?"

Mackenzie questioned me with a look.

"You know? Scooby-Doo?"

She shook her head and shrugged.

"It was the lighthouse keeper," I said, doing my best impression of Fred. "Old man Caruthers."

Xu Yin shook a fist in the air. "And I would have gotten away with it too, if not for you meddling kids."

The doctor, busy checking my vitals, chimed in. "Rut roh raggy."

Mackenzie only scowled at us in confusion.

"Didn't you watch cartoons as a child?"

She shook her head. "I never saw the point."

"The point is fun," Xu Yin commented.

"Regardless," said Mackenzie. "Our killer is flesh and blood."

"When were you going to tell me about the night vision goggles and the ghillie suit?"

"I'm telling you now," Mackenzie said.

"It would have been nice to know before," I growled.

"I didn't know before," she said. "I only suspected. I first developed the theory during our attempt to summon the ghost. The killer tried to use the gas on us then and I must have got a partial dose, which is why I ran off. I couldn't describe the effects I was feeling then, and didn't understand what had made me act the way I did, but I was starting to form a theory after we found Xu Yin. Then, when the killer attacked us in the crypt, I quickly pulled my sweater up over my nose to avoid the worst of the gas."

"Why didn't you warn me?"

"I was too busy trying to calm down Xu Yin so she didn't go running off, and in the confusion, you got away."

Xu Yin came to her defense. "It took her several minutes

to calm me down. I was freaking out. It was the same feeling I had the first time I saw the ghost. By the time Mackenzie helped me relax, you were long gone. We only found you because we heard you shrieking for help."

"I wasn't shrieking," I said. "I was shouting. There's a difference."

"Either way," said Xu Yin, "you sounded like a scared little girl."

I ignored her and asked, "Did either of you find my gun? I must have dropped it when I ran out of the tomb."

Mackenzie shrugged. "Sorry."

"Great," I said. "How come every time I work a case with you, I have to report a missing firearm?"

"This time it's not my fault."

"That's not going to help when I'm sitting in front of a review board."

"I'll have uniform officers search the tunnels for your missing service weapon," Mackenzie said.

I took a minute to sort through everything Mackenzie had told me and then asked, "Why is our killer dressing up like a ghost?"

"I think I know," she said.

"How?"

"The same way I know who the killer is."

I said, "You know who did this?"

Mackenzie nodded.

"Let's nail him to a wall."

Mackenzie looked aghast. "We're going to arrest him," she said. "We have to. It's the law."

"It's an expression," I told her.

She bought her phone out and made a note of that.

Xu Yin said, "Can I go with you?"

"Absolutely not," I said. "We've put you in enough danger. I'm going to have to explain all this to my CO. When he learns we took a middle schooler on a murder investigation, he's going to flip his lid."

Mackenzie made a note of that as well and before she could ask, I said, "It means to be very angry."

She nodded and typed.

"I'm in high school," Xu Yin said. "And maybe I want to be a cop some day? This could be like a ride along."

"And some day when you're eighteen and you've filled out all the necessary release forms, you can go on a ride along," I told her. "For now, we're taking you home."

"Fine." She stuffed her hands in her pockets and rolled her eyes.

61

"What is this?" Nicky Cipriani asked as we walked through the door of the interview room. Uniformed officers had picked him up leaving his office and we'd let him sweat in the box for forty-five minutes. He sat in a chair that had a short leg, making it hard to get comfortable. I know, because I had removed the hard plastic foot on the bottom of the chair leg. It forces the suspect to keep shifting their balance and the metal makes a harsh squeak on the cheap linoleum. Cipriani said, "Am I in some kinda trouble?"

"That's putting it mildly." I took the chair across from him and fixed the big contractor with a hard stare. I was painfully aware of the fact that this evil S.O.B. had drugged me and tried to skin me just a few hours earlier. He would have done it too, if Mackenzie hadn't stopped him. I was wondering what kind of drug he had used on me and if it had any long-term side effects.

Mackenzie stood just behind my shoulder, her hands locked together and her fingers twisting. She blinked a few times and said, "Where were you today between noon and four?"

"I was at the office," Cipriani told us.

"That's a lie," Mackenzie said. "We already spoke to your secretary. She told us you left the office just before noon and didn't return until a few minutes after four."

Cipriani hunched forward, causing the chair leg to let out a scream. It didn't seem to bother him, but Mackenzie winced. "Okay, I was out of the office, but I don't see why you're so interested. I haven't done anything wrong."

"Give it up, Cipriani," I said. "We got ya dead bang on murder and assaulting a police officer."

"Whoa, whoa, whoa!" He held up both hands. The chair leg shrieked again. "Murder? Hey, I never murdered no one."

"Then where were you?" Mackenzie asked.

He hesitated.

"We know you've been masquerading as a ghost," I said. "We know you killed Chin Mei Tsu for her map of the tunnels. We know you killed John Chen when he discovered the tomb, and then you went after Xu Yin and her friend to scare the rest of the residents away. You wanted to make sure no one else got anywhere near that treasure."

"What tomb?" Cipriani said. "What treasure? I don't know anything about any of that. And I certainly didn't kill anybody."

"Then why not tell us where you were this afternoon?" Mackenzie asked.

I said, "Because he's lying."

"I'm not lying." Cipriani shook his head. "It wasn't me."

Mackenzie brought out her phone and placed it on the

battered table top. It had a picture of the metal tripod along with the rope used to bind my feet. She said, "Recognize this?"

He leaned over for a look and the chair leg squeaked.

Mackenzie's face bunched in pain, and I realized my interrogation method, which worked so well for neurotypical cops and criminals, was backfiring with Mackenzie in the room.

Cipriani shrugged. "It's a skinning tripod."

"You used it to skin all three victims," Mackenzie said. "You wanted the residents of Chinatown to believe an angry spirit was behind the murders. You knew it would drive them from the neighborhood in fear."

Cipriani was shaking his head. "I'm telling you, I never killed anybody."

Mackenzie said, "Then why did I see the exact same tripod in the back of your pickup truck parked outside your office yesterday?"

"I *have* a skinning tripod," Cipriani admitted. He pointed to the photo on her phone. "But that one's not mine."

"It's the exact same model," Mackenzie said.

"They make more than one!" Large beads of sweat were collecting on his forehead and rolling down his cheeks. He said, "Mine's still in the bed of my pickup. You can check. I have a hunting trip planned this weekend. I put it in there 'cause I didn't want to forget it."

"You been doing some hunting, alright," I said, "but not bucks."

"I never killed anything besides deer and I mostly just spend my time in the woods drinking."

"Sure you do," I said. "Sure. Couple of bucks. A little old lady with a map to buried treasure. A couple of cops."

"I keep telling you, I didn't do none of those things," he whined. "I don't know nothing about no buried treasure. I wish I did."

"Then tell us where you were today," Mackenzie said.

"He's guilty," I said and stood up. "We've got everything we need to charge him. Let's take this to the DA and throw the book at this scumbag."

"Wait," he cried. "Wait."

I stopped and turned back.

Mackenzie leaned forward, balancing on her toes.

Cipriani shifted in the seat, making more noise, and said, "Look, if I tell you where I was all afternoon and it ain't, strictly speaking, legal, am I going to be in trouble?"

I said, "No" at the same time Mackenzie said "Yes."

Cipriani looked between the two of us, sweating like a hog at the trough. His eyes were bulging right out of his skull and his chins bunched like he was about to cry.

I turned to Mackenzie and motioned her into the corner. The interview room was small and we had to whisper. I said, "If he's not our guy, then let's find out and cut him loose. I'm not interested in petty crime."

"What if it's not petty?" Mackenzie whispered back. "What if he was robbing a bank?"

I stuck my fists on my hips. "I seriously doubt that. He was probably with a hooker."

She thought that over and said, "That's a crime."

"Not a crime I care about."

"You should."

I held up a hand. "Let's stay focused on the murders.

We can crusade against prostitution once we've put an end to homicide."

"That doesn't seem likely to ever happen," she said, "but okay."

I dug a nickel from my pocket, took a minute to wedge it under Cipriani's chair leg, and then said, "Okay, where were you?"

"And you ain't gonna charge me?"

I held up three fingers. "Scout's honor."

"I was straightening out a few fellas owed money."

"I don't understand," Mackenzie said.

"He moonlights as a bookie," I explained.

"Hey, hey," said Cipriani. "I never said anything about bookmaking. A few goombas owed me some money and I went to collect."

"Any of these goombas in the hospital right now?"

He shrugged. "Teddy Druthers broke his thumb doing repairs around the house recently."

"I bet," I said. "And I suppose these guys will confirm your whereabouts?"

"You better believe it. I never hurt nobody."

"Not even Teddy Druthers?" I asked.

Cipriani spread his hands. "The idiot's clumsy with a hammer. That ain't my fault."

Mackenzie was pacing the interview room. "It's no coincidence that the killer used the exact same model tripod."

"Like I said, the company makes more than one. It's one of them, whatcha call it? Profit schemes."

Mackenzie's fingers flicked the hem of her slacks. Her face was tight with concentration. She said, "There's a connection."

"Not with me," Cipriani said.

"Somewhere," Mackenzie told him without stopping.

"Hey, all I know is that I didn't kill nobody and I was nowhere near Chinatown this afternoon. Can I go now?"

I sighed and said, "Yeah."

"No." Mackenzie shook her head.

"No?" Cipriani and I said at the same time.

"No," Mackenzie told us.

I crowded Mackenzie back into the corner. "He's got an alibi. This guy didn't do it."

Mackenzie took a fistful off her own hair and tugged.

"What are you doing?" I asked.

"She alright?" Cipriani said. "She ain't having a seizure or aneurism or something, is she?"

"She's fine," I said, not knowing if that were true. Mackenzie had turned to face the corner and was tugging hard at her ponytail. She started to hum loudly.

"Maybe she needs a doctor," Cipriani said. He was on his feet now, alarm written on his face.

"She's uh... stimulating the hair follicles," I lied. "It helps the brain to concentrate."

"No kidding?" Cipriani said. "I never heard of that."

"Yeah," I said. "It's a well-known FBI trick."

I put my hands on Mackenzie's shoulders and pressed down hard. Whispering in her ear, I said, "You okay, Mackenzie?"

It took a moment, but she finally let out a breath and relaxed. Her hand let go of her ponytail. She stood there a moment, face to the wall, then spun around so fast I was forced to leap back. "When did you go hunting last?"

"Must have been late August," Cipriani said. "Why?"

A light danced in Mackenzie's eyes. "You took Bruce MacNab with you?"

Cipriani's brows went up and his jaw wagged. "That's right. He was very interested in learning to skin a buck. How did you know that?"

"You're free to go," Mackenzie said.

62

We had spent the next morning on the phone with the DA, procuring search warrants and I parked the Mercury across the street from the Happy Time Dumpling just after two o'clock. Thunderclouds boiled overhead, promising rain. A ghostly wind whipped along the concrete canyons of Chinatown. People hurried along the sidewalks, shoulders hunched and chins tucked. A sleek red Maserati was parked in front of the restaurant and a black Lincoln was nosed in close behind. MacNab and his lawyer were already there.

Mackenzie and I got out and hurried across the street. I reached for the door and Mackenzie strode in with a determined frown on her face. The smell of deep fried dough washed over us. My feet made wet peeling noises on the sticky floor.

Bruce MacNab and his lawyer were seated at a table in the empty dining room. Momma Lo and grandfather sat across from them. Xu Yin's mother had a pen in one hand

and spectacles riding low on her nose. She was just about to put pen to paper.

"Do not sign those!" Mackenzie blurted.

Bruce MacNab turned and his eyes narrowed. "And why ever not?"

"Don't sign," Mackenzie told Momma Lo.

"We've already reached a deal." Bruce had a smile fixed on his face but it was a plastic grin, held in place through sheer force of will. "I've met her asking price, which she raised three times I might add, and we've agreed to the sale. We're just waiting on signatures. Now if you'll excuse us, officers..."

Mackenzie shook her head. "Don't do it."

Xu Yin pushed through the beaded curtain from the kitchens. "What's going on?"

"Mr. MacNab is trying to swindle your family out of a fortune," Mackenzie said.

MacNab chortled but the truth was written all over his face. "This is ridiculous. We've got a deal. You already agreed to sell. Please sign the papers."

Momma Lo hesitated.

"If you don't sign, the deal is off and you get nothing," MacNab said, an edge to his voice. "I'll buy out one of the other corner lots and you can watch while your business goes under. I'm giving you a chance to come out ahead. Now sign the damn papers."

Xu Yin hurried forward and snatched the pen from her mother's hand. "Don't sign it, Momma. Not yet. Let's hear what Mackenzie has to say."

"Mr. MacNab won't be buying anything today," Mackenzie said. "In fact, he's going to jail."

"Jail?" MacNab snorted. "What a load of crap. I haven't done anything wrong."

I said, "How about three murders?"

His face turned white. "I don't know what you're talking about."

"Sure you do," I said. "You were offering the locals money to hold out against your father. You *wanted* his deal to fall through so you could make one of your own. We asked around. We've got a dozen witnesses willing to testify, under oath, that you were bribing them to hold out. We spoke to your father. You were supposed to be convincing them to sell. Instead you did the opposite."

"One of the first people you spoke with was Chin Mei Tsu," Mackenzie said. "An old lady who liked to talk and she was going senile. She mentioned Shang Guo Chew's grave to you. She told you about the map, told you it led to the final resting place of a dethroned Chinese emperor. You knew the secret was worth a fortune, but your father was about to buy up the land."

MacNab was shaking his head. "This is all wild speculation. You don't have any proof. You're desperate to hang this murder on someone. You haven't got any suspects and you're trying to frame me."

"You found the tomb," Mackenzie said. "You knew how much the find was worth, but only to the person holding the deed. You used the Chinese ghost story to kill John Chen and Jennifer Kwan, spreading fear, causing your father to lose interest, and driving down real estate prices at the same time, which would allow you to buy the property cheap. I checked the county records. The tomb is directly underneath this dumpling shop, which makes this lot worth millions."

"I don't know what you're talking about," Bruce MacNab blustered. He turned to his lawyer. "This is libel. Slander! Can't you do something?"

The barrister started up from his chair and cleared his throat.

"Sit down," I told him. "You'll have your work cut out for you over the next few months. Your client is going to stand trial for murder."

"I hardly think so." MacNab was on his feet now, a vein throbbing in his forehead. He jabbed a finger under my nose. "You haven't got any proof."

"We have a search warrant for your apartment in Manhattan and the house in the Hamptons," Mackenzie told him. "Investigators are going through your apartment as we speak."

I said, "They found several very old, very valuable Chinese vases."

"Along with bottles of acid," Mackenzie said. "We had the tub in Chin Mei Tsu's apartment tested. That's how you got rid of the skins. You melted them with acid so it would look like the work of a ghost."

MacNab licked his lips. The blood was draining from his face.

"It was an ingenious crime," Mackenzie told him. "You used hallucinogens and a ghillie suit along with night vision goggles to convince the people of Chinatown that there was a ghost."

"Hallucinogens?" Bruce said. "Do you even hear yourselves? No one is going to believe that in court."

"Oh but they will," I assured him. "I had a taste of your product. You majored in Chemistry at university and even bragged the first time we met that you were a bit of a chemist."

I pointed to the picture window.

Bruce MacNab turned.

A pair of uniformed officers going through the trunk of his Maserati.

"Hey, that's my car! They can't do that."

"I'll want to see that search warrant," the lawyer said and I obliged him with a copy.

Outside, one of the uniformed officers held up an aerosol can.

I said, "Is that what you used to drug me?"

MacNab started to open his mouth but his lawyer laid a hand on his arm.

"You almost had us fooled," Mackenzie said. "But you made one mistake; you couldn't resist taking some of the artifacts from the tomb. Without those we might not have a case."

I said, "With them we've got you dead to rights, Bruce."

"You're under arrest," Mackenzie said. "Please turn around and place your hands on your head."

63

We spent the rest of the day on paperwork. Murder investigations require mountains of it. There's a reason cops refer to them as *murder books*. They're kept in large three-ring binders and generally have more pages than a Steven King novel. And when the chief suspect is society's upper crust, you'd better make sure you cross the t's and dot the i's or the defense will tear you apart on the stand. So I was at my desk in the bullpen, filling in forms, making notes, and cross referencing our work.

Mackenzie had disappeared for the better part of an hour. I assumed she was taking a sensory break, probably needed to escape all the noise and took a walk outside. I used the opportunity to refill my coffee and check the score of the Giants game. It was after six in the evening. Bruce McNab was in custody; an antique Chinese teapot along with night vision goggles had been discovered in his Manhattan loft. The DA was already talking plea bargains.

The snot-nosed little brat was rich and his daddy had a long reach. He'd probably do a dime in a white-collar institution undergoing psychiatric treatment. The thought left me feeling sick to my stomach, but at the end of the day we had caught the killer and closed the case, and that's all that mattered.

I clipped the last of the pages into the binder, signed my initials and closed the book. "Done and done."

Mackenzie had returned. She took a slim folder from her coat and dropped it on top of my desk.

"What's this?" I opened the jacket and found the employment records and security checks on a rent-a-cop working for the armored car company. His name was Jason Tilly and he'd been with the company six months.

Mackenzie said, "Armored cars are notoriously difficult to rob. They're basically mobile bank vaults with armed security. Working on the hypothesis that the robbers must have an inside man, I searched for connections, cross-referencing new employees with known bank robbery crews."

I sat up a little straighter. "You found a connection?"

She nodded. "Jason Tilly's sister, Agatha Tilly, is married to a John Rappaport. Rappaport did seven years on attempted robbery and was released just four months ago."

"Good work," I said. "I'll have unis pick up Rappaport and Tilly first thing in the morning. I owe you."

She shrugged, as if to say, *nothing to it.*

And just like that, we had closed two high-profile cases in one day. I would have gotten there eventually, but it would have been weeks of sifting paperwork and digging through everybody's background.

"Come on, Sherlock," I said. "I'll give you a lift home."

We took the elevator down to the parking garage and I patted my pockets in search of my keys. At first I thought I'd left them upstairs but Mackenzie produced them with a flourish.

"Did you steal my keys?" I asked.

She nodded and pointed.

The Mercury had been repainted, bumper to bumper, and a new windshield installed. Instead of dull beige with rust spots, it was now bright yellow with a black racing stripe down the middle.

A slow smile worked over my face. "You had my car painted?"

Another nod.

I stood there a moment, lost for words, trailing my fingertips along the glossy finish. "Mackenzie, this is... I don't know what to say. Thank you."

She had her hands clasped together, torturing her fingers. "I hope the color is to your liking."

"The color is great," I said. "But this must have cost a lot of money."

"I've come to understand that it's customary to do something nice when you have a favor to ask."

"You want to ask me a favor?"

She nodded.

I looked over the gleaming body of my Mercury and said, "Must be some favor. You didn't kill anyone, did you? Is there a body in the trunk? You want me to help you hide it?"

She frowned and shook her head. "Why would I kill anybody?"

I held up the hang ten sign.

"Oh," she said. And then, "Ha."

Her dry emotionless laugh made it even funnier. I smiled and said, "What do you need?"

"A partner."

I leaned my forearms on the roof of the car. "You want to partner with me on a permanent basis?"

"We work well together." She stared at her sneakers. "You don't seem to mind that I'm autistic and you understand things about neurotypical behavior that I sometimes miss."

"Sometimes?" I arched an eyebrow.

"I think we'd make a good team." She cocked her head to the side. "What do you say?"

I crossed around the car and stuck out a hand. "Put 'er there."

She frowned at my outstretched hand. "Put what there?"

I laughed, took her hand, and pumped it. "It means I accept."

The End.

A WORD FROM KIMBERLY CLAIRY

Autism is not an illness, but it is a disability within this fast paced culture, as it effects how the person processes and communicates information. But, with sensitivity and the right supports those with autism can succeed and can live meaningful lives, I know because I am doing it!

Who am I?

I am not a diagnosis.
    I am not a label.
    I am not autism.
    I am not a failure.
    I am not worthless.
    I am not stupid.
    I am not a mistake, nor am I my mistakes.

I cannot be measured by a size, a number, an expectation or a list of rules. My purpose and my worth are not tangible things. They just are. And they are infinite. I may not see them sometimes or believe they are there but they are. They are simply because I am.

Who am I?

I am brave.

I am strong.

I am creative and innovative.

I am compassionate, kind, gentle, and caring.

I am honest and sincere

I am carefree, playful, funny, quirky, unique, genuine, and innocent.

I am a thinker, I love to solve problems I think outside the box.

I am perceptive and intuitive.

I am social, but in my own way.

I am full of energy, helpful and accepting of all people

I am Kim!

I like to climb and build and create.

I thirst to be outside to smell the fresh air feel the dirt beneath my feet...to touch the wise trees and hear the orchestra of birds, crickets, rustling leaves, and the pitter patter of my moving feet.

I enjoy yoga, walking, running, stretching, twirling, jumping- being in my body with my body, one body one mind.

I yearn to help others, to love unconditionally, to accept non-judgmentally.

I have autism.

I process things differently.

The world moves very fast, and I am often unable to keep up but that is ok, I don't have to.

I see the details and can figure out things others often can't because I notice.

I create my own solutions.

I think in pictures, my words are visual representations.

I can't always verbalize my thoughts. I can be slow to learn or mishear what is said.

This can be frustrating; but patience, persistence and not giving up is key.

I note beauty in everything, everyone, every animal.

I feel and see emotions in colors, shapes, and textures.

I don't like loud or busy places because they make my ears bleed and my eyes burn.

Certain noises, tones, and pitches are deafening and I have to cover my ears or wear headphones.

I walk and sometimes listen with my eyes closed. This way I can hear and see what is happening.

I need deep pressure to calm down. I may hum loudly, fidget, or smell things in order to focus.

I can act a little immature or childlike at times and I may do strange things...but that is ok because otherwise I would not be able to interact and be with the world, with you, with me

I am not a diagnosis

I am not a label

I am not autism

I am not a failure, worthless, or stupid

I am not a mistake, nor am I my mistakes
I am none of those things.
I am Kim
And
That is enough.

DID YOU ENJOY THE BOOK?

Please take a moment to leave a review on Amazon. Readers depend on reviews when choosing what to read next and authors depend on them to sell books. An honest review is like leaving your waiter a hundred dollar tip. The best part is, it doesn't cost you a dime!

ABOUT THE AUTHOR

I was born and raised in sunny Saint Petersburg, FL on a steady diet of action movies and fantasy novels. After 9/11, I left a career in photography to join the United States Army. Since then, I have travelled the world and done everything from teaching English in China to driving a forklift. I studied creative writing at Eckerd College and wrote five books in the best-selling Jake Noble Series before releasing the Mackenzie and Cole series. When not writing, I can be found indoor rock climbing, playing the guitar, and haunting smoke-filled jazz clubs in downtown Saint Pete. I'm currently at work on another Mackenzie and Cole paranormal mystery. You can follow me on my website William-MillerAuthor.com

facebook.com/authorwillmiller

twitter.com/man_author

instagram.com/wmiller314

CAN'T WAIT FOR MORE?

Sign up to the Mackenzie and Cole Fan Club and I'll notify you as soon as the next spine tingling mystery is available.

Sign up to receive all the news about Mackenzie and Cole!